Viva Byron!

Other Books by Hugh Thomson

The White Rock: An Exploration of the Inca Heartland
(Weidenfeld & Nicolson 2001)

Nanda Devi: A Journey to the Last Sanctuary
(Weidenfeld & Nicolson 2004)

Cochineal Red: Travels Through Ancient Peru
(Weidenfeld & Nicolson 2006)

Tequila Oil: Getting Lost in Mexico
(Weidenfeld & Nicolson 2009)

50 Wonders of the World
(Quercus 2009)

The Green Road into the Trees: An Exploration of England
(Preface/Random House 2012)

One Man and a Mule: Across England with a Pack Mule
(Preface/Random House 2017)

The Map Tour
(Andre Deutsch 2018)

Hugh Thomson

Viva Byron!

Byron lives on…

His fictional adventures
in South America

A 'what-if' novel

Castle & Maine
Oxford

Castle & Maine Publishing

ISBN 978-1-0686342-2-2

2 4 6 8 10 9 7 5 3 1

The great object of life is sensation – to feel that we exist, even though in pain. It is this 'craving void' which drives us to gaming – to battle – to travel – to intemperate but keenly felt pursuits of every description, whose principal attraction is the agitation inseparable from their accomplishment.

Byron, letter to Annabella Milbanke, 1813

When a man hath no freedom to fight for at home,
let him combat for that of his neighbours.

'Stanzas', *Jeux d'Esprit*, 1820

PROLOGUE

It is difficult to approach close to the painting. The room is roped at the doorway so paying visitors may view it from afar, while not able to finger the porcelain or make off with the silver, always laid on the long dining table for a party of ten.

But the group portrait is so large it dominates the room. Painted in the late Spanish style, with a heavy lacquer, it shows a dark interior illuminated only by shafts of light from the windows, much like the room within which it is now placed. Yet there all resemblance ends – for outside the windows of the painting, palm trees are rising from bougainvillea and bright tropical flowers; beyond the trees there is the hint of a distant sea. Whereas the visitor to Kingston Lacy, unless lucky enough to come on the rare sunny day that Dorset can provide, is likely to look out on a landscape of mist, cloud or drizzle settling around its oaks and beeches, even if some of the trees are unusual foreign specimens.

To one side of the painting, a man with striking green-blue eyes, dressed in an equally striking bright orange shirt, is holding up an ornate decanter of crystal to the light. The painter has shown the light from the decanter diffracting and playing across the man's face. The observant visitor might notice the same decanter standing in the room they are in now, on a sideboard under a small picture of a woman selling oranges; the unobservant have it pointed out to them on an information board identifying the man as William Bankes, who collected the antiquities which decorate this, his ancestral home.

In the centre of the painting, sitting on a hard-backed chair, looking directly at the viewer, is a young woman with a dark, Latin complexion and strikingly fair hair. As she is sitting, it is hard to tell how tall she may be; but she wears a bold red dress that, along with Bankes's orange shirt, dominates the painting chromatically. Beside her is a young girl of about four or five, wearing a puffed-up pale skirt that is perhaps the painter's way of paying homage to the princesses in Velasquez's celebrated *Las Meninas*. The young girl has a petulant expression, understandable if she had been asked to pose for some time.

Off to one side of the painting, isolated from the others and standing by a desk, another man, wearing black, almost merges with the shadows – were it not for the loose white shirt that escapes from his tightly tailored jacket, and the intensity of the gaze he has fastened on the desk and the objects scattered across its surface. These are illuminated by the light of a single candle: a miniature globe, a pair of riding gloves in a light brown kid, three octavo volumes bound in gilt, and a skull.

CANTO I

To John Cam Hobhouse, from George Gordon Byron

Ravenna, August 20th, 1819

My dear Hobhouse – I have not lately had of your news – and shall not reproach you because I think if you had any good to send me you would do so. – I wrote to you twice or thrice from Bologna – and am at present in Ravenna – address to me however at Venice.

– My time has passed viciously and agreeably. At the advanced age of thirty-one, so few years – months – days – hours – or even minutes! – remain to me that '*carpe diem*' is not enough. I have been obliged to crop even the *seconds* – but who can trust to tomorrow? – I cannot repent me (I try very often) so much of anything I have *done*… as of anything I have left *undone*.

Alas! I have been but idle – and have the prospect of early decay – without having seized *every available instant* of our pleasurable year. This is a bitter thought – and it will be difficult for me ever to recover the despondency into which this idea naturally throws me. – Philosophy would be in vain – *let us try action*!

And now what do you think? I have two notions – one to visit England in the spring – while the other – is to go to South America…

But 'South America' comes out blotched. Each time Teresa shifts in her afternoon sleep – which she does often, impatiently, as if a cat dozing in the sunshine – she jogs against the cushion; a hard cushion of the sort the Italians like on their sofas, with an inlaid wooden panel, giving a flat – if small – surface on which to rest the writing paper.

The afternoon light reflects up from the tiles of the loggia and shines through her blonde hair against the turquoise floor. She is sleeping fully clothed in case any servant comes knocking importunely on the door. And if any did – they would find him resting his lame foot on the sofa – and writing a letter:

> Europe is grown decrepit! – Besides, the same things happen here again and again. But those fellows in South America are as fresh as their New World – and fierce as their earthquakes. – I'm enamoured of Bolivar – and his dashing General Paez. My grandfather spoke truth about the South Americans.

His grandfather. Vice-Admiral John Byron. 'Foul-Weather' *Jack*. Who had beaten along the South American coast for years – shipwrecked so often he became a hero. Nothing the British public liked so much as a man who wasn't modest about his failures.

Or dislikes so much as a poet who – whisper it – is said to have slept with his sister and every willing boy who crossed his path. Who lives in a decadent palace in Venice. The *Blackwood's* review of *Don Juan* – in the last mail packet from England – calls him an unrepenting, unsoftened, smiling, sarcastic, joyous sinner. Before they ran out of adjectives. In the following fusillade, they said they had never read such an infusion of genius and vice.

'*Genius and vice*'. Well at least Murray ought to sell a few copies on that! Society ladies might not leave his book lying open in the drawing room – friends tell him there is an Eleventh Commandment to all women not to read it – but they could hide a discreetly bound copy in plain leather under their bedsheets. An idea he enjoys.

He looks down at his hand holding the pen. His writer's hand. It is corpulent, bloated. These years of exile in Italy have made him fat. When did he add eating to his family of vices? Only thirty-one – an age which seems *maudlin* – and he can no longer see his knuckles. Lucky his few remaining readers – those not offended by *Don Juan* – know him from those portraits commissioned back in London when he was thin enough to wear loose white shirts – and had cheekbones. Without the premature crow's-feet.

What would his Admiral grandfather have said? He is sure if Jack Byron had lived long enough to meet him – they would have understood each other. Not least because they each had suffered. His grandfather at sea and he on land.

Although as he looks at Teresa, he has to admit he hasn't suffered much. Or at least, no more than could be said to be necessary to become a poet.

A small pustule of brown ink spills from the pen because of the steep angle. He adjusts the lectern cushion. No point in sullying the fine Lucchese furniture. The sofa belongs to Teresa's husband, the Count – so, strictly speaking, is not his concern. But still. It is one thing to enjoy another man's wife; quite another to damage his sofa, particularly one that may have been in the family for several generations.

The paper better positioned, he adds a last note to Hobhouse:

> – Yes – I want to embark and possess myself of the Andes! – or a spacious plain of South America with volcanoes but not too many earthquakes.

> – believe me ever yrs. most truly – Byron

Would Hobhouse understand? That for him to leave Italy is a *necessity*. And that South America could be the best place – by far – for him to go.

Unlikely. Even though he'd hinted already – when Hobhouse asked who he considered the world's greatest man. He had replied, with unaccustomed deliberation, 'Once I thought it was Prizefighter Jackson – but now, undoubtedly... Simon Bolivar!'

Bolivar, who wanted to liberate an entire continent. He had just beaten the Spaniards at a great battle in the Andes – Venezuela was almost free – a whole new country, Colombia, had been created – and the rest of South America would surely follow. The Bourbon kings of Spain and its Empire kicked in their tender silk-stockinged shins.

Bolivar as the first man of his nation – another Washington, as he had acclaimed him to Hobhouse – a leader in talent and truth. Bolivar riding with his generals and his men to the applause of the street. While he, Byron, had been idle in Italy, chasing women and getting fat.

Although with Teresa, he might have stopped chasing and found – by accident – the perfect companion for such a journey and adventure.

She opens her eyes and looks at him with that languorous expression, halfway between impertinence and amused indifference.

'Writing again? I hope that's another letter to me.'

'Why should I write to you, *amor mio*, when you are lying beside me?'

'Because you might be planning to leave me. And because if you're not writing to me, you could be writing to another woman.'

'A woman called Mr Hobhouse?

'I'm sure these Englishwomen can dissemble and pretend to be men if they choose. But since you're awake, perhaps you can tell me in person how much you adore me.'

His saddle-horses have arrived; those for the carriage are to come separately. They take advantage of the cool of the evening to ride out. He has not seen Teresa on a horse before. While she calls herself 'an equestrian' – *una cavallerizza*, more liquid in Italian – she would not do well round Rotten Row in Hyde Park, and he likes her all the better for it.

Teresa rides a horse as an afterthought to conversation, which is continuous and often delightful. Even her pauses – pregnant with innu- endo, *insinuazione* – sound good in Italian.

The sandy paths through the light shade of the Ravenna pine forests are perfect for riding. But as they crest a hill – at walking speed, for they have grooms with them, not least to be decorous – she loses control of her mount – who starts to run after his own stallion to bite him. Teresa, alarmed, screeches in her high hat and sky-blue habit – embarrassing both him and the grooms – who have their hands full to keep her from tumbling or her clothes from being torn by the trees and thickets of the pine forest. She is left with light scratches on her arms, about which he is concerned.

'Your horse provoked my own.'

'And how did it do that...?'

'By being so self assured and philosophical.'

Then she laughs, and he feels a moment of pure and reckless happiness – like a child already tired of the party but who insists on having yet one more game. And they spur the horses on.

To John Cam Hobhouse, from George Gordon Byron

Palazzo Mocenigo, Venice, October 3rd, 1819

He pauses before he begins the letter. This is uncharacteristic. As a rule, he likes the headlong charge.

But writing that address is a reminder of how determined he has become to leave Italy. Not that he hasn't enjoyed himself; yet he has been *indolent*.

He shifts his weight on one of those delicate Italian chairs that break easily so he can see the Grand Canal curving round the bend to where it joins another, smaller waterway, the Ca' Foscari, a junction famous for the ripest, most inventive obscenities the Venetian dialect can provide. Those right-of-way arguments had once given him endless enjoyment – he had lobbed in comments as well from that same bay window, just to bemuse the boatmen. But now their noise and squawking annoy him. Like fishwives at the Rialto.

Three years in the city with only the occasional *deviazione* away. The pleasures have faded. Everything in Venetian life – its gondolas, its laziness, the crumbling buildings. He has become tired, even, of the view from St Mark's down to the Grand Canal, one he had always thought would provide infinite amusement.

When he first swam the whole length of the Canal – and over from the Lido – what a triumph of a race that had been. He had left Mengaldo floundering so short – knocked up, exhausted – hallooing for the boat like a huntsman who'd lost his horse – that by the time they reached the Canal's entrance, the *Cavalier* was a full five hundred yards behind and had – *given up*. Just desserts for a gelded mountebank – so boastful about his exploits with Napoleon – so servile in the *salons* and *conversaziones* of Venice. So desperate to make the acquaintance of a British *Milord*.

Alexander Scott had kept pace – at least as far as the Rialto – but then he too had taken to a gondola. Also *defeated*.

He alone had kept going, to cheers from the Rialto Bridge – emerging finally at the furthest scrag end of the Canal – having stayed in far longer than the other two – and swimming easily. The whole distance computed by the Venetians at some four and a half Italian miles, which – while short-changed doubtless on honest English miles – had given him enormous pleasure. In the water from half-past four till a quarter-past eight – without touching land or resting. And still, as he enjoyed describing to Hobhouse, with the energy to enjoy a woman in the forenoon and another in the evening, against the walls of a side canal, at ten of the clock. With the swimming in between.

But on his most recent swim – to raise his spirits – and on his own, for now no one will take up his challenge – he had been assaulted by the *smells*, both various and particular. Some made him retch. Burning caulk and bilge from the Arsenale ships – rotting fish and fruit as he passed the Rialto – sewage washed in from the side canals by Cannaregio and the back of the city. And he was not noticed any more as he swam. He had become part of Venice's decayed furniture, as if he were another piece of floating debris.

What had the vitriolic review in *Blackwood's* said? That Venice was… the lurking place of the selfish and polluted exile of this *miserable* man who had exhausted every species of sensual gratification. That he had drained the cup of sin to its bitterest dregs. That they wished no such being as Byron – had ever existed!

Murray refused to publish his response. But then Murray, like all publishers, was craven. Writing to him – as a supposed exile who had lost touch in Italy – to tell him – *pompously* –the British public were now *too refined* for what he, Murray, saw as the excesses of *Don Juan*. To justify the cuts he wanted. What cant! He knows the British public. And they have a stronger stomach than Murray allows.

Still, it adds to a growing, instinctive feeling – that he would be happy never to set foot in England again. And the thought comes back to him – repeatedly – like the aftertaste of cheap wine. Why be a servile brother of the *quill* – with the hacks of Grub Street – when he could be a far nobler brother of the *blade*? Prove that a poet could be a soldier.

He wants a life of action – yearns for it. Enough of writing to Murray every time his sensitive publisher wants Juan to put his breeches back on – or not take them off in the first place. When there is a clarion call across Europe – and across the Atlantic – from people tired of worn-out kings and foreign powers.

He could leave Europe for a New World writ large and fresh. Take on an adventure – as Teresa is always urging him to do. Live by the imagination – as he always urges himself to do.

What would it matter if he never wrote another line? A man was born passionate of body – why he likes to swim – for his damaged foot to be weightless in the water. So he can feel full-bodied – living as he should. Not pacing out a half-life in the shadows of a Venetian palace with the cries of monkeys in the rafters and of the dogs from the flooded lower floor.

He has been bilious all summer – but also excited and agitated – exhausted mentally and bodily. That phrase of Swift's flies about his head and continually haunts him – 'that I shall die at top first'. Die just when he should be living most, at the height of his life.

He feels *constrained* by Venice – an empty oyster shell – without its pearl. The *foppery* of the place! When you start to recognise all the prostitutes in a city – when they all to a woman call you by name as you pass – it is time to leave. Though since meeting Teresa, he has foresworn them – most anyway were fireships who would leave a man burning. He knows which ones were feared by men, which the prime articles and which ones the biters. Some with a spirit of anarchy he admires.

He hears the first strike as the Santa Maria della Salute tolls its slow, hourly tribute to plague victims of the past. To see a city die daily, as Venice does, is a sad contemplation.

Enough to drive a man to drink. Or more drink. But he is determined not to have any.

The bell gives its last peal. *To hell with it*. He shouts down the hall for Fletcher to bring red wine – the Cahors and not that Italian filth.

Then he settles at the window, to continue the letter to Hobhouse – a more serious one than he is accustomed to write – but scribbling fast, dashing off his thoughts, as he knows what he wants to say.

Dear Hobhouse

My South American project, of which I believe I spoke to you (as you mention it) – was this. – I perceive that advantageous offers were – or are – to be held out to settlers in the Venezuelan territory, let alone the New Granada that has been christened again as Colombia – oh brave new world!

– My affairs in England are nearly settled – or in prospect of settlement. In Italy I have no debts – and could leave when I choose.

Fletcher arrives with the wine. He has a manservant's keen instinct for how long to delay any given command – the necessary gap between servility and surliness. And at this hour of the day, Fletcher may well have been partaking himself. It would be hard to tell.

The light reflects off the waters of the canal and into the bay of the apartment window, playing round the red liquid in the glass. He drains it fast. He begins to underline words for emphasis.

– I *assure* you I am *serious* – and that the notion has been about me *for a long time*. – I should go there with my Contessa from Ravenna – who is nineteen – she says – and with my natural daughter Allegra – now nearly three – and pitch my tent *for good and all*.

– I want a country – and a home – and if possible – a free one. I am not yet thirty-two years of age – I might still be a decent citizen and found a house and a family – as good – or better than the one I had before.

There is no freedom in Europe – that's certain – it is besides *a worn out portion of the globe*.

– I won't go to South America to travel but to settle. – Do not laugh at me – you will – but I assure you I am quite in earnest if this thing be practicable. I want to go there as a settler – and as I say, above all, a *Citizen*.

He likes the idea of being a citizen. A Citizen. A *citoyen*. In a republic. How often has he discussed the notion with those agitating in Italy for freedom from the Austrian yoke? Although he also likes the idea of still being a *Milord*. But then both may be possible.

When he sees South America in his mind's eye – in the chamber of his green imagination – he imagines a landscape of rich fecundity – a jaguar draped over a log in the foreground – bright red tropical flowers behind. A few beautiful young natives, both male and female, bathing. The reality – he knows – will likely be different. But then it is not his place or destiny to live by the distortions of any reality. It has always disappointed him.

He falls asleep on the floor, sodden with wine. Fletcher finds him and, with due consideration, props his head against the stone of a nearby pillar.

Fletcher always looks reproving if he drinks. He knows why. Because unlike Fletcher, who can empty a hogshead without the slightest change in disposition, he, after just a few glasses, becomes *querulous and quarrelsome*. Laudanum has a similar effect. The only thing that puts him in high spirits (absurd, but true) is a dose of Epsom salts, taken in the afternoon.

He wakes to find Mutz licking his face. He looks the dog in its sad eyes; its mongrel face.

He surveys the damp, sodden ground floor with dismay. His bulldog Moretto also comes splashing across, as if to be fed. The cranes look *disconsolate*, topknots hanging lank down their necks, like dissolute monks; the sound of the monkeys high above in the *palazzo* rancorous – not 'charming', as he had recently described them in a letter to Hobhouse.

A wild disorder often pleased – but not today. He feels unaccustomed dismay, with the equally unaccustomed realisation that he is beginning to experience the same emotion more often.

Winter is approaching and the water laps against the doors of the *palazzo* with increased urgency. At intervals, the waves are forced even higher by large cargo boats which discharge their vegetables and wares at the Rialto market.

The floor smells of old tallow, of animal excrement, of *neglect*. Worst is the rotting fruit that has floated from the Rialto and lodged under the jetty-boards, so impossible for Fletcher to remove. The water smacks against the bottom of the staircase as he hauls up to the safety of the *piano nobile*. Moretto pads beside him, the bulldog's feet much steadier than his own.

It is not the way he wants to present himself to his friends back in England. Or to present himself to himself; not the way he will write to them. But at least he can now go to sleep in a bed.

From the quayside near the Madonna dell'Orto, the Adriatic looks sheet-grey, as if it were the Atlantic – with a fog. The sea bells toll from the Murano lighthouse; its faint oscillating beam sweeping the water is only just visible across the channel.

The winters in Venice are as sharp as needles – and he has counted out too many of them. The only warmth left in the city comes from the Tintorettos, like the one in the church near where the painter himself – 'il Furioso' – had lived. The shafts of light illuminating the Virgin on the stairs – the deep reds and velvets of the cloaks, and the gold and silver of the steps – the Egyptian obelisk behind – the deep vantage point and the drama of the scene. He can see why Bankes is so desirous of acquiring it.

He will seek out the priest and ask, as he has been charged to do.

To William Bankes,

Palazzo Mocenigo, Venice, January 3rd, 1820

Dear Bankes

A tertian and malarial fever which has troubled me for some time – and my daughter Allegra being ill over Christmas, the poor child – prevented me from replying before to your welcome letter. I have not been ignorant of your progress nor of your discoveries – and I trust you are no worse in health from your labours.

The address of my letter will have explained to you why I cannot join you at Trieste. I was on the point of setting out for England and then South America (before I knew of your arrival) when my child's illness made her and me dependant on a Venetian proto-medical quack. So I remain.

It is now seven years since you and I met – which time you have employed better for others and more honourably for yourself than I have done.

Should you come this way – and I am still here – you need not be reminded how glad I shall be to see you; I long to hear some part from you. I can assure you I am as much the humblest of your servants as at Trinity.

At least you have had better fortune than any traveller of equal enterprise (except perhaps Humboldt) in returning safe; and after the fate of other explorers, like Burckhardt, left dead on their field of endeavour – it is hardly less surprise than satisfaction to get you back again.

Meanwhile I have made enquiries for you about a Tintoretto you could purchase – from a Jewish dealer in Cannaregio

– it is not as fine as his Siege of Constantinople in the palace of the Doge – but it will serve – an Apollo – tho' whether with such fine *Hyacinths* around him as we found in Cambridge – or incitement to the '*coitum plenum et optabilem*' – you must judge.

Believe me ever and very affectionately yours –

Byron.

Fletcher is good at placing people. He needs to be. The carnival of characters who arrive asking for admittance to the palazzo would not disgrace the *commedia dell'arte*. Vociferous women – creditors – literary admirers from England – or worse America – with their persistence – let alone emissaries from the Count concerning Teresa. All need tact and discrimination and the occasional firm word.

He likens it to being a publican – an Admiral of the High Seas as they call them in Deptford – where he would have worn a blue apron to give his statements even more authority. At least he can have Moretto in the doorway beside him – not that the bulldog is capable of denying entrance to the most undeserving charlatan – although *they* are not to know that.

But he finds it hard to place the lean, saturnine Englishman who has just arrived with his carpetbags and has a velveteen blue cloak around him that trails the dust of many a foreign floor. The man's skin is weather-beaten like a sailor's, but his neckerchief is of finest silk and he has a shock of tousled red hair. He is also unsettled by the man's eyes, which are acute and questioning – and of a startlingly clear blue with a green cast. Not a man to take lightly.

'My apologies, Mr Bankes, but his lordship is still asleep.' It is past noon so he does say this apologetically, as if responsible for his master's habits. 'Would you care to wait in the hall?' – This even more apologetically – as it would have to be in an area both dry and free of animal excrement, of which there are few.

Bankes is already moving past him with his bags, and then again, without question or apology of his own, advancing up the marble staircase to the *piano nobile* and on through the billiard room. It is with impatience that their visitor throws open the doors to his lordship's bedroom – and, finding it empty, continues on to the adjoining dressing room, to burst in there with equal impetuosity, Fletcher trailing behind, making distressed noises like a sheep that has lost a lamb.

An hour later, his lordship is out of the bath and consuming a delicate breakfast of raw egg, a cup of tea without either milk or sugar, and a dry biscuit. Bankes recalls his eating habits as eccentric even when a student – and has time to study the man whom he has not seen for many years.

He has grown fatter, both in person and face – having lost that refined, spiritual look which Bankes remembers from earlier times. So the diet of raw egg may be necessary. The addition of straggling whiskers – a recent acquisition, it emerges – is not an improvement. Apparently he had been told by a Italian that he had *una faccia di musico*, a musician's face – said surely with a winning smile of deprecation – and this had convinced his old friend to emulate such *artistes* and add whiskers. A mistake, in Bankes's view. Together with the length of his hair, down well below the neck, and the foreign style of his coat and boots – all this makes him seem – well, *much changed*.

The man is still, however, eminently handsome. Whatever his features have lost of their high, romantic character – that pale intensity – they have become more mischievous and arch for the waggish wisdom – and play of humour – which so suits his friend's various, prodigal nature; while it occurs to Bankes that the new roundness of his contours – which had startled him when he saw his naked lordship in the bath – has increased the striking resemblance of his old friend's finely formed mouth and chin to those of the Belvedere Apollo – a useful touchstone to Bankes of male beauty.

His friend is eating breakfast standing up, another affectation that Bankes remembers from their days as students. But at least that means they can be on their way faster.

He finds he is struggling to keep up. Bankes's tall figure strides ahead through the marketplace of the Rialto as if in the Levant – or Egypt – brushing off beggars, barging people – so unlike those diffident English travellers who shy from physical contact. Moving more like a horse than a man. Not the sort of person to make allowance for his companion's lame foot. Never was.

Indeed, Bankes has not altered at all. He is more conscious of the changes within himself.

After his precipitate arrival, his old acquaintance had demanded they spend the whole of the previous day in the Doge's Palace, declaring most paintings flaccid, meretricious or affectedly lachrymose. That Canaletto was just 'a picture book artist', apparently, and Francesco Guardi much better, an opinion offered, he suspects, because Guardi was so less well known.

Then Bankes kept him up half the night talking of travels in Africa and the Levant – wonderful accounts. Stories that make him feel as if, while Bankes has lived in the world, he himself lives only at one remove – through writing.

When he told him of his own plans for South America – Bankes had been direct and immediate. His pale green-blue eyes up close into his own face.

'You should take the following. If I forget anything – I will send you a list. Gifts and bribes for those you need to suborn. Mercury – laudanum – razors. Boots of the sort they sell in Piccadilly for the wet Highlands of Scotland. You will not find anything to read unless you reach Peru, where the bookshops of Lima are well-stocked. Indeed Lima, I am told, has *everything*.

— 'The sea voyage is – of course – far longer than that you took to Lisbon. For the passage – you will need your own provisions. I would not take a woman – but if you must – and I see that you are set – then make sure to take a large zinc tub, so she can perform her toilet and ablutions. Or she will make your life an even greater misery.'

He had not liked – or dared – tell Bankes his plans to take not only a woman – who is in some ways taking him – but the monkeys – dogs – and cats. Perhaps the eagle and the fox. Perhaps even his parrots – although there must be plenty out there anyway. Like coals to Newstead.

'And then your manservant can use the same tub to wash your own clothes. In carbolic soap against the fleas. If you trust to the ship's crew for your laundry – you will set foot in this new country of Colombia – or *Columbia*, however you pronounce it – wearing nothing but a singlet for your modesty. A fine sight that would be. A *Milord* with just a shirt and a lobcock!'

Bankes had smirked, strode to the window and flung it open imperiously – letting in the Adriatic wind as if he were standing on the foredeck of a frigate already. The green *marmorino* of the room shimmered around him.

'Go soon. Go soon while it is still summer there – as it is winter here. And before you succumb to *doubts*.' Turning to look at him –

look *down* at him – as he lay on the decaying sofa with his old mastiff drooling from the side of its mouth. He was conscious of the spectacle he must have presented. As fat as the old dog.

'In a New World, as it still is – and one roused by liberty to a new appreciation – the possibilities are *without limit*. Read the accounts of Inca Garcilaso de la Vega. Of Cieza de Leon.' He rolled the names sonorously. 'Telling of that New World before the Spaniards came. But never believe the account of any native you meet – unless you hear the same account from a separate personage. Find your way by instinct and by the stars.'

Bankes had always led him astray – the godfather of all mischief. At Trinity he had introduced him to choirboys – gambling – and sodomy. He was two years older than Byron and still it feels he will always be the senior.

'If you get fever – cease travelling and find a local woman who knows a remedy. Record everything meticulously. Come, let me show you.'

Bankes had excavated in one of the capacious carpet bags strewn on the floor of the *piano nobile* since his first arrival. He pulled out a pile of manuscripts and spread them on a table – first wiping away any dust or breadcrumbs that had escaped Fletcher's notice.

'Look. Here – I have noted every last stone of antiquities I saw in the Valley of the Kings. The exact heights of obelisks. The markings. Belzoni may have written his name on the wall of the burial chamber at Chephren – as the first person to enter – but what matters is *observation*. Not *ownership*. "Survey mankind from China to Peru."

— 'What you see today may soon be gone. Remember those mounds at Troy you told me of. Look around in Venice. A dying city. A city in decay.

— 'You may – you *will* – encounter and find things in South America that have *never* been written about. When you went to Greece, all you were doing was follow in the footsteps of other writers – carving your name in the stonework, like a schoolboy adding his initials to a desk. But out there, you will have a *tabula rasa*. A blank canvas, like the English painter we saw down at the quayside painting the light across the lagoon.

— 'I might even accompany you.'

This was a statement, not a question. 'I have long wanted to see the pyramids of Peru. The streets and palaces of Cusco, so fine in their day they put Seville to shame. Streets so clean you could eat an orange off the pavement. That's what the chroniclers say.'

He had nodded. He had never read those chronicles – or heard of Garcilaso de la Vega. But he did not betray his ignorance to Bankes; and it was an ignorance that would be swiftly amended.

Now, as they stride through the Rialto, Bankes turns briskly. 'For the Tintoretto, we can cross the bridge or take a boat?'

But before he can reply, Bankes has engaged a gondolier and indicated that he, Byron, will pay the fare.

In some ways they are reassuring and familiar – yet the old leather trunks covered with dust and dirt – are those *owl droppings?* – fill her with dismay. A cloud of small moths fly up when they are opened. The bodies of others lie scattered across her mildewed clothes. A fine shawl has holes in it from the moths. The trunks have been lying in the Count's attic since she arrived as a young bride. It has taken persistence from both her and Fanny even to find them in the face of intransigent disapproval from the Count's own servants.

The trunks have always travelled with her, from her family home to the convent school at Faenza and the years boarding at Rampi's – Madame Rampi with her insistence on *une éducation forte* – 'a young lady *of any education* should speak French.' Back home to Ravenna – and then, in a bewilderingly short time, here – to the Count's large, dark mansion, where as a bride she was expected to follow intricate expectations and *rules* he had elaborated over two previous marriages.

Inside the first trunk she discovers a few possessions from home and school – an old family Bible, rosary beads, some textbooks on rhetoric and grammar. The Bible and rosary beads will not come with her. It is unlikely the bishops and priests of South America will receive her with warmth, as a runaway wife – and now the companion of a poet supposed to be the devil incarnate.

But other things can certainly come. She imagines one cannot obtain Italian books easily in the *terra incognita* to which they are travelling. Or for that matter anything much – perhaps she should take more trunks? She will ask Fanny to obtain some.

She opens everything in her room – her *armoire*, her desks, the cabinets beside the bed, the heavy cupboards that line one wall, so that their doors all stand open, at an angle – as if with wings ready to fly.

It is easiest to start with books. The whole of Dante – of course. The leather-bound edition her father gave her before she went to college. Pietro Aretino, whose 'immoral books' she had left in the trunk in case the Count disapproved – as he most likely would – though the Count is hardly in a position to judge other men for immorality. The *Animali Parlanti* of Giambattista Casti, as she liked the conceit of a parliament of animals who could talk.

So what else?

She has many of *caro Giorgio*'s own books. But she decides to leave them behind – as they are in English. He will doubtless bring them anyway – and think it *absurd* of her to be reading them. Of course, he will be bringing many books on his own account – has threatened to bring the complete ninety-two volumes of Voltaire, as essential for travel. It is hard to tell sometimes when he is serious.

More appealing is Madame de Stael. A copy of *Corinne,* bound in faded purple plush, hidden beside the bed – in a drawer the Count had never dared to open. Although what if he had? He would have read a story about a young Scottish Lord and his love for a beautiful Italian poet – although he might also have read Byron's inscription. She reads it again – needlessly, as she knows it well.

My dearest Teresa – I have read this book in your garden; – my Love – you were absent – or I could not have read it. – It is a favourite book of yours – and the writer was a friend of mine. – You will not understand these English words – and *others* will not understand them – which is the reason I have not scribbled them in Italian – but you will recognize the handwriting of him who passionately loves you – and you will divine that over a book which was yours – he could only think of love.

In that word beautiful in all languages – but most so in yours – *Amor mio* – is comprised my existence here and hereafter. – I feel that I exist here – and I fear that I shall exist hereafter – to what purpose – you will decide – my destiny rests with you – & you are a woman nineteen years of age – and two years out of a Convent. – I wish that you had stayed there with all my heart – or at least that I had never met you in your married state. – but all this is too late –

I love you – and you love me – at least you say so – and act as if you did so – which last is a great consolation in all events. – But I more than love you – and cannot cease to love you. – Think of me sometimes when the Alps and the Ocean divide us – but they never will – unless you wish it…

Corinne – with the question Madame de Stael asked, 'Ought not every woman, like every man, to make a way for herself according to her nature and talents?' – and its loathing of the dull domestic duty which could prevent any woman from doing just that.

On the floor are empty hat boxes – which remind her. Should she bring some? – Byron is bringing a fur cape. And his Hussar uniform.

Some pale sarsenet dresses for the heat, as she likes the feel of the light silk across her body. Though while the elaborate sleeve puffs are newly fashionable in Italy, would the style have reached the Americas? Well it would now...

Her sky-blue riding habit, of course. Both saddles – one embossed with the family crest, a present from her brother. She had hoped Pietro could join them, as an ardent revolutionary eager for such an adventure. But he wants to stay with their father and force the Austrians out of Italy. She fears for him sometimes.

Her riding boots, which Fanny has polished to a fine sheen so the leather is as smooth as peach. And her other shoes. She should bring plenty of shoes. And *more boots*. Who knows if there are cobblers in Colombia, or wherever they find themselves? She needs ones with subtle elevation.

It is all more difficult and complicated than at first appeared – when she had pressed her *caro Milord* at a propitious moment, as they lay together at the inn on the way from Ravenna to Venice – the idea he had toyed with – as with many of his projects – but which could be made to happen.

He once told her that a man's choices were only limited – by his imagination. She had reminded him of this. How else had their own attachment begun? Their carriages travelling separately in the way convention demanded – though annoying how the other guests at the inn had included, by complete coincidence, none other than Countess Benzoni. The greatest gossip in Venice and with her own *salon* to dispense the tattle. But it is to escape such attentions – and whispers – and inquisitions – and insinuations – that she wants to leave for the other side of the world. Enough is enough.

Fanny bustles in, already talking, as much to herself as to her mistress.

'They will no longer cook for us. I will make you some broth myself. And then we should leave, Contessa. Let us go to Venice. As soon as we can. *Prontissimo!* Have you decided what I should pack?'

'No. It is too difficult to choose.'

'It is not difficult, with respect, Contessa. Bring everything!

—'I do not think you will ever return to this place. I will bring linen bags from your father's house, and I will scent them with the lavender and rose petals from his garden for the sea journey, and then when we arrive you will have clothes that always remind you of Ravenna.'

Captain Brigstable surveys the unlikely-looking spectacle.

On the quayside are four mules, each of them carrying leather trunks that look to the captain of the *Santa Rosa* as if at maximum capacity – almost two hundred pounds an animal, he suspects. He is a keen judge of weight and ballast.

Then there are four smaller trunks already placed down on the quay. A large canteen arranged on its side so cutlery does not fall out. A zinc tub for bathing. This last draws his displeasure and concern. A bathing tub on board is an incongruity that will cause annoyance both in its storage and deployment.

Two trestle beds have been erected, presumably while his passengers awaited the boat. On one of them lies a pale-faced Eng-lishman, with short black hair, a striking profile and high black riding boots prominent as he lies facing the waterline. From the slight bend in the mattress it is clear the man, who he presumes his principal client, is not light.

On the other bed sits – more sedately – a young woman with light hair and a dark complexion, wearing fine clothes that are unsuitable for travelling by sea. She is cradling a bulldog and a small child in a yellow organza dress, who stares solemnly at him across the water.

A tall and lean man in an old blue coat is sitting on a folding camp stool nearby, leaning forward as if inspecting the boat as it arrives.

Behind them – as though in conference or on stage – stand a burly manservant with a florid face and a maid. Behind this group again is a young pageboy sitting on a wine crate of the sort used to transport claret or Cahors from Bordeaux, filled with books; the boy presumably there to say goodbye to his mistress, as he does not figure on the cargo list of passengers.

More bedsteads have been leaned against a nearby wall, ready for departure, along with some large canvas sacks which bulge in different and suggestive ways. There are high narrow saddles which he recognises as English ones. But what draws the captain's attention most – and his concern – is the quantity of livestock. Dogs – cats – several birds of a sort he does not recognise – and, to his *particular* alarm, various monkeys.

He descends to the quayside to remonstrate. Or supplicate.

'My lord – my most humble apologies – but you must understand my crew will not – will never – accept such animals on board.'

He knows of old the answer this is likely to provoke – and the English Lord turns a sardonic, hard eye towards him.

'The monkeys? As I presume all sailors will welcome cats – and tolerate dogs. We can of course leave them behind. They have many admirers in Venice. Fletcher, can you take them to the Countess Benzoni?

— 'That may delay our departure a little – although you have already delayed it somewhat, Sir, by your late arrival, although I understand the contingencies under which you operate at sea. My grandfather was a sailor. Jack Byron.'

This comes with a sharp look for recognition. Captain Brigstable has little interest in naval history, only in current requirements and contingencies, so does no more than nod his head slightly, as if in acknowledgment.

'Your delay is anyway immaterial, as we are awaiting the baggage.'

The captain gives a bemused wave around them.

'But this is the baggage – I presume – my Lord?'

'No, no,' said the Lord thus addressed, with an amused glance at the tall man sitting on a chair, who is still appraising the captain and his boat in a way that speaks of both familiarity and judgement. 'These are just the travelling requirements of myself and my companion, Mr William Bankes.' At this, Bankes gives a slight nod in the captain's direction.

'The Contessa's baggage has yet to arrive – with all her linen too – and let me assure you it will make this seem – a mere *bagatelle*!'

For the first days of the journey, he stands often at the mizzen shrouds, staring out over the waves. Sometimes Moretto sits patiently beside him on the deck, ears pricking whenever a distant seagull skims the waves – but otherwise he is alone. He does not like being an object of curiosity – either for those other passengers whose company he will have to bear until Gibraltar – before they depart further across the Atlantic to South America – or for the crew themselves.

Not that the sailors pay him much attention. They are more concerned with a perpetual game of abel-wackets, in which, to the amusement of all present, the loser is struck on the palm with a heavy knotted rope – the same rope used to measure the speed of the boat 'in knots' by paying it out in the wind to see how many fly up. The business of the game itself seems largely irrelevant. They play the cards with such speed and ferocity he has never ascertained the rules. Nor dare ask. What matters is the *punishment* for the loser – and that they should laugh off the loss and the blow.

He stands closer to overhear their conversation – not hard, as they bellow at a volume that would overcome a full force gale, let alone the gentle billows of the Mediterranean.

'Strange fish indeed on board this ship. Captain Queerness and Captain Sharp. There's scholars and coggers and cheaters, and ones that will cag for months before they die of the barrel-fever when they get ashore.'

The most voluble of all is a young man from Cork, scarred ferociously on his cheek when he had been chalked, according to Fletcher, in a fight outside a pub.

They tell tales of 'air and exercise' – of beatings, prompted by one just carried out before all hands for some minor infringement – and of a man 'being in his attitude' when drunk. He will use that phrase with Bankes. 'Perhaps you have forgotten the events of that occasion,' he will say, 'because you were *in your attitude*.'

He had his hair cut before leaving Venice and his whiskers removed. They had been a mistake. Fletcher performed the operation with a mixture of reluctance at standing in for a barber – and pleasure at restoring his master's appearance. Now he feels the sea breeze sharply on his shorn face and neck; his senses quicken. Ever since he had first taken the Lisbon packet and left England, all those years ago, his senses have always quickened at sea.

Turning, he sees Teresa towards the other end of the ship. She holds Allegra carefully within the folds of her fine Venetian cloak. They shelter in a lean-to the captain and his crew have cobbled together – in a considerate way – below the bridge and to starboard, so to the lee of the prevailing winds. Even so, there is plenty of what sailors describe as 'weather'. He has often thought it remarkable how women keep their clothes intact and clean in conditions which would leave a man's in tatters.

It is at Teresa's insistence they have brought Allegra. He thought perhaps she should stay at the convent school – or return to her mother – although Claire Clairmont was such an odd-headed girl – with the wild spirit that had attracted him – he had not liked the idea of entrusting Allegra to her care, or to that of Shelley. Though was South America the place to take a small child?

But, as Teresa argued, if Allegra was prone to the malaria common around the Adriatic – the doctors had worried she might die from the last attack – and her English constitution gave little protection against such diseases, any more it did him – better to take her away. Although at times she does not seem that English – speaking nothing but Venetian – reciting her Catholic rosary taught her by the nuns – and saying 'Bon *di* Papa' to him in a droll way. He thinks she has a good deal of the Byron about her already. Is that good or bad?

Allegra calls Teresa '*Mammina*' – perhaps easier as she cannot pronounce her 'r's – and frowns and pouts in a way that reminds him of his sister, Augusta. She has the same blue eyes – light hair growing darker daily – a dimple in the chin – a scowl on the brow – white skin – sweet voice – and a particular liking of music – and of her own way in everything. Was it any wonder she reminds him so much of himself?

He feels pleased – overjoyed – Allegra is with them. It had been worth it just for the look on Bankes's face when he told him that, along with everything else – he would be bringing a three-year-old girl.

Bankes had given him the sardonic glance which always prefigured one of his barbs.

'So – *your cheeks once paled from early riot – have bloomed in calm domestic quiet.*'

As Bankes knows well, there is nothing he detests more than having his own poetry quoted back at him – unless it is to have his poetry *misquoted*, particularly as it would appear churlish and priggish to point this out.

'Not quite what I wrote. But I agree with the sentiment, if not the source.'

And he does.

Late one afternoon, as they near Malta and see the lights of Valetta – the sailors say they feel a barrel-fever rising – his own spirits lift and he goes to surprise Teresa in their spacious cabin with its wide windows looking aft.

'Did you know I have my own list of rules for you?'

'Really, my lord?' She arches an enquiring eyebrow at him. 'And what rules might those be?'

'My own rules are these,' he says, punctuating each with a luxurious and stolen kiss.

'First, you should stay in bed at least until noon – particularly if with your lover and loyal *cavalier*.

— 'That you can – if you like – read aloud a passage from Dante or Petrarch – or whichever poet you choose – in the hour before sunset, which we are approaching now.

— 'That on no account should you spend *too much time* on household matters – as intrinsically dull.

— 'That separation from you inconveniences me greatly – in ways you understand.' This said with his hand up her petticoat.

She pushes him gently away, although not far.

'Perhaps I shall have my own rules for you as well.'

'And what *rules* might those be?

'I won't tell you yet. You will have to wait to see – what they are.' And she laughs in his face.

It had been the Count's lists that had infuriated her most. – His *rules*.

He remembered once waking in Venice from a delirium brought on by malaria – to find Teresa on one side of the bed and Fletcher on the other – with her waving the paper of 'conditions' at him – drawn up by the Count to ensure her *complete docility*, as she put it.

'*Rule One*,' she almost shouted – Fletcher's presence causing her not the slightest hesitation – '*Let her not be late in rising, nor slow over her dressing, nor fussy over lacing and washing.*'

Teresa's expression was so aggrieved – and the rule so *nugatory* – he could not but laugh, albeit a weak, sickbed laugh – which infuriated her more. She read out the rest – some seventeen rules – from household matters to how she should compose herself with the Count during the day. That she should not be '*conceited or impatient*' – that she should be '*prudent in her economies – and satisfied with her rooms and furniture*'.

One clause in particular caught his attention – from the concentrated fury with which Teresa read it aloud. She was allowed '*to submit her own views and reflections, sweetly, modestly and tentatively,*' and even answer the Count's arguments. '*But – if my arguments do not convince her, she shall refrain from insisting, and yield with...*' – Teresa's voice rose to a crescendo – '*good will and good temper*'. Words spoken with less than good temper already.

How little the Count knew his young wife. And how hopeful, when he declared, '*you can easily change your adult habits, which have only lasted a few years, but I cannot change mine – for they have lasted more than forty!*'

Towards the end, the Count got to the crux – the sticking point – the very matter – of *The Rules*. Teresa waved the paper at them both. Fletcher took a step back from the bed.

'*That she should receive as few visitors as possible,*' – meaning in particular, of course, any passing British Lords – '*be completely docile and...*' – buried away at the end – '*give no one else preference over her loving husband*'. What an Italian formulation.

The Count had in effect given his Contessa a clear alternative – her husband or Byron – to which she had replied instantly. She said that in that case it would be – Byron! As the Count should have realised, the lover generally having the preference in these matters – and no woman likes being put in the position of making *a final decision* when a useful ambiguity could have continued.

Later, she had sent the Count her own list of rules, magnificent in their insolent brevity.

'CLAUSES IN REPLY TO YOURS,' she had styled them, like a lawyer – beginning –

Clause 1 – *To get up whenever I like* –

Proceeding to dismiss his requests with further insolence – demanding he give her a horse with everything necessary – including a riding habit, in the colour of her choice – and ending, underlined forcibly –

Clause 8 – To receive – without discrimination – *any visitor I want.*

When the Count came to him, crying about it – he told the man that if he abandoned his wife, then he, Byron, would take her undoubtedly – both as a duty – and through *strong inclination*. That Teresa deserved happiness.

The Count waved this aside as an irrelevance – and curious conceit – but made it clear, without the slightest embarrassment, that for a suitable loan – and Byron's recommendation to the British Government that the Count become British Consul in Ravenna, with an honorarium – a proposition so preposterous he almost laughed in the man's face, not least the idea the British government would follow any recommendation of his! – but had acquiesced out of the politics and humour of the situation – that, *if all this would occur*, the Count would, graciously, relinquish his wife.

Although for the sake of honour, he said, the Count needed them to 'pass over the Alps' – to leave the country forthwith. Or at least when their affairs were in order. And when Byron had made that letter of introduction for him.

To John Cam Hobhouse, from George Gordon Byron

Gibraltar, January 28th, 1820

My dear Hobhouse – We have been sadly flea-bitten at Gibraltar – the dirtiest, most *detestable* spot in existence. So much so that we have elected to stay on the ship while in harbour.

We sail tomorrow, I hope, south to the island of La Gomera in the Canaries before attempting the Atlantic passage – having been detained by lack of wind and other necessaries.

Those being at last procured, by this time tomorrow evening we should be embarked on 'the *vide vorld of vaters vor all the vorld* like Robinson Crusoe' – if so be that our Capt. Kidd – one Captain Brigstable – our gallant or rather *gallows* commander understands plain sailing and Mercator, and takes us on our voyage according to the chart.

For my part, I have no wish to see the tight little island of Britain ever again.

Address to me at the port of San Sebastian in Gomera.

– yrs. most truly – Byron

Hobhouse would still not want him to go. None of his friends would. But by the time he gets a reply they will be underway.

When they wake the next day, the water in the port is preternaturally calm and he can hear Spanish voices carrying across from the quay.

'You're miraculous,' he says, brushing back a strand of her light hair and tucking it behind her ear. '*Miracoloso*. Or should that be *miracolosa*?'

'*Miracolosa*, with an *a*. You should know that. Unless you want to be waking up with a boy. In which case it would be *miracoloso*, with an *o*.'

She pauses.

'So do I have your promise? On your honour as an English gentleman and a *Milord*?'

'What promise?'

'That is not encouraging. Your promise you will write no more of *Don Juan* after these first four cantos.'

'You have my *unwilling* promise – as I do not believe, in the way Murray believes, that the British public is so scandalised as to ostracise me – or us – from any further social encounters as punishment for Johnny's exploits. And I have no intention of ever again *being* in British society. Will the ladies of Colombia not talk to us because of my scandalous writing? I doubt it.

— 'Moreover you are confusing *my* Don Juan, who is more sinned against – or at least sinned *with* – for the Don Giovanni of the Opera who has such a reputation as a seducer. My Juan is a great deal younger and an innocent in a complicated world – whereas Don Giovanni is a sophisticated, much older libertine at large. You see, with *Don Juan* I am true to Nature in making the advances come from the females.'

'Are you suggesting, my Lord, I made advances to you – rather than being the hapless victim of your intrigues and English cunning?'

'Not at all. You were lodged in a tower at Ravenna and I rode up on my horse to rescue you. A hapless princess.'

'Did you, *Milord*? That sounds improbable. Although I am glad you consider me a princess – or perhaps it suits you to forget I was – and am – a *Countess* – with the attendant inconvenience of a Count. Who at one point petitioned the Pope to put me in a convent because I was associating with an undesirable English *Milord*, who was not only a foreigner – but a Protestant.'

'*La mia amante*. I forget nothing. *Niente*. And if it pleases you, I will pause in the adventures of my Don Johnny, not least as we are about to begin our own. As long as you allow me to ask you at some stage if you will reconsider.'

'That I will grant you. Although it will be *un miracolo* if I do. A miracle, so *miracolo*, with an *o*.' She does an '*o*' with her mouth. And bites his finger.

He can hear the business of the ship about them as the seamen make the ship ready to sail. Orders bellowed. Crates being lowered heavily on deck, then dragged across it.

Her *appetites* – he swore no one could consume a peach with more zest. In the past, he had disliked the sight of a woman dining – had proclaimed no woman should ever be seen eating or drinking – unless it be lobster and champagne, the only true becoming feminine viands. Which he likes himself. But he can watch Teresa eat anything.

Is it being a Catholic? Which enables her to behave with such passion and then let that passion subsume peacefully between them, like a pillow regaining its shape? Where an Englishwoman might sometimes faint – or conveniently affect one – he had never seen an Italian girl do so outright. They just called on their saints to give them strength.

The English women he has known – like Lady Oxford or others in society, let alone his wife – had acted as if any intimate act should immediately be forgotten, and more formal conversation necessary. No wonder he had so often experienced that *triste post coitum* the ancients spoke of, melancholy after the act of consummation just when he had hoped to feel elevated.

Teresa's Catholicism gives her an assurance beyond her years. There is much to be said for a religion which enables you to act as badly as you want – then have complete absolution from a priest behind the anonymity of a screen. So much better than the Calvinist crucible in which a man – or a woman – must carry their sins like a knapsack upon their back, getting heavier and heavier.

Perhaps he should become a Catholic? Now that would really annoy the Scottish reviewers at *Blackwood's*. Their batteries would be opened – but he could fire broadsides back. He would no longer be able to take the Oath of Allegiance; so would have to renounce his seat in the House of Lords. And cause a stir of the sort he enjoys. Cause an *uproar* about Catholic Emancipation – bizarre that centuries after the Reformation, Catholics should still need to hide away. He could create a scene that made the Gordon riots look tame.

He reaches over to stroke her breast; the hardened nipple. Pleasures of the flesh – perhaps if mankind spent more time in bed with their lovers, and less time frigging their consciences, the world would be a better place? Or certainly a more enjoyable one.

As they sail from Gibraltar, they pass a great thrashing of the waters where the currents from the Atlantic meet the Mediterranean. He brings Allegra out onto deck so she can see the great feeding fish, the tunny, bulk themselves out of the sea and then flop down – chasing, so Bankes tells him, the smaller fish attracted by the turbulence of the currents.

She is entranced, as he is, by the *energy* of the moment. The swirling profligacy of it all. And then later, as they sail out further through the gates of Hercules and into the wide Atlantic, by the dolphins that play around the bow.

CANTO II

To John Cam Hobhouse, from George Gordon Byron

San Sebastian, the island of La Gomera, February 12th, 1820

You must imagine – if a man full of Westminster matters still has that *capacity* – a volcano in the sea with its mountaintop perpetually wreathed in cloud.

This island of La Gomera has a volcano so high it makes any English or Scottish mountain look more like a mountebank. It is *immense* – and yet the island is small. As a consequence, by the time the folds of this volcano have reached the sea, there is little left in the way of level ground. In this way it differs from the larger island of Tenerife we see across the sound that divides them – all the Canary Islands not being far apart. Many of the others can be seen from a viewpoint high on the island that I want to go to with my Contessa – as I still call her even though her Count has been left far behind – indeed, because her Count has been left far behind.

The island furthermost west – towards the Americas – is called El Hierro, the iron one, and they tell me has a giant crater worthy of a Cyclops. Perhaps these were the distant islands towards which Odysseus and his men sailed when they passed the Scylla and Charybdis of the Straits of Gibraltar? – Certainly Gibraltar is such a dank, dismal affair – no right-minded sailor would ever want to fall into its whirlpool.

This island is full of airs and graces – and both Calibans and Ariels. The native inhabitants toil ceaselessly in the fields with their mules – a fine animal which we neglect unaccountably in Britain. Teresa finds she is more at ease riding one than the flighty and underfed horses – although the governor's uncle has lent me a black stallion normally kept for his personal use.

The Spanish overseers treat both men and mules with equal indifference – presumably in the same way that has made Bolivar's cause so attractive in the Americas.

Meanwhile Fletcher has discovered the joys of Purl-Royal – the Canary wine flavoured with wormwood – which may turn the last of his flaxen locks grey.

In San Sebastian, there are few houses of any antiquity – although this is the port from which Columbus once sailed – reluctantly, I am informed, as it took him from the arms of his paramour – Beatriz de Bobadilla, known as *the Huntress* at the Spanish court before Queen Isabella ejected her for hunting King Ferdinand too assiduously. The Huntress was sent to La Gomera, where she married the governor – who died, conveniently, killed in fighting when the natives rebelled – so she was ready for a *dalliance* with Columbus.

Rather than staying a few days – he stayed in her embrace for months. Whether his crew reacted as Odysseus's when that Greek hero *dallied* so long with Circe is not recorded – or whether they were turned into pigs for that matter. Or like Fletcher took solace in the Purl-Royal.

The natives take touching pride in Beatriz's transgressions – I wonder if they would do so if Columbus had not achieved fame?

We have been put up in the Governor's residence, for reasons which are complicated but satisfactory – as his house sits on a clifftop above the harbour and affords a fine prospect of Tenerife – and the harbour below.

He breaks off as he feels the Sirocco wind, direct from the African coast, bringing a fine dust and fierce heat. It has been blowing for days, one of the excuses the captain gives for why they cannot sail.

Teresa sits a little back from the balcony-window, out of the sunlight, using a large Venetian fan with a peacock motif to cool herself. She wears fewer clothes than usual, which he appreciates. He has also engaged a local boy to pull on the rope outside the room. This works a large ceiling fan that whirls ponderously above them and, while making little difference to the temperature, provides a soothing, peaceful sound he finds conducive to thought.

The room has a balcony which looks east out towards Tenerife across the sea; a prospect he enjoys on his own at dawn while Teresa is asleep and then together with her towards the close of the day as the air cools, when the distant mountains of that island turn purple.

He likes to rise early while Teresa is still in bed after the night's exertions and alarms – there is a bird that seems to call the hours – and write on the balcony with its bougainvillea and frangipani – a taste of the New World to come, as they tell him these flowers have been brought back by sailors on their return from the Americas. There are dragon trees in the gardens, their trunks smooth as an elephant.

He can look at the sea for hours – just as he remembers Shelley lay on his back in the Alps and stared at the clouds, to Mary's impatience. He likes to watch the waves shimmer and beckon in a way that never happened with the monotone Adriatic back in Venice. This is a long, slow, withdrawing sea which draws its strength from shores the other side of the world. The mutability of the sea, constantly changing. He feels at home on the sea, or near it, in a way he never does when far inland.

He turns back to the letter:

> I like to sit idly – surely not, you say! – on the quay and watch fishing boats as they arrive and depart. In doing so I am

merely following the customs of the place – as most of the menfolk like to line the harbour walls and discourse.

Although we are off the coast of Africa – they are more Mohammedan than African in appearance, with a lighter skin – as is apparent when the Spanish slaving ships make an entry with their cargoes. They pursue that horrific and barbarous practice with even more assiduity than our own West Indian merchants – the ships bound for their dominions in the Americas – and no Wilberforce or Burdett here to protest.

One must suppose the inhabitants share a great deal of Spanish blood that visiting sailors have left over the centuries. They are handsome in appearance – like the Othellos I saw in Venice. Bankes has – as you may imagine – already made *enquiries*.

As to the women – they seem heavy and thickset – but come alive in the Spanish manner when the opportunity for coquetry and badinage presents – to the extent Teresa feels the need to assert her domination over my own inclinations – not that she should be concerned, as I find myself curiously quiescent and uxorious.

She has flourished like a Miranda in her own island – full of noises, sounds and sweet airs. A light plays over her head that I find transfixing, and not just in the bed – a capacious one, again in the Spanish manner – although their idea of a matrimonial bed is to yoke two single ones together – as if there should always be a gap between the parties. This causes the annoyance of having the sheets in compartments, which is like sleeping with a woman and still wearing your breeches.

The Governor's Residence is so close to the clifftop that much of the garden has crumbled away – and it appears the houses of some of his predecessors perished in that manner.

When the time comes, this too will slip over the edge and a new building – in similar fashion – be built further back.

The Residence makes a fine impression from below – while still extant. This picture of the Spanish presence slowly falling over a cliff is remarkably *apt* for their precipitous decline in the Americas. Although of course not a thought I have shared with the Governor, who presumes that – as an English Lord – I have royalist sympathies and will be supporting the Spanish crown when I arrive in Colombia. A notion of which I have not disabused him.

Our ship is in the harbour below – the necessary repairs being attended to by the captain. Bankes presses him daily on the likelihood of our departure, with some asperity – but I am content to be delayed in this goodly isle – '*those were pearls that were his eyes*'.

Yours ever – Byron

One day, when the Sirocco is at its worst, he engages horses – a large handsome chestnut for him, a bay mare for Teresa which Javier – the groom – assures them is of a disposition – *muy mansa* and tame – suitable for a Contessa, and more reputable than the mules she has hitherto favoured.

They ride out on a road fringed by banana trees, with coconut palms rising yet higher above them. Vines tumble over the palisades marking out the yellow wheat fields, while ferns moistened by small clearwater springs cover the walls, and there are orchards of orange trees loaded with blossom. Higher up, he can see small chapels on hilltops that have been cleared devotedly by the islanders, with cypresses planted around them. A sylvan scene.

On the lower slopes of the volcano, grey-green agave plants are interspersed with prickly pear. When Teresa asks if the prickly pear is edible, he reminds her they may be a fruit much like a woman, said to be delicious but with prickles on the exterior.

'So unlike men, who have prickles both on the exterior and the interior,' she responds sharply.

They discover from Javier that the plant comes from Mexico.

'Those who returned brought it,' he says with an expansive gesture that sweeps towards the sea and the waves and the Americas which lie somewhere over the horizon.

They dismount so Javier can press the grey powdery mildew that lies on the cacti to reveal dead cochineal beetles beneath, which feed only on these prickly pears. 'Pinch one, so,' he demonstrates, 'and this red is like blood.'

He has heard of cochineal, but never seen it in the raw. This is the red he knows from the paintings of Titian and Tintoretto in Venice. How strange a red dye extracted from dead beetles found in the New World should transform Italian painting – from the austere style prac- tised by the early Renaissance masters to the richness that came later. That let cardinals dye their cloaks a more vivid scarlet; and soldiers parade around in cherry picker trousers.

And it is a red that comes from death – from the corpses of insects that have themselves killed the plant they feed on, for many of the cacti have become grey and desiccated from their attentions.

He at once thinks of the story he will tell Bankes on their return that evening. He asks Javier to collect some cochineal to take back.

But first Teresa, on a whim, crushes some of the cochineal beneath her fingers and smears it over her own face. Then she approaches Byron, holding him close, and smears it over his.

'*Caro mio*, now you look like one of the savages we will find in the Americas,' and the groom looks away, at first, embarrassed and unsure, but then back – with unabashed fascination as Teresa daubs her lips with cochineal and brushes against her lover's face so he, Byron, is streaked further with the red, in the way an actress paints.

As they ride further up the side of the volcano, they enter a peculiar and unexpected forest – with what appears like a sea mist hanging over it, for the volcano is often in cloud. There is suddenly a welcome coldness. It reminds him of Nottinghamshire; he almost expects to hear the rooks calling. Although here, the trees rise more than a hundred feet above them – and from the branches hang wide webs of grey moss, as if spun by an enormous spider. Javier tells them it is called *barba de la selva*, beard of the forest, a phrase he repeats to himself and enjoys as they ride.

There are other plants of profusion and oddity, tumbling into the mist on either side of the path – some poisonous and not to be touched. Most irregular of all are the giant heathers, as if the straggling plants of his youth in the Highlands have been given an elixir and transformed into trees the size of rowans.

The path narrows to an old mule track used for transporting bananas and papaya from the fertile side of the island to the more barren one. As it winds around the contours of the slope they catch glimpses of the volcano ahead.

'Does not Corinne climb Vesuvius with her lover, the English Lord?' remarks Teresa. Corinne, the independent and free-spirited heroine who believes in the power of art and literature and love; *Corinne* which is almost their novel; *Corinne* as one of the few books she has still kept on their travels, as most were so dull she gave them to Captain Brigstable; a gift he seemed to accept with polite enthusiasm.

'Indeed. As I remember, they have a long conversation on the slopes of the volcano. Or rather, Lord Oswald spends a great deal of time talking about his past – and Corinne listens with interest.'

'How familiar that sounds.'

'I hope not too familiar. And he does confide in her his *innermost secrets*, which he has told no other soul.'

'That is better and as it should be. Although sometimes I feel the secrets you tell me – are ones you have *practised* on other women. Because you tell them so well. And because you enjoy trying to shock a woman by talking of the dark depravities of your past.'

'Have I not succeeded in shocking you, *carissima*? I must try harder. Difficult to shock an Italian woman, given your Borgias and Medicis – who behaved so badly even Lady Oxford would blush – and she is a woman who professes to have seen the world.'

'And has seen Lord Byron naked – so I would have thought is *un-shockable*. For I seem to remember you telling me, when confiding your own *innermost secrets*, was she not the older woman who you led scandalously astray from her duty to her husband and children?'

He flicks playfully towards her rump with his horse switch, although gently so as not to connect, in case he flicks the horse accidentally and the mare sets off at a gallop down the slopes of the volcano.

'As so often happens – and as occurs to my Don Juan – it was *she* who led me astray. Just like the Italian aristocrat I once met at a midnight *conversazione* at the Palazzo Benzoni. Who engaged me in conversation on the balcony while her husband was with old friends inside. Who had the audacity to accept my invitation to join me in my gondola the following day.'

'Poor Giorgio. Forever led astray by the seductive powers of these dangerous women when all he wants to do – is be studious, learn Albanian and practise his pistol shooting. *La vita deve essere così dura...* Life must be so hard...'

They pause to drink water from metal flasks wrapped in wet cloth to keep them cool. This gives the opportunity to rest his bad foot out of the stirrups. After the long ascent, it has begun to chafe. They have a clear view of the cone of Gomera's volcano, which rises barren above the surrounding forest.

'I once saw Humphry Davy give a demonstration of a volcano's power in London. At the Royal Institution in Albemarle Street.'

Teresa looks blank. The names mean nothing to her. He tries harder.

'He showed how combustible potassium and magnesium emerge to the surface of a volcano – and react with air to cause lava flows that explode down the side – *un'esplosione* like the one that covered Pompeii. He did it with a small model in a most dramatic fashion. Several ladies of a tender disposition fainted.'

'I would not have fainted. Unless I was with the right companion to catch me. But this volcano,' she gestures ahead of them, 'it is long dead? There is no smoke.'

'Not dead but sleeping. Like that volcano in the East Indies which erupted a few years ago. I forget what it was called. And we are much the same. Emotions long dormant can come to the surface, suddenly, for no apparent reason.

— 'I once tried to go to Iceland to see the volcanoes. And I have seen Stromboli – but only from the sea when sailing down the Italian coast. It is a shame we could not have passed that way from Venice, as you would have enjoyed the prospect. Some of the finest swimming I have ever had was under that volcano, when the coxswain rowed me out in a jolly boat and my only companion in the water was a turtle.

— 'Shelley made a pilgrimage to Vesuvius, the lucky man, and climbed it – *at night* – with flames reaching out against the skies.

— 'I have often reflected that as citizens of the earth, we too are *volcanoes* – for we have elements within us that cannot be revealed – until we combust and overflow with emotion.'

The horses are close beside each other, with the guide a little way ahead, facing forwards, so he raises her hand in its kid glove and fixes her with a gaze unusual in its intensity, and leans towards her so he can lower his voice.

'*Io invece per te la sento proprio così.* I feel that way about you.'

Teresa blushes, uncharacteristically.

They hear mules coming towards them, bells tingling. 'How charming they should wear bells,' says Teresa, to fill the moment, and he points out they are merely to find the animals should they should get lost – as in this forest they sometimes must. The muleteers look askance at the pale English *Milord*, with his face smeared red and his equally decorated Contessa – although she tips her hat daintily over her head to conceal the marks of the cochineal, out of a modesty that is only intermittent.

And indeed, becomes more intermittent as they reach the high vantage point looking down over the other islands, which they admire, and turn to the north of the island along a coursing stream, called El Cedro after the cedars that line its banks. They stop beside the water. Once the picnic is unloaded, he dispatches Javier to a safe distance to graze the horses – with instructions not to return too soon.

They spread out smoked goat's cheese, figs, dried ham and a bread scented with wild fennel seeds, together with a carafe of white Forastera wine – Bankes has declared, in his categoric way, that wines grown on volcanic soils taste better – and then he helps himself to her as well.

She laughs and takes more cochineal from the saddlebag and smears it over him in defence, around his neck and nipples after he has torn off his shirt. And he replies in kind – threatening that unless she is naked, it will ruin her clothes – until they are covered in the red dye and must bathe afterwards in the nearby stream, and laugh as the waters run red.

In the process, and in the excitement, he has ripped her sky-blue riding habit of which she is so proud.

'Never mind,' he says when she protests, 'we will have one made for you in San Sebastian before we sail.'

And they do, using the old riding habit as a template for the new one, with a longer train so it flies up behind her as she rides. But Teresa chooses a cloth dyed from the same cochineal they had seen on the cactus and smeared over their faces, a scarlet of startling intensity, just like, in truth, one of those cardinal's cloaks.

'You will be hearing my orisons next,' he says.

'I would not be able to wear this in Venice. No respectable Venetian lady ever could. But in a new world, I might as well wear what I wish.'

She buys him red ink, *sangre de drago*, dragon's blood, made from the sap of the dragon trees, so he also can write whatever he wants, without fear of reprimand or censure.

He feels an unusual lightness within – and senses she shares that. One day, sprawled beside a river, they hear a flock of birds singing, with a lulling, swooping note – and then Teresa sees one, hopping along by the water – an elegant bird which looks as if it is wearing a grey morning suit with a bright yellow waistcoat. 'For all the world,' he declares, 'as if he were walking up to the altar in St James's Piccadilly.'

Has the canary bird given the islands their name? Or have the islands given their name to the bird? It is impossible to know. Nor does he care. But as he looks at Teresa, with her loosened hair, which is also golden, he feels a rare epiphany – a moment of pure happiness of the sort he is unaccustomed to experiencing.

He finds the black sand on the beaches of La Gomera both attractive and repellent, a mixture characteristic for him.

Just before dark, he takes Teresa along the beach closest to San Sebastian, while there is light still in the sky – being the east of the island, there is no sunset, but instead a moon rising above the mountains of Tenerife across the gulf. A full moon. A wolf moon, as they called it when he was a boy at Newstead and saw it across the moors.

He wants to see her skin gleam against the black sand by moonlight, like the black natural hair of a woman against her pale belly – a fancy which she is complicit with, indeed curious about, and he disrobes her more carefully this time, so nothing should rip, putting her fine silks on a rock. But then he tears his own clothes off with abandon – his loose white shirt, his breeches and lastly, absurdly, his white linen hat of which he is inordinately proud, as it is so much finer than the straw 'Panama' ones worn by the Spaniards.

He once had relations with an African woman in Venice, on pure white sheets, the black against the white, and Teresa's skin against the fine black sand, pressed down into it by his own white body, excites him equally. He tells her so, expecting her not to like the reference to another woman.

She surprises him, as she often does. 'And are the mulattas made –
differently – from us in the female parts?'

'The same. Although of course none can compare to yours—' but
before he can continue, she laughs and throws black sand in his face.

He pulls her protesting into the sea – protesting lightly in the way
of a woman who wants to be taken there. And after emerging from the
surf, they eat their food naked and hold glasses of wine up towards the
moon to watch the orb reflected in the liquid of the goblet, made larger
and rounder.

As so often, she has the last laugh. For when they return that night,
he finds black sand has entered every crevice of his clothes – his white
shirt stained in a way that will have Fletcher clucking like a school
matron – worse, his linen hat compromised irrevocably by grains of
black sand too absorbed within the mesh ever to be removed.

'But *Milord*,' – she calls him *Milord* only at the moments of least
respect and most familiarity – 'now you can enjoy the fine contrast of
black against white whenever you look in the mirror – and see your
hat. You will have no need of me at all.'

Bankes beckons him aside in the heavy wooden corridor of the
Governor's Residence and leads him, without speaking, to a reception
room he has not seen before. It looks formal, with a table too large to
fit comfortably into the room, as if for one of the interminable admin-
istrative sessions of which the Spaniards are fond.

The shutters are fastened with bolts, and Bankes produces a candle
which he lights from a flint in his pocket. Bankes has poachers' pock-
ets from which he often produces such useful objects. He holds the

candle under a dark portrait, made even darker by layers of grime and varnish; just visible is the face of a young girl, perhaps eighteen or so, selling oranges, with a pitcher of water beside her – and a much younger boy with an urchin's grin who turns away, as if he has seen something off the corner of the canvas. It is a small painting, no larger than a woman's dressing mirror.

'This,' says Bankes triumphantly, 'is a *Murillo*.' – pronouncing the '*ll*' ostentatiously, in the Spanish style, as a rolled '*y*'.

He looks at Bankes with an expression he often adopts with his friend, when he does not quite admit ignorance but has to supplicate for further information. As if he too is looking for something out of the corner of the frame.

'But they don't know that. So it is hanging here, in some unused room. They only know and value his religious paintings, which they can keep for their dark churches, but Murillo was also, like Velasquez, a painter of *life*.'

He is aware that Bankes has a collection of Spanish paintings at his house in Dorset; that he is one of the few to indulge in a taste for such art, when most in England prefer the Italian school with their brighter palettes. And that he is still nursing a resentment he had not bought the Tintoretto in Venice, when a price could not be agreed and it was even unclear who owned the painting in the first place.

'I will buy this,' says Bankes, with an expression he recognises from Cambridge days. An expression which, even then, before he came into his inheritance, Bankes had worn for buying horses, paintings – or for that matter the favours of choirboys. A look of acquisition.

'Buy it? But is the Governor selling?'

'I told him I wanted it for the frame,' – which, now he looks at it, is ornate in the baroque style and heavily gilded – 'that I might have it painted over with a portrait of myself, commissioned when I get to the New World, where such frames may be difficult to find.'

'So you will bring it with us? Might it not be easier to send straight to England – or collect on our return?'

Bankes gives him a sharp look, of the sort his friend reserves for a foolish question.

'We will not come back. The trade winds take us from here to the Americas.' – patiently, as if to a child – 'But the returning winds go further north, directly to England. I have learned after years of collecting – that no one takes better care of your possessions – than yourself. This picture will take its chances in the New World with me.'

Bankes holds the candle up against the painting again. There is a bowl of water on the table beside the girl in the picture. It shimmers by the light of the flame.

One night after they have set sail again across the Atlantic, a storm starts up. Teresa clings to him in alarm as the stateroom furniture is swung from side to side. Allegra shelters in their bed, her head buried in the sheets to pretend nothing is happening. Moretto and Mutz howl in alternate waves that batter the senses. Fletcher tries to lash a heavy chest to the wall, but the lighter zinc bathtub is impossible to contain and flies about the cabin with a will of its own.

'You should not be alarmed because – you will not know this – I was born in a caul.'

Teresa is not so much reassured as mystified.

'A "caul"? What is a caul? A "coal"? Or were you called to be born? Explain.'

'A caul is the sack in which a baby is enclosed in the womb – and which breaks on birth, almost always. But not in my case. To be born in a caul is exceedingly rare – and brings with it one signal piece of luck.'

'*Che cosa?*'

'That no man or woman who is born in a whole caul – can ever be drowned at sea. That is an ancient wisdom.'

Teresa is unimpressed.

'Is it? Well, I'm sure it will give us great satisfaction,' – her voice rising – 'to appreciate, as the rest of us drown – that you cannot be one of our number!'

By dawn the sea has again calmed. Bankes affects not to notice there has been a storm at all and strolls around the stern, as if exercising a dog.

But he himself is alarmed. When Captain Brigstable emerges on deck – and he asks, as a ritual between them, if the Captain has yet had his *morning meridian*, a cue for rum to be brought by Fletcher from their copious supplies – he makes circuitous inquiries.

The Captain says it may take three more weeks to reach Colombia. Or twice as long if they meet more storms and have to bear off to run with the wind.

Bankes had told him Columbus had once done the crossing from Gomera in just twenty-two days. But that was exceptional. Perhaps spurred on by his love-tryst beforehand. Beatriz de Bobadilla may have given him her Huntress's wings.

They may be at sea for a while. The storm has made him conscious of the risks to which he has exposed both Teresa and Allegra – let alone the uncertainties of what lies ahead in revolutionary Colombia.

Has he done the right thing to bring them?

He watches Bankes at a distance playing abel-wackets with the sailors. It is noticeable some of the men are hesitant, because Bankes is vicious in the way he whacks the rope over their knuckles if he wins, which he usually does.

He envies him his certainties.

When he goes back below to the stateroom, Teresa is sleeping off the storm as if she had stayed up all night for the Venice carnival, Allegra curled beside her.

It was Teresa who had been so insistent they come. Indeed, had been the only person who supported the plan; had helped initiate it as they lay together at that Padua inn, escaping the attentions of her Count.

Was it really only a year ago he had met her? At a midnight *conversazione* in the Palazzo Benzoni, the *salon* which all Venetian society attended. 'Lord Byron – let me introduce you to Contessa Teresa Guiccioli.'

She had arrived with the Count, startlingly older as her husband – three times her age. But then she was only nineteen. Twenty now. Or is she? He suspects she is creative with her birth date, as with other things.

Everything had happened so fast – in so compressed a period – only recently, with the long crossing, has he had time to reflect – to unpack all that transpired. As he lies on the broad daybed below the wide windows, in the full morning sun as it chases them across the Atlantic, he remembers that first evening. How the Count and his Countess had come on from the theatre to the *salon*. The Count swept in to meet friends – old men on dark velvet sofas. He himself had been standing by the entrance – bored, in the shadows – and when she stayed to take in the cooler air – he talked to her.

Their conversation had been shorter than he liked – as he was yet to gauge how alert or inattentive the Count would be – and it was never good to offend a rich, unprincipled Italian nobleman. The Count was said to have killed one previous wife – there had been several before Teresa – and murdered a nobleman who dared sue him – so having a foreign dissolute knifed in an alley would be light work.

His first – and fast – impressions had been accurate. She was pretty – of course – but in an unexpected way for an Italian girl, with blonde hair on olive skin, a striking combination. – And she had the bold forwardness of the *ingenue*. He could tell she could be at one and the same time a great coquette – extremely vain – excessively affected – clever enough – and yet be without *the smallest principle*. Enough complications to arrest him – and make him want to arouse in her the passion he could tell lay not far below the surface. For that she certainly had – passion, and a good deal of *imagination*.

She had already been married a year. What had Hobhouse always said? Back in London. When they were cutting *swathes* through society. 'New brides always wait a year.' Quite long enough. Particularly when – in this case – married to a husband who was sixty if a day.

Then, out of boredom and devilry – how *Blackwood's* would have felt vindicated – he suggested – as they stood on the balcony at that first meeting, close as there was little space – she come to him in his private gondola *the very next day*, during the Count's siesta. A bold dare he thought she would dismiss out of hand – and she accepted, with alacrity.

Complicated months of intrigue followed, moving between Venice and the Count's house in Ravenna. Intrigue which he liked – he relished nothing more. *Dalliance* in the reception rooms of the Count's house, knowing servants could enter at any moment – as he was entering her – delicious – and dangerous – it gives him happiness still to think of it – and *alive* in every sense, not just for the pleasure, more than ecstatic, but for the danger from those curious servants.

At first, he was only her *cavalier servente*. That strange Italian phrase, both complicit and suggestive. A man a woman took as an *'attentive companion'* – with useful imprecision as to whether a Galahad or a Lancelot – a faithful knight or a faithful lover. In either case, it was for the husband to decide to ignore. And for the woman to initiate.

But shortly after it began, they had both been – what? Surprised by love? Betrayed by love? Something that started as *amatory business* – a thing apart – had turned into something else.

In Ravenna, they read *The Divine Comedy* together from the same book, like Francesca and Paolo. And although those lovers of Rimini – who Dante placed in Hell – had been *sufficiently naughty*, Teresa and he made sure to be a good deal worse. That day they read no more.

Of course he realised then – realises still – she could be trouble. Has always sensed that since the first meeting. Part of the connection between them – the *attachment*. That she could be imperious and *exigeante*, as Italians say. That there would be quarrels ahead. That she might deliberately flirt with other *cavaliers* to encourage his jealousy; had certainly done so.

She reminds him sometimes of an Italian Caroline Lamb – but a prettier, not so savage Caro. She has the same aristocratic disdain of public opinion – without the *mad recklessness* that had made Caro impossible.

Teresa's convent education adds spice to the various occasions. It has left her not at all innocent – or innocent in ways that make him laugh – and well versed in Dante. She can recite much of *The Divine Comedy* by heart; and has brought her Dante on the ship. He can see the book now beside their bed. He likes – no, adores – to listen to her cadences of *ottava rima*; how she rolls her 'r's in a way no English tongue could manage. To be called *caro Giorgio. Car-r-r-o Giorgio.*

His letters to her in Italian, when they had been apart – he in Venice, she in Ravenna – had a naked sentimentality he could never have exposed to the cold light of English prose. Like a schoolboy – with a schoolboy's jealousies and concern this could be the only love of his life. *L'ultima mia passione* – 'my final passion'. He had not felt like this since certain schoolboys at Harrow.

Forse se ti amassi meno, non mi costerebbe tanto a spiegare i pensieri miei…

Perhaps if I loved you less, it would not cost me so much to express my thoughts…

She had returned that emotion – at great risk. Many an Italian married woman found herself in a nunnery for breaking the conventions of a *cavalier servente*. Let alone a countess. She had been brave on his behalf – was being brave now.

And he had loved her even more because she was vulnerable. Not just because of her Count who might have turned vicious in a moment. But she gets ill, frequently. At times, he feels concerned – and worries she may go the way of everything he had ever cared for. Like everything for which he has felt real attachment. 'War, death, or sickness did lay siege to it, making it momentary as a sound, swift as a shadow, short as any dream.' Blown away by some arbitrary storm – that might arrive at any time. Just as little Allegra had come so close to dying in Venice.

He watches Teresa as she sleeps during the day, catching up on all she lost during the turbulent night, with the small child in a blanket beside her. It occurs to him he has never spent so much continuous time with a woman before. There had always been *interludes* – many necessary, given the inconvenient presence of husbands; and some welcome, given the ferocity of female desire and conversation. As with Caroline Lamb.

But with Teresa, he finds he enjoys the simplest of pleasures that had previously eluded him. Waking beside her and feeling her body next to his, as the ship rocks them together. The rhythm of her breathing. Her Acqua di Santa Maria Novella perfumes which he can smell suffusing the stateroom with cedar, lavender and bergamot.

'And what did the elephant do next?'

Allegra is insistent – although she knows the answer perfectly well, as he has told the story every day since the storm.

'The elephant started throwing things with his trunk.'

'Like this?' She hurls some toys out of the zinc tub, now lashed to the deck as a temporary nursery and with only a few dents from its night in the tempest. The metal sides catch the light so it reflects around them – and dazzles – as the ship shifts in the sun with the waves.

Allegra enjoys throwing the toys. Sometimes Mutz will collect them back for her, if the dog has been allowed on deck. He tucks her Kaleidoscope into his Marseilles vest for preservation, as he knows how upset she would be if it were lost in the melee she is creating. One of Brewster's new Kaleidoscopes, all the rage in Venice before he left – and too fragile for ejection from the tub.

'The elephant bellowed.'

Allegra bellows.

'And then the Austrian soldiers —'

'How many?'

'And then a *great many* Austrian soldiers advanced along the quay – with the gondoliers watching from the water – and tried to get the elephant to go into a sort of Noah's Ark they had lashed to the jetty for just this purpose.'

'But there would need to be two elephants to go into Noah's Ark.'

'If you keep interrupting I won't finish the story. But you're right – and that's why the elephant wouldn't go into the Ark on his own.'

He is sitting curled up in the zinc tub beside her, in his vest and loose nankeen trousers, so he can demonstrate with toy soldiers and a model boat that Captain Brigstable has lent them, used to instruct midshipmen in the setting of sails.

'Instead the elephant chased at the soldiers…'

Allegra has been waiting for this. She crawls screaming round the tub until she comes nose to nose with the toy soldiers.

'…And the soldiers were so frightened they fell off the pontoon and into the water…'

Allegra knocks them over.

'…where the gondoliers rescued them.'

'Did the soldiers have to pay the gondoliers?'

'Yes. Everyone *always* has to pay gondoliers.'

'Were they very, very wet?'

'They were very, very wet.'

'And what happened to the elephant?'

'That I don't know.'

But he does know – and after passing Allegra the Kaleidoscope, so she can put it to her eye and scan the horizon like the captain, he remembers that day in Venice.

When Tita – such a fine, feminine name for a hulking man – had taken him out in the gondola – and he had fallen asleep to the gentle sound of Tita's blade sliding artfully through the water, in the agreeable way to which he was accustomed.

As they passed the Riva, the devil's own row had broken out – for that was when the large bull elephant had broken loose, its trunk swinging over the water.

How the beast had escaped was a mystery. Another gondolier nearby – they queued up to watch the spectacle – informed Tita, perhaps with exaggeration, perhaps *not* – that the animal had consumed the contents of a fruit shop – lashed out at a keeper so badly it might have killed him – and – the detail both gondoliers agreed most shocking – broken into a *church*. Which church was unclear.

The elephant was taking amusement in flinging great beams of wood in all directions, becoming more furious at the efforts made to contain him – and displayed the most extraordinary strength. He pulled down all before him, like Samson in the temple.

After the Austrian soldiers had tried to catch him – and *failed,* to Allegra's delight – there was a stand-off, as in a prize fight, while the elephant quietened and bided his time, and everyone kept a distance. A stand-off that would last for a while.

He had left. But later, Fletcher told him the elephant had been killed, at last, by a cannon brought from the Arsenale. The first shot missed but the second entered – and then, Fletcher added, to show his intelligence was *detailed* – made its exit through the skin of the beast's shoulder. '*A mortal wound.*' Furthermore, the reason the elephant had gone mad in the first place was that 'my Lord, it is the *rutting* month' – how Fletcher caressed the phrase – 'and He went mad for want of a She' – this last said with studied deliberation.

He still feels an unconscionable anger well up at the thought. How this elephant should have been so constrained – its power and majesty diminished – by pygmies who like the Lilliputians in Swift were trying to contain their Gulliver. And had shot him.

'Do you want to see through my telescope, Papa?'

'Of course.' He takes the Kaleidoscope and twists it to see the colours rotate against the sun.

'Mr Johnson, Sir, would you say that if a man is tired of the sea, he is tired of life?'

He puts his hand inside the top of his frock coat and tries to sound both pompous and profound at the same time.

'Well, Mr Boswell, I would say this. That if a man is tired of the sea – he is probably looking forward to port.'

'That is very good, Sir. I will write it down.' Bankes pretends to scribble on the ship's rail.

'Moreover, I would declare – I would rather be in London for an hour than on the Atlantic for a week. Or for that matter three weeks. After a while the *prospect* of waves can pall. It is not a view that commends itself to more than a single glance.' The ship gives a lurch sideways in the Atlantic swell and his weaker foot slips slightly, but he regains his posture and stares fixedly ahead to where a thin grey sky rests between the clouds and a rolling sea.

'And what, Sir, do you think of the recent efforts of Lord Byron? Would he be worthy of inclusion in your *Lives of the Poets?*'

'Lord Byron!' he snorts. 'Sir, I have the good fortune to be long dead, so as not to have to contemplate such an inclusion and the questions it might present. But should I have to consider the merits of his writing – I would conclude that the noble Lord has at least the grace to acknowledge the *superiority* of Pope, which is more than many of his upstart contemporaries in the Lakes – who not only would I exclude from my *Lives of the Poets*, but, in Mr Southey's case particularly, consign to the deepest pit of the literary inferno.'

'Is that not harsh, Sir?'

'Harsh? The man presumes, Sir, without the talent to merit the occasion or his position.' He gives a mild snort of satisfaction at the neatness of his own epigram. 'And the notion that he should be a Poet Laureate? An absurd post – which merits no due consideration whatsoever – held by an absurdity. Come Sir, have a care not to provoke me.

— 'The morals and character of Lord Byron do not bear *scrutiny*. But then nor do those of many of our most admirable writers. Richard Savage, who I knew well, was a fine writer but a terrible man. Rochester even worse, and yet wrote the most tender of lyrics. However, one thing for which Lord Byron must be commended. I gather he kept a bear when a member of Trinity College? – an estimable achievement.'

'Some have compared you to a bear.'

'I am not sure if *some* have – but *you* have, Mr Boswell, in your five-volume *Life of Samuel Johnson* available from all booksellers in Piccadilly, from which I understand you have made a pretty profit.

— 'I could not help noticing, also, how in your recollection of our conversations you take a certain *liberty*. You have improved the tone and tenor not only of what I said – but of how you might have replied. I imagine the same might transpire to Lord Byron if one of his close companions – say, Mr William Bankes, although he sounds *highly* disreputable – chose ever to commit his memory to paper…'

But Bankes is suddenly impatient of the game. In addition, he has just seen what he thinks a frigate bird skimming a distant wave, a sign landfall cannot be far away.

To John Cam Hobhouse, from George Gordon Byron

Cartagena, Colombia, April 21st, 1820

My dear Hobhouse – or should I now say *Honourable Member* – we have crossed the Atlantic – to the Americas – and are in the new Carthage! Cartagena *'de los Indios'* to be precise – though no Hannibal is here.

Even Bankes does not know why they called it so. A Carthage to hold against the Roman Empire of Europe perhaps? – Cartagena – The great port of entry for Spain to the Americas – or perhaps soon of *exit* for the Spaniards – is in the part of Venezuela they now call 'Colombia'.

A large marsh surrounds the city which makes the air fetid and unhealthy. We may not stay long before we remove ourselves inland as – if we are not taken off by the sword – we are like to march off with an ague in this mud-basket. It is one thing to die martially – quite another 'marsh-ally'.

While the port remains – just – in the hands of Spanish royalists, it is unclear how much of the new country Bolivar and his rebels hold – although we suspect most of it.

We arrived in time for what Spaniards call *Semana Santa* – the week before Easter. To the delight of both my Contessa and Allegra, we have had nothing but fireworks and processions, bread and circuses. Allegra thinks this is to celebrate our own arrival – an impression I am happy to foster. She is quite recovered from the tertian fevers of Venice – but as this place has an equally unhealthy climate, I do not want to tarry long, despite its varied delights.

For the final celebrations on Easter Sunday, they decked the altarpieces with flowers so wild they would make a Hampshire parson blush. Heliconia with bright red spikes and what Bankes identified as *plumeria* – but in Italy they call *frangipani* – after the Marquis of that name who created a perfume from the flower when it was brought from the Americas. I would like to have a perfume named after me and sold in Jermyn Street – and perhaps you could have an *agreeable* soft soap named after you and your speeches.

Even the beggars dressed up for Easter – with crowns of thorns around their heads – while Pontius Pilate – a large and capacious black gentleman – patrolled the streets wearing a striped silk suit – young acolytes fanning his ample form. The apostles sat at a table laden with sweet custard apples, mango and papaya.

At sunset they hung effigies of Judas from the lamps and filled the stuffed dummies with rockets – so they explode! – though whether they put in thirty pieces of silver for the beggars to collect after they combusted, I do not know – it would have been *just*.

The Judases were disguised as Frenchmen – as the Spaniards here dislike the French heartily – understandable given Bonaparte's occupation of their country and throne – and the correct suspicion they have been supporters of Bolivar's band in their republican mischief. I have not been able to toast Napoleon in public in my usual way – you will be sorry to hear (might you be arrested again if you tried that in London?). Elsewhere in the country – where Bolivar holds sway – it is said they are burning Judases dressed as the Spanish Viceroy.

To our amusement, they found it difficult to light the Judas figures. For the straw had become so damp they burned but slowly. Allegra was much diverted by the spectacle and even Bankes managed a smile. He has much *licence* here as you may imagine. Although he is concerned the picture he acquired by Murillo may atrophy in the damp – he keeps it in a room at the top of our lodgings so the wind will blow through and not allow moisture to settle…

Perhaps, like a Judas, I am not burning well – for you must excuse the sad state of this letter – if it arrives at all, which must be improbable – so damp is the air – or *húmedo* as they say – my Spanish coming along fast, like a down-at-heel Italian without quite the spring in its step – but full of that soft bastard Latin I like so much – '*which sounds like it should be writ on satin*' – who wrote that?

So damp is the air that the ink from my pen is spreading on the paper like the aquatints my Contessa uses for her *picturesque* scenes – of which she is finding many – as Cartagena – like Venice – obliges with vistas down every alley.

Although she does not include the ladies of the street in her compositions – so must have searched hard to find a prospect which does not contain them – for they are more numerous than you may remember even in Venice. Not that a new and *upstanding* Member of Parliament would partake in such activity – or ever be upstanding in any but the most correct manner.

Yours

B.

He is swimming in the Pacific Ocean. The water is more ochre and gold – perhaps even brown – than blue. Is this because an estuary near-by feeds in fresh water which changes the colour of the salt?

After the long sea confinement – the frustration of weeks sur-rounded by water, yet unable to swim – it is good to feel his chest open out. The powerful swell lifting up as the waves surge to crash against the beach.

A line of pelicans overhead, less orderly than geese. Sometimes the line splinters, as if a military engagement when the cavalry might divide. He wonders idly – an impossibility that might become a possi-bility – what it would be like to ride with Bolivar, or the dashing commander Paez and his men? A line of horses galloping along a beach. Or across the savannah. It would, at the very least, be a good way to see the country. Hard to gauge from the royalists in Cartagena how much real fighting has taken place. Or whether resistance has melted away.

He is wary of the currents, as Bankes has told him there may be a riptide, having had *intelligence*, perhaps from the young fishermen he likes to consort with in Cartagena harbour. So it is best to swim along-side the shore, just behind the breaking waves. Alone, as Bankes –

strange for someone so adventurous – is unable to swim, however fond of recounting how he once floated in the Dead Sea.

Fletcher is waiting on the shore with dry clothes. He takes off the old nankeen trousers that have accompanied him on so many swimming expeditions, light and absorbent. He uses a velvet cloak to dry – and notices a small wader bird advance on elegant hindlegs with an acute, questing bill as if *enquiring* down the shore. If Allegra were here – or Teresa – he would laugh at it with them. But Fletcher is not of that disposition.

'They tell me there are sharks in this water.'

It is unhelpful – if characteristic – of Fletcher to mention this now, when he has finished swimming. But it allows him to affect an insouciance he would not feel if he were about to enter the sea.

'As long as they eat my bad leg – not the good one – I might even be obliged.'

From a sack, Fletcher produces a phial of Rowland's Macassar Oil so he can darken and thicken his master's hair again after the water has rinsed it.

'Your *massacre* oil, sir.'

'Indeed. Then you better go ahead and annihilate me.'

Fletcher snorts. No man can be a hero to his valet, as the Germans liked to say. But then no valet can be a hero to his master either.

She is awake. She listens to the incessant rain and the processions which carry on for days after Easter, without rhyme or reason, despite the torrent.

The natives of Cartagena enjoy the rain. They laugh and play their drums louder. But she is... *disconcerted*. She did not expect to find something so mundane as *rain* in the New World, which can at times seem oddly like the Old World – but then, at other times, be completely different.

Although Bankes has told her – or did he tell Byron and she overheard? – this is just the beginning of the season of tempests. And why the first ones receive such a welcome after the long drought of the winter. Here, the seasons move to a different rhythm, with no difference between summer and winter as far as the heat, but only in the quantity of rain.

Fanny complains the washing never dries, and of the constant dampness which seeps into her bones, she says, like mildew. But she has bought rosewater in the market and bowls of this help perfume the air better.

The market is a great pleasure for Fanny. She proclaims it better than even the Rialto for the profusion of fish and foreign wares – silks from China which have been brought first to Mexico and then down to Cartagena. Silks of a richness – and cheapness – that means Fanny herself can walk festooned with the finest of them. She has taken to wearing an orange turban wrapped round her head which Teresa thinks ludicrous – but Fanny says will make her appear more like a native when it comes to bargaining.

When the *Cartageneros* stroll along the port's walkways at sunset, as Byron and she had just done, the women show off Chinese fans, waving them with agitation when someone is close whose attention they want to attract, whether male or female. The men meanwhile are in the most resplendent of uniforms, including those, says Byron, who have not lifted a sword either for or against Bolivar – but do not let that be an encumbrance to their display of military valour.

She had not been able to resist pointing out – that his own Hussar uniform might also be said to be *unearned.* Perhaps why, piqued, he has tonight retreated to his own bedroom in their capacious house – a house far larger than most *palazzos* in Venice. She knows how sensitive he is to such imputations.

But she likes being alone inside the white muslin nets which hang around her bed to avoid the mosquitoes she can hear whining and calling beyond. She takes pleasure trapping these between her hands – for they fly slowly and uncertainly, as if they too find the air heavy and damp – and further pleasure in seeing the *mancha*, the spot of red they release when crushed – from her own blood, she supposes, although they may have fed on others before her.

Perhaps one has come from Byron's bedroom and brought his blood with it. Like that curious poem he told her about in which a flea shares two lovers' blood and brings them together. She laughs as she remembers how she covered his face with red from the cochineal beetle in Gomera. There is cochineal red everywhere here in the city, even for the cheapest of rugs and hangings, so the rooms feel rich and the views through the windows of distant cool azure-blue sea more acute.

That is by day. Now, as she looks out through the *tempesta,* the water froths black and unimaginable. She will get Fanny to buy more candles, at her market, so she can have light all around the bed.

It is a strange sensation, walking the streets of Cartagena. For no one knows or cares about her. In Venice, she could not move without whispers getting back to the Count; in Ravenna, to her family. She had felt constrained, curtailed.

But in Cartagena, there is little curiosity. The port is a place where everyone passes through from one world to another. A carousel. A portal, like the entrance to Hades. Is she like Persephone going down into the depths? And will she return? She is both free – and lost.

By day, she is drawn to the sea wall and the arches that run beneath it, each one a private space for a pair of lovers to linger well into dusk. To walk past them is to have an almost theatrical display of the attitudes of courtship – supplication, enjoyment, completion.

Byron and she find an empty arch, on a late morning of overpowering sun; the cool of the shade is welcome. They play out some of these comic tableaux – he on his knees before her with upturned gaze, as if singing; then with his arms around her, as if caught in the middle of a dance – a dance which he could never do; and finally, with an operatic gesture, as if to fling the flowers she carried against the smell of the Carthaginian sewers above the arch – so they would carry, like a bridal bouquet, towards the seagulls who might or might not catch them.

Bankes takes them to see fine merchants' houses, through old doors with bronze Islamic studs which, he says, show Moorish influence on the Spanish conquistadors – along with elaborate wooden *mudejar* balconies. Although Byron is more interested in how feasible it was for the Don Juans of the day to climb up to them.

There are clusters of white bougainvillea against walls painted either bright yellow or pale blue, both of which can dazzle in the strong sun. If the climate were more agreeable, she could imagine living in such a house, with orange trees in the patio and water playing from the fountain.

One day of that light drizzle the inhabitants call *llovizna,* a wonderfully soft, onomatopoeic word, Bankes brings them to a house painted deep turquoise, and tells them it is to be prized for its contents – unusual praise from a man so proud of his own collections. From outside, it looks just another private house, albeit a large one even by the handsome standards of Cartagena merchants.

But past a lobby lined with a startling array of nude female statues, they enter a warren piled high with books. Bankes threads his way to the corner. From a far recess, working at a desk scattered with bills, a man with a piebald face, pockmarked skin and wild grey hair flopping across his forehead rises to greet them.

Teresa is alarmed and takes a step back, knocking over a pile of leather-bound volumes.

'*No importa, no importa,*' says the man. 'I have sufficient, as you can see. Welcome to the Casa Turquesa. My name is Sangucho – like the soup – and my bookshop is at your disposal, indeed *convenience.*'

Bankes has not wasted time with such preliminaries and is already making a discovery.

'Look, here is the whole of Humboldt.' He waves at a long shelf which contains dozens of books.

'He came here,' announces Sangucho. 'Twenty years ago, when he arrived from Cuba – to this shop. Before he began his great journey to Ecuador and Peru – the journey that was to produce so much. But he did not then have the fame he later acquired.

— 'I liked him. His face was marked, like mine, by the pox, although you do not see that in his portraits. He came with Bonpland, his secretary and his' – Sangucho turns to shield his remarks from Teresa, who has anyway found a shelf of Italian literature – '*amigo especial*. His special friend.' And makes a crude gesture with thumb and finger. Both Bankes and he look askance, as if such notions could not be entertained by English gentlemen.

'We have his works in French, in German, in Dutch – but they are only starting to appear in English, so you must choose your language.'

Bankes has seized on a large volume of engravings which sits alone on a table – and needs to, given its size and weight.

'His *Atlas Pittoresque du Voyage.* I have heard tell of it but never seen a copy.'

Bankes turns the pages with the concupiscence of the collector. 'This is a book so expensive I doubt even I could buy it,' he murmurs, more to himself than the company. 'It would cost more than a Murillo or Velazquez.'

He looks over Bankes's shoulder as his friend leafs through pictures of ruins above high canyons, or of the two explorers deep in the jungles of the Orinoco River. The figures of Humboldt and Bonpland are miniscule against the landscape.

He suspects that perhaps this may be the greatest benefit of the New World – that once again man can appear small in proportion to the enormities of nature.

Teresa appears engrossed in her Italian books, just as Bankes is by the Humboldt. Sangucho takes him by the arm, in an unnervingly familiar way, and leads him to another book-lined room.

'We sell many copies of your *Childe Harold*,' says the bookseller, confidentially.

'You know who I am?'

'Of course. The copies are beautifully made,' and Sangucho reaches up to present one from the shelf. He notices, to his annoyance, that he has been positioned next to Southey. And that it has been published in bound vellum.

'But these are not Murray's?'

'They are *copias piratas*. Pirate copies that have come my way – pirate like your Francis Drake.' Sangucho laughs, with a smile that is a little piratical itself. 'There is a long tradition here of such copies – and as a result we have a profusion of books.'

He says sharply, 'So the writer – in this case *me* – receives no money from the sale?'

Sangucho shrugs, less than apologetically, almost with pleasure.

'I sell them. I do not publish them. And you are a *Milord*. Do you need the money from a few sales in a remote country?'

'Well, maybe not,' he huffs a little, aware he is standing on his pride and may appear priggish. 'But it is the *principle* as well.'

'How interesting to hear of *principles* from the author of *Don Juan*. We sell that as well – but in the cabinet of erotic literature I have in the furthest room. For those with special tastes...'

He has no wish to see those books – doubtless French – which have been designated bedside companions to his *Juan*. But it occurs to him this will be a good story to tell Hobhouse. Or tease Murray with the news. Not least because a casual perusal shows the copy has been far better made than Murray achieved back in Piccadilly.

'Tell me,' he asks Sangucho, adopting a similar tone of confidentiality, for he has always been a good chameleon in company. 'When Baron Humboldt came here, did he show any *affiliation* to Bolivar's republican cause? It is hard to tell from his writing.'

'He had to be careful – as did we all – and, *Milord*, as we all *need* to do still. Who knows if the Spanish King may return in greater force, particularly if Peru is threatened? Send an army of *reconquista* as they did against the Moors.

— 'When Humboldt arrived, those were different days. Besides, he travelled under the express protection of the Spanish crown. The Bourbons were his patrons. So he had to be, shall we say, *circumspect* in any criticisms he made.

— 'It is different today. Only now can I keep copies of Thomas Paine's *Common Sense*, of Rousseau or of Voltaire. Of Montesquieu. Of writers who the Spaniards have always suppressed.

— 'If the Viceroy was not so preoccupied with the forces of Bolivar, he might send his men over here to burn such revolutionary authors – or to obtain a private copy of *Don Juan* for his own use.

— 'You look *sorprendido*. Surprised by my shop. Perhaps you thought not to find such quantities of books in the New World? Many make that mistake when they arrive. They forget – more copies of *Don Quixote* were sold in Lima than ever were sold in Spain.'

'All *copias pirata* I suppose?' he asks with asperity.

'*Copias piratas*, not *pirata*,' corrects Sangucho mildly, with a schoolmasterly attitude he recognises from previous dealings with booksellers and publishers. 'But yes, *probablemente*, they would have been *copias piratas*. There has always been a voracious appetite for reading here, both because of the weather' – he cocks his piebald eye outside; it is raining more heavily – 'and because those who come are *dreamers – los aventurosos*. Often that is *why* they have come – they have read the Inca Garcilaso de La Vega, or travellers' tales, like Humboldt's, which fuelled their curiosity. Perhaps why you came yourselves?'

'It may be why Bankes came. I came for other reasons.'

'If you travel to Santa Fe de Bogota – to find Bolivar—'

'How do you know I have come to find Bolivar?' he interrupts.

'But of course you have. If you travel to Bogota to find Bolivar – and then on with him towards Ecuador and Peru – the journey may take months. It took Humboldt a year and a half to cover that distance – stopping, admittedly, to reflect and for *descrubrimientos cientificos*. His scientific discoveries. You will need a trunk full of books for such a journey. Perhaps you would like me to make a selection?'

'Yes,' says Bankes, who has joined them. 'I would.' Bankes is inclined temperamentally to buy anything that is offered and glances cautiously at Sangucho.

'What would your best price be for Humboldt's book of engravings?'

Sangucho turns to look at Bankes with indulgence and acuity. 'You are aware in Europe it sells for three hundred guineas.' This is a statement, not a question.

Teresa has joined them. 'You could buy a *palazzo* in Venice for that. One of the smaller ones, belonging to a lesser family.'

Bankes whispers a price he is prepared to pay into the bookseller's ear.

'Perhaps – let us talk again.'

He has listened to this with amusement and interrogates his friend with an eyebrow, more in enquiry than reproof, which would anyway be futile.

Bankes is somewhat defensive. 'I could remove and frame each engraving to produce eighty pictures – perhaps line a whole room at Kingston Lacy – a room filled also with other possessions I bring back from our travels.'

'You could,' he agrees, feeling amiable; nothing is more conducive to making a writer warm-hearted in his dispositions than to discover a book of his being sold – and sold well – in an unexpected location. Even in a pirate edition.

And one of the things he likes about Bankes is how often he makes the possible become the probable; something he wants to emulate.

To live with *every sensation* – to delight as much in a boxing match – or a gallop – or a cat stretching – or the feel of your mistress's flesh against your hand. To live in this world and beyond it – to speculate on the past and future of the world – but above all to live in the moment! To reject the *cant* and hypocrisy of that tight little island he has left behind, where happiness is measured out in prescribed spoonfuls and the gossip added with silver tongs – its draughty halls and lugubrious matrons. The more he contemplates the distant prospect of his native home – the more he dislikes the view.

Whereas he delights in the Cartagena fish market. He watches fishmongers throw huge tarpon about on the floor – tarpon who could thrust up through the water and leap clear – along with sharks and other spectacles of the sea – hammerheads; enormous squid; bright blue parrot-fish; large tunny, red snapper and a profusion of delicate, delicious white fish such as seabass.

The only fish on an English table came cooked to dry extinction and then smothered in parsley sauce as an embalming liquid. Fanny has shown the cook here how to prepare the seabass in the Italian style, baked in salt to preserve the flavour and stuffed with fennel and lemon.

Crowds of pelicans stand alongside the barefooted local boys and amuse him by the brazen way they seize on the scraps of fish they can steal.

'You would make a good pelican,' he tells Bankes.

Although there is another animal for which Bankes has an even greater affinity.

It is curious, but Bankes presents a magnetic attraction for cats. Any cat that sees Bankes on their wanderings through Cartagena will approach to investigate and purr and rub against his leg. Sangucho has also noticed this phenomenon.

When he asks Bankes, his friend pauses as if this is something he has never considered or noticed.

'Perhaps they recognise in me a fellow spirit?'

'Perhaps. Or perhaps it is not a matter of *spirit* so much as *civet.* Perhaps they smell on you some essence to which they aspire. Perhaps a wild cat once sprayed on your traveller's cloak?'

Bankes's traveller's cloak has many smells, of uncured goat, of dust and of heat, and could quite possibly contain the spray of a civet. Fletcher has tried to wash it on numerous occasions – but been beaten back.

'Or perhaps you were licked by a lion in your sleep as you lay in the Egyptian desert?'

'I have lain with both lions and lambs, as you know.'

'I know. Biblically. But perhaps also it is because you have the eyes of a cat?'

For Bankes's eyes often intrigue, being almost green and setting off his red hair. His friend turns and yawns, stretches, then yowls softly in a feline way.

'I hope your claws are clipped,' he says.

'I always retract my claws,' says Bankes. 'But you have, in your customary way, and with an excess of imagination, confused the *civet* cat, which is a particular species, with the *domestic* cat. Domestic cats such as these do not spray civet, or for that matter find it attractive. Only civet cats do. It is true, tomcats may mark their territory with a spray – but that is different – and certainly not civet.'

'I stand corrected.'

'You do.'

One game that delights Allegra is to find as many animals as possible frozen on the doors of Cartagena houses. There are lions, lizards, octopuses – even a hippopotamus – the occupants competing for the most elaborate fantasy that a door knocker and blacksmiths can provide.

Some are heavy, and would need two footmen of substantial size to lift and let go, the resulting thud reverberating through the large mansion.

'And why is that lion so high?' asks Allegra; it is true, not even a giant of a footman would reach it.

'Ah,' explains Sangucho briskly when asked, as the font of all Cartagena wisdom. 'The lion shows it is the house of a general. And the knocker is high because it is presumed that anybody visiting – would be on a horse.'

'But of course,' says Bankes. 'How stupid of us not to have realised.' Sangucho looks inclined to agree.

He notices the breasts of the mermaid knocker near their own house are worn almost to the ribs by incessant handling, whether from prurience or because they are the easiest part of the knocker for a footman to grasp.

He has started to tell Allegra a story each night before she falls asleep – begun whimsically at sea, when she has tired of elephants, and continued on land after her increasingly strident demands. Called '*El Guapo and the Saint*' – *guapo* a Spanish word meaning 'handsome' which amuses her because – *guapo guapo guapo* – it sounds like a frog croaking – the story is a bowdlerised version of his *Don Juan*; so Murray would approve. A dashing young hero meets a saintly woman, Santa Margherita, who gets involved in his adventures, saving El Guapo from the consequence of his many mistakes.

It had come about because of Allegra's interest in saints after her Catholic convent – and from his own wish to describe a real saint, not the nuns' plasterboard ones. And from her insistence, if Papa is a poet and a *storyteller* – as he had told her once and she has a retentive memory – then she should *hear* his stories. Should she not, being his daughter?

A real saint must care deeply about their fellow humans, and also animals. To Allegra's amusement, each time he told the story Santa Margherita acquired an additional animal – so she and El Guapo were soon travelling the world with cats, dogs and exotic beasts like monkeys and a bear – in a way not so different from their own. Allegra had to recall each animal at the outset – as in the game where participants extend the list between them of what they are packing to travel, each having to remember all that has gone before. One of the few he had ever played with his own mother, who liked the *accumulation* involved.

One evening, having left Allegra to sleep, he hears excited voices coming from her bedroom towards midnight and goes to discover the cause.

Allegra's face is pressed close against a jar with small holes in it, glowing with an intense light that flickers across her face.

'Should you not be asleep?' he asks, feeling an unfamiliar sense of paternal responsibility.

'I have brought her glow-worms,' says the voice of Bankes from the shadows. '*Elater noctilucus*, which the locals call *cocuyos*. Fireflies. They use them as lighting in the poorest houses where they cannot afford candles.'

'*Elater noctilucus,*' repeats Allegra, looking so solemn he bends down to whisper in his daughter's ear.

'*Glow-worms. Glow-worms* is easier and has a ring to it.'

> '*Ye living lamps, by whose dear light,*
> *The nightingale does sit so late —*'

Bankes picks up:

> '*…Ye country comets, that portend*
> *No war nor prince's funeral.*'

He looks inside the jar. The phosphorescent insects are bright against its black sides, like stars.

Bankes and he stand on the balcony at the side of the house over-looking the harbour, sharing another of Bankes's cigars. Although hours before dawn, there is a profusion of lights from the small fishing boats leaving the harbour that want to avoid each other.

'I have heard tell,' says Bankes, 'that out at sea the captains of some ships use only *cocuyo* lights from the fireflies so as not to attract pirates, as they are bright enough to see around a ship – but not so bright as to be visible from too great a distance.'

'Indeed. I will remember that – should it ever prove of use.'

'Did you know some of the sparks emitted by the fireflies are for the purpose of mating – for attracting individuals of the other sex?'

Bankes pauses for a moment to see if he too has attracted attention.

'And of course,' – when Bankes says 'of course', it is to indicate that it is only obvious to Bankes – 'you realise female fireflies sometimes lure the male of the species – and consume them?'

'How different from females of the human species.'

'You would know better. But I am aware that the female praying mantis consumes its partner during the act of conception.'

'Is that true? Although now I think about it, carnal knowledge of the flesh has always seemed to me a moment of *significance* – which should be marked by some appropriate signal. Even if cannibalism seems extreme. I have occasionally felt myself to be consumed.'

'Perhaps you should learn to identify which flashes signify genuine desire – and which an intention to consume a mate.'

'Now that is an alchemist's stone which men – and women, for that matter – have long desired to discover, with a similar chance of success. But I would hope the human heart capable of emitting sparks of true light and desire – or else what would be the point of living?'

Bankes inhales heavily on the cigar so the tip burns red, and blows the smoke upwards. They watch it disperse in the light sea breeze from the port.

Bankes can be exhausting. Stimulating, but exhausting. It was one thing to have his conversation in bursts. But when he *sustains* – when he *rattles* –when he cannot let go of a subject –like the iniquities of James Silk Buckingham who had, he thought, plagiarised his research in Egypt – or the absurdities of Hester Stanhope, with her gawky manner and high-pitched voice which Bankes would imitate with a screech like a parrot – knowing full well how she had irritated Byron when they met in Athens – then he would plead tiredness, or the need to practise shooting in a field.

Bankes does not accompany him on these missions as he claims to be so good a shot, it is not necessary.

'I can hit an egg four times out of five, at a paced-out distance of twelve yards.'

'Of course you can. But will you have missed the chicken?'

It is true some of Bankes's stories are of interest – like how he was smuggled into Mecca as a half-witted pilgrim with poor Arabic. But they do not bear the frequent *repetition* – repetition such that he has begun to note the slight variations with which Bankes embellishes each retelling. About which he can tease and bamm him mercilessly. Or at the very least, supply the ending to each story before Bankes does.

Teresa has noticed Bankes is always writing. He records every-thing with meticulous thoroughness. When he learns that a certain species of turtle will return to the same beach where it was born and give birth itself – he enquires for the precise dimensions of that turtle when infant and when fully grown – about the olivaceous colour of its shell – why precisely it should be called 'Ridley's Turtle' – and who the original Ridley was – although this last proves difficult to elucidate.

She asks Byron when they are alone what Bankes does with these writings.

'He has always taken *notes*. He did the same in Egypt. He showed me a trunk of his manuscripts when he arrived in Venice. But he will never finish a book or publish. It would mean going back – to spend time revising. And that is not in Bankes's *capacity*. He would rather make new discoveries than advertise old ones. A strange mixture of industry and indolence.'

'How sad. *Triste*. It seems such a waste.'

He shrugs. 'The world needs only so many books. Sangucho's shelves would collapse under the weight of Bankes's enquiries, just as they are at risk of doing from Humboldt.'

Sangucho has become a regular visitor at the house. He has taken to bringing books as unsolicited presents and has an eclectic approach to those he chooses for his European visitors.

He gives Bankes a treatise on the use of quinine to treat malarial fevers.

To Teresa, he presents a novel by Jane Austen, just shipped from England, 'so she can know the English better'.

'Impossible,' says Teresa, 'for they always say the opposite of what they mean.' But it proves a book which furnishes Teresa with much amusement and which she takes to quoting at the dinner table.

'*There are certainly not so many men of large fortune in the world, as there are pretty women to deserve them*. I agree. She writes with perspicacity.'

'You mean, "she wrote". She died three years ago. One of Murray's authors, so I know about her – or indeed I do now, because her identity was only learned after her death.

— 'I sometimes wish I too had published anonymously.'

Bankes snorts. 'No you *don't*. You might not always want to dance – but you enjoy being at the centre of any *salon*, with the eyes of the world upon you.'

He ignores such impertinence. 'I am surprised, Sangucho, that you have not brought out a pirate edition of this novel?'

'Give me time, *Milord*. It has only just arrived.'

He himself receives from the bookseller some curious picaresque tales by Lazarillo de Tormes from the age of Cervantes – tales of pickpockets and thieves who thrived in Madrid and the strange comradeship between them, which pleases him greatly – as his pleasure does Sangucho, who likes to give him worldly advice on how best to proceed as a writer.

One evening, as they sit around the fireplace, lit more for comfort than heat, Sangucho confides, 'What you must do, *Milord*, is *flatter* your reader into thinking themselves your equal – make them your con-fidante – as if you had stayed up all night together drinking – or perhaps in your case in a brothel – and now wish to tell them a story.

— 'Someone like Humboldt is of course magnificent for his range and his enquiry. But he is a professor behind a lectern. What you could do – is write a book for all those who *dream* of journeying to South America. Just as *Childe Harold* was enticing for your pallid English readers who desired to travel around the Mediterranean, but were unable to do so – because of your adored Napoleon.

— 'You could describe South America at this, the moment of its liberation. For we all realise the Spanish rule is *over*. What Bolivar has begun in the north he – or someone else – will repeat all over the continent. The Empire is a rotten coconut shell. One push' – and the bookseller presses a large finger against Byron's temple – 'and it will go right through.

— 'Who will write the story of what is happening? Not the Liberator. He is not like Napoleon who wanted nothing so much as write his memoirs.'

Sangucho pauses for effect. 'I know Bolivar. I know Bolivar *well*.' At this intelligence, Bankes crosses over from the window to join them.

'Bolivar is a man with a fixity of purpose,' and Sangucho holds them with a stare as if to interrogate their own.

By this time, Sangucho has had glass after glass of *viche*, a fiery but deceptively white drink of pure cane spirit, and he fancies if he were to hold a match to the bookseller's mouth, it would ignite.

'Write a *true* book. Write about the things Humboldt could not mention because he travelled under the protection of the Spanish monarch – about *why* Bolivar needed to liberate the Southern Americas. And do it for me, *as your reader,* now you have drunk with me past midnight – even if you have not drunk with me in a brothel – yet.'

Bankes interjects: 'I agree. You need to write again. It engages your attention in a way nothing else does. I have noticed. Why not make an account of our travels, as Sangucho suggests?'

Sangucho pursues the thought. 'And I will publish it here, in fine octavo volumes, perhaps bound in armadillo or some appropriate American hide – like caiman – as *A New Atlas of the Americas.*'

Teresa arrives, having put Allegra to sleep, just as he replies.

'Travel books are dull. My friend Hobhouse wrote one about our journey to Albania. All he could ever find to say was that – the landscape is *agreeable.* And anyway,' – in the soft, offhand manner when he wants to make a particularly serious point – 'I have come here to live – perhaps to fight if called upon to do so – but not… to write.'

'So for your *Don Juan*, do you plan more than the four cantos you have published? Or should I say – our *piratas* have published!'

'Four will do for the while,' and he glances at Teresa. 'Four, with perhaps a brief epilogue. But for a while I want to exist in the world, not on the page. So the *piratas* will have to wait.'

'You are forsaking literature? I doubt that will last long. Men give up on all women – when just one leaves them. But only for a short while, *Milord.*' Sangucho gives a deep bow, as a compliment, to Teresa, who is amused. 'Then their minds are changed for them. Perhaps you will return to writing when whatever small literary disappointment you have experienced passes. And maybe what you need – is a new, more sympathetic publisher!'

Bankes laughs. As one of life's perpetual purchasers, he likes a good vendor. And he knows that Sangucho has hit a nerve.

'And if that time comes – let me know. I would happily publish an account of your travels – which in your hands could never be dull or merely *agreeable* – particularly if they include a personal description of Bolivar and his generals – and the war. For that is missing in Humboldt – he came too early, before the fireworks when they burned Judases dressed like the Viceroy. And like all Germans, he describes *everything* – in multiple volumes – whereas you would only describe the things that did not bore you – or therefore, the reader.

— 'And yes, absolutely, you should certainly join Bolivar in combat. The book might be much improved if you did.'

'Really?' he says, 'You would like me to risk my life to advance a book you might want to publish?' He raises an eyebrow that would have made Murray quail.

'Of course,' says Sangucho, unabashed. 'Even better if you were to *die* in the process – although only if you have sent me your manuscript first. A publisher can have no greater pleasure than editing a manuscript when the author – like your poor Jane Austen – is no longer present to object to any changes.'

Teresa shouts in mock outrage. She would have stamped her boot if the heels were not so high. '*Basta*! – Enough! That is not amusing in the least! It would be inappropriate anyway for *Milord* to die anywhere – but in my arms.'

'Can I not have a say where I should die?'

'No,' says Bankes. 'You cannot. No man can determine the place and time and manner of the end of his own life – unless he takes it himself. It would be intolerable if we were to know when and where we were to die.' And he gazes mordantly into the embers of the fire.

'In that case,' says Sangucho, filling their glasses with the white cane spirit and flinging what remains onto the flames so they flare up for an instant, 'let us drink to life and *joder a los demás*!'

'What,' says Teresa, sipping from her glass, for she has acquired a taste for the *viche* spirit, less sweet and cloying than Sambuca, 'does that mean?'

'It is best left untranslated,' declares Bankes, primly.

'No, it is not,' he says, having heard Sangucho utter the phrase before. 'It means "Enjoy life and let the rest of them go to hell!"'

— 'Which is an excellent sentiment, and one I have tried *always* to follow.'

He is alone on the balcony at the end of the day, the smell of frangipani and almond trees released by another drizzle of the *llovizna* that so often comes in the late afternoon.

Teresa has a gift, he has come to realise – a gift of when to be with him and when to leave him alone, instinctively, without asking. A rare gift. Some women – like Caro Lamb, constantly importuning – or his wife, who lacked the gift to such an extent he would have to be almost rude to have a moment's peace – had driven him to distraction; and certainly the destruction of any friendship or love. What was that line of Othello's – 'leave me but a little to myself'? And that had ended badly.

Nor is Bankes better. There are times when he would give his right arm – or his damaged right foot, at least – for his friend to *shut up* and leave him alone.

But Teresa has a sixth sense as to when they should be together, or when apart.

'*Mio Giorgio?*'

She comes to him now, on the balcony, to watch the lights of the fishing boats as they head out for their tarpon, their *corvina* and their sharks, under a moon that lights up the bay.

He is pleased to see her. For she also has the gift of knowing when to rejoin him. To stand together in silence. The night sky stretches around and above them like an illuminated canopy, and he puts his arm around her.

'So are you pleased we came?' she asks one night, when they are alone, with Bankes away patrolling the streets of Cartagena for his own pleasures.

He pauses. It is a more complicated question than might appear.

'I feel we are at the doorway – of a great enterprise – and of course I am delighted to be with you, *mi cariña*. But we are only at the portals of the adventure. Sometimes I feel this is like Venice – that I am almost in that city, still, and preparing for our departure. Is this Dante's purgatory? Are we just in the first circle? And what, come to that, do you think Dante would make of the New World?'

'He would find it similar to the old,' observes Teresa. 'Both saints and sinners – the blessed and the damned – Guelphs fighting Ghibellines – royalists against *patriotas*…

— '*Maestro, che è quel ch'i' odo? E che gent'è che par nel duol sì vinta?* You remember the lines.

— *'Master, what is this I hear? What people are these that live in such pain?'*

She sees what he means now Byron has remarked on the similarity with Venice. Not that Cartagena has canals. But like Venice, it has the same setting by a sea without any corresponding maritime energy. A familiar inertia and slow decay. She knows Byron takes a piquant pleasure in finding such *transience* in human affairs; it is not one she shares.

That Cartagena had once been important was indubitable, when it had been the gateway for Spain to all its dominions. But that had brought a dark side; the entry point for thousands of slaves disgorged as cargo from Africa and led south, in chains, to plantations and the mines. Some still arrive in the port, to her great distress. A barbaric and horrible custom, which the Spanish overseers treat as normally as if selling goods on the Rialto.

The population of what Bolivar and his generals have christened Colombia – an interesting and strange neologism, Sangucho has noted, given how loyal Columbus was to his 'most Catholic monarchs' – were as much African as native or Spanish as far as she can tell.

Bolivar has promised freedom to the slaves and enlisted many in his army. But some are still to be seen on the streets of the city – streets that are phenomenally muddy. It is a dirty city. Perhaps why the inhabitants like to promenade along the high seawall, stone-laid and away from the mud, for their evening *paseo,* with a fresh breeze from the ocean.

There is a charming custom, which Sangucho explains to him, of the *piropo* – a compliment half whispered, half left behind a shoulder as a man advances past a pair of ladies – or indeed past one, if she is bold and immodest enough to be walking on her own. This comment will be addressed to the lady, but should not be salacious – rather *suggested* in a Latin and courteous manner.

So Sangucho says a man might say, *si tu cuerpo fuera cárcel, yo fuera tu prisionero...*, 'if you were a gaol, I would happily be your prisoner...,' or more directly – and perhaps passing more slowly – 'how come a star is shining down here in the daylight?'

As Bankes walks with him on these evening perambulations – although they are not yet adept at whispering *piropos*, and perhaps in Bankes's case this is to the good, as some youths of Cartagena might not care to be so propositioned – Bankes points to deterioration in the buildings they pass. The cracks not just in the façades – which are many – but the way whole houses have tilted on their sides, as if their foundations were slipping into the sea.

A few years before, the royalists had recovered the city from Bolivar and his *patriotas* by putting it under siege – a siege so harsh, they learned, that the inhabitants ate even the water cobwebs from the cisterns – and signs of damage from that siege remain. Bankes has found a building with a cannonball still lodged in the masonry – the walls so soft and decayed, they absorbed the shot like a sponge. Bankes promises he will return with Allegra, for it might amuse the girl; he likes to present the world to her as a cabinet of curiosities.

There are more troubling signs of the city's decay – rats in the street, despite cats and dogs so combative the air is filled with the sound of rendered animal flesh – and it is filled too with noxious smells that make Venice seem ambrosial in retrospect. The vultures land as ungainly heaps of wings on the city walls, like black umbrellas collapsing. They can afford to be clumsy and uncoordinated. Such is the extent of the vermin and refuse throughout the city, even the stupidest vulture will never go hungry – like lawyers, he observes to Bankes.

They have taken to the local custom – he enjoys doing so – of holding a perfumed handkerchief to their noses as they walk. He notices many men use this as a way of disguising the passing *piropos* they make to women – as however innocuous, they may not be welcomed if noticed by gossiping strangers – or by jealous husbands and lovers who have been known to follow at a distance and accost anyone they suspect of delivering a *proposition*.

He has suggested to Teresa she might like to patrol the battlements on her own – not escorted by Fanny or himself, as would be proper – and Bankes and he might follow at a distance – to accost any Spanish gentleman who dared slip a *piropo* in her direction. He would, he says, remind such a gentleman there was a reason English *Milords* were called *piratas* along the coast since the days of Raleigh and Drake – and that Bankes and he would be ready to produce cutlasses to resolve the matter.

'A cutlass!' exclaimed Teresa. 'Perhaps a pocket knife would be more apt. I have seen you slice up an orange very prettily.'

— 'You should, anyway, be *flattered* if I should receive such compliments. Remember nothing is expected in return – not so much as a glance or acknowledgement. I think it is a charming habit. You should be more offended if they do *not* give me such a compliment.'

'Really? Perhaps I should sharpen my cutlass. And my pocket knife as well.'

On another evening they gather inside – again with Sangucho – in the room with big bay windows that overlooks the sea, from which they can watch the bats flying along the seawall.

Bankes has taken to wearing loose-sleeved shirts favoured by the locals and called *guayaberas*, in extravagant shades of lilac, gold and even pink – although, as his friend, he feels he must advise against the pink, which does not favour his redhead's complexion. He has also suggested that such shirts may end in the used clothes shops of Monmouth Street if Bankes ever returns to London.

Sangucho has found for Bankes the best of local tailors who produces ever more embroidered creations, with gold thread picking out the seams and rich silk linings to the collars.

'So would you wear this in Kingston Lacy?' he asks Bankes about the most recent and striking creation, a black shirt with a gilt collar and a red rose embroidered over the shoulder.

'Why not? Perhaps when I am receiving in the Inca reception chambers I intend to create alongside my Egyptian dining room.'

He does not let even the trace of a smile cross his face, for his friend is sensitive to any imputation of questionable taste, even though more than capable of criticising others. Instead he spins the miniature globe on his desk, a present from Sangucho to go with the beautifully bound books he has already given.

Teresa approaches – diffidently, as she remains wary of Bankes, however *louche* his shirt – and asks if she may feel the texture.

'It is fine – but not linen or silk,' she admires.

Sangucho appears at her elbow, as if the tailor himself.

'They use sea cotton mixed with a small quantity of linen. Pure linen, in this heat, would not fare well,' and the bookseller looks at him as if to continue a conversation, because Sangucho has admonished his habit of wearing white shirts of pure linen, cut loose and flowing, which by evening are drooping – *'flojo y triste'* as he puts it, floppy and sad – like flowers without water – or perhaps like flowers with too much water, for it is impossible not to sweat profusely in this heat.

'Would you like one yourself, *caro mio*?' asks Teresa, with a trace of mischief, and looking fresh herself, for Fanny changes her clothes every few hours.

'Would you have me in a pale blue? Or daffodil yellow like a Lakeside poet?'

'No, no, in the purest black, with our monogrammed interlocking initials around the cuffs – but done discreetly, so no one can notice – unless, like me, they know where to look.'

She says this so winningly he finds it hard to refuse her suggestion – and besides —

'A black shirt will make my skin appear paler than it is after these months of sun. And perhaps I will wear it for the portrait I have commissioned of us all.'

He likes to surprise Bankes. And he has surprised everyone present.

'A portrait?' asks Bankes. 'And who, pray, might the artist be? Will you invite the Royal Academy to send somebody?'

'A singular protégé of Sangucho's, who has brought him to my attention. You will like his work – all dark shadows in the Spanish style you so admire. His name is Johannes Meer Guylten.'

'A very Spanish name.'

'His father was Dutch and settled here with a Creole woman.'

'Is the intention that I am in this portrait? And if so – where will it be set?

'All of us will be in the painting and we will be in here. I will be at the desk writing – or at least contemplating writing, which is my natural state. You will be admiring an antiquity that Sangucho is displaying to you —'

'I had not realised I would be present,' interrupts the bookseller.

'And which antiquity?' asks Bankes. 'I trust I can choose. I would not want to be admiring some Dutch porcelain doll.'

'But of course. And *mi Contessa*,' – she looks alarmed – 'you will be kneeling in front of a small nativity scene we will also commission, praying in the most becoming and devout manner – and wearing a mantilla of black Spanish lace. Perhaps with Allegra beside you and perhaps —'

Teresa interrupts. 'I will not wear black Spanish lace, which is for widows and grandmothers. I will wear my riding cloak of red, and this painter can find a colour of a suitable red to match for his palette, and he can paint me as a Venetian painter would, which is in the centre of this portrait!'

And she catches his amused expression – and laughs at having been caught. She should know better than to think he would ever want her to wear black.

Allegra has some small protrusion in her thumb and Teresa, with infinite care, is trying to peel back the skin and see if a splinter has entered. She is using tweezers with bone handles given to her as part of an *equipe de toilette* by her grandmother, one of a set of three, each with different widths. She is using the smallest to try to pinch the flesh on either side of the inflammation on the girl's skin. Allegra is reacting with unexpected stoicism, so intent is she on what Teresa is doing.

The same case contains a hairbrush with a tortoiseshell handle and stiff unforgiving bristle, which reminds her of the convent school where the nuns used such hairbrushes as discipline to wreak out girls' hair, particularly if they were in need of correction or salvation. Because of this, Teresa, who occasionally needed both, is cautious with the tweezers.

Bankes, who is watching, offers the use of his magnifying glass, which he positions above the girl's thumb. This ensures Allegra holds her hand still as she is a little scared of Bankes – as perhaps are they all – so Teresa can press down and squeeze with her own thumb and forefinger.

'Here it comes —' and Allegra gives a little cry, either of surprise or pain, as a black thorn rises up from the pressure exerted by the tweezers. Fanny makes an admiring noise in the background. The spine is surprisingly large to have been buried in such a small piece of flesh.

Bankes holds the magnifying glass so Allegra can see and admire the spine in all its enormity.

'As Milton said of paradise, "no rose without a thorn".'

He would correct Bankes, as he has the line wrong, but holds back. Any correction will merely encourage further comment from Bankes's sharp tongue.

'That would be dangerous to leave in place,' observes Teresa, and Allegra looks solemn – but then laughs.

'Would a rose grow from my thumb?'

She had picked it trying to smell the roses in Sangucho's garden when he had invited them all to tea. This had been a formal invitation, delivered by Sangucho's manservant in a strikingly white jacket that offset his dark skin. 'At *la hora inglesa* of four o'clock, the English hour, could I have the pleasure of your company...'. Given a chance, said Bankes, Sangucho would have had the card engraved.

They had all sat on formal chairs with gilt backs that looked incongruous against the grass. The manservant, wearing gloves, handed them cucumber sandwiches – though the cucumbers were so large and fecund, the slices flopped out of the bread. Allegra preferred rolls filled with the soft white flesh of coconut and a dab of guava jam.

It amused him to see Bankes trying to look manly and severe in his usual way when eating an oversized cucumber sandwich.

'You would look more at ease if you were eating a side of beef,' he said, at which Bankes had the grace to laugh.

'And of course I have added cold milk,' announced Sangucho, 'to go with your black tea, even though we do not, as a rule, drink it or keep dairy cows. But I asked one of my maidservants, who is nursing a child, to express it from her own breast, so it is of the purest quality.'

Teresa – who had been given a cup first, as senior lady present – almost choked as she drank, although she tried to do so in a polite way.

'This has human milk!'

Sangucho gave the pause to which they were accustomed from him, prior to the delivery of some *bon mot* on Voltaire, or the iniquities of Napoleon, or the correct way of preparing his namesake soup, the *sangucho*.

'You *believed* me, Contessa. Of course not. It has the milk of cows, gathered fresh from the market.

— 'But what is so interesting is that you *chose to believe* it was possible I would have put a maidservant's breast-milk in your tea. For you are all of that travelling capacity in which you believe *anything* anybody tells you about this continent, as if a place where the miraculous were always true. And sometimes it is – but sometimes it is not.

'You will discover,' – and Sangucho's voice changed timbre from that which he used to deliver a *bon mot* to that in which he presented an essential truth – 'that the chief interest in travel comes from the discrepancy between what you expect… and what you find.

— 'Santiago,' – this to his manservant – 'will you please ensure young Señorita Allegra has another *rollo de coco* – and perhaps you would escort her to the kitchen, where the cook has prepared ices of passionfruit, custard apple, lime and mango. I think it important she should make her own personal choice of flavour – and bring us out a selection on the silver tray ready for that purpose.'

It is a vision he thought he would keep with him as they made their journey into the wild areas of the continent that lie ahead – his daughter, blonde hair cut short by Teresa, advancing across the immaculately cut lawn with a tray of ices – Sangucho solemnly making a selection and telling her that later he will take her, as a reward, to see the birds' nest in the hibiscus with its turquoise eggs – telling her that turquoise is his favourite colour – why his house is called La Casa Turquesa. Sangucho's manservant standing by throughout with white linen napkins so each guest can wipe their lips judiciously after tasting the ices – which are, Teresa declares, of a richness and variety that surpass even those of Ravenna.

'Curious,' said Bankes. 'I would not have expected a custard apple to produce so exquisite a taste.'

'Even more curious,' he told Bankes, his lip curling, 'is that you should have *expectations* of how a custard apple ice might taste in the first place. What else do you spend your time thinking about? Passionfruit confiture?'

'Well,' Bankes had rejoined, on his mettle, as if tasting sour rhubarb and not the fruits of the jungle, 'at least one can eat and enjoy a custard apple. Unlike the poetry you have spent so many hours on as your concern. Which cannot be eaten. And only, at times, enjoyed.'

'*Touché.*'

'But Mr Bankes,' asked Allegra, looking up at him, 'have you not tried all these ices before?'

Allegra has a touching faith, not wholly misplaced, that Bankes has done everything it is possible to do in this world. She likes to hear him tell of how he has seen both hippopotamuses and giraffes.

'I have never eaten such ices,' declared Bankes, with his hand on his heart and to the great pleasure of both Allegra and Sangucho.

'Come,' said Sangucho to the girl, 'as a reward for having dispensed my desserts so admirably, let me show you something.'

Then he leads her, with the rest of the party following, and Teresa holding a parasol over the little girl's head to protect her from the Caribbean sun, to a large hibiscus. Halfway up the plant is a small nest.

'If you would like to lift her up' Sangucho suggested. And Byron held Allegra so she could see inside the nest, which had three turquoise eggs.

Beside the nest was a rose which attracted Teresa's attention.

'I did not know that roses could grow here.'

'Everything grows here,' says Sangucho, with a bracing wave of his hand that takes in the hibiscus, the palm trees and the frangipani hanging in swathes like heavy drapery from the walls of the garden.

'That is not strictly true,' said Bankes. 'But it is an admirable sentiment.'

And Allegra reached out to the red damask rose so she could smell it, and in touching the stem, had pricked her thumb with the thorn.

Bankes grasps him by the arm and leads him past the startled dogs into the deep shadows of the house, of which there are many. He likes to do this over many matters, whether it is the quality of the coffee or chocolate they are consuming – or to apprise him of some antiquities he has found and wants to keep in the house, which is rapidly filling with such acquisitions.

Bankes brings his piercing eyes even closer towards his own than usual.

'We cannot stay.'

'Why? Have you committed *delinquencies* again?'

'Because we *can* stay. Because we could spend months in Cartagena considering the possibilities. Or you could. I know you too well. This could become another Venice. A place where it is easy to be indolent, with agreeable company at times. With now Sangucho rather than Murray supplying you with the latest books and magazines from London. And this climate is bad. The Contessa and Allegra may sicken from tertian fever. Particularly when the heat and rain increase in the summer.

— 'We should – we *must* – take a boat up the Magdalena River to Bogota. Not because it is in the mountains and cooler – but Bolivar may be there and it is the centre for all we need to achieve, surely. What is the point of lingering – on the *periphery*?

— 'Did we not say that we would help his cause, if necessary? Or do you want to be on the side of the Royalists here in Cartagena, not that they are very present? So far, what have we heard from Bolivar? A clandestine note from a private secretary in which he acknowledges our arrival. Which doubtless gets sent to every Irish wastrel off the ship who might take up arms for the Liberator. He has an agent in London who sends such mercenaries.

— 'We need to go and see him. In Bogota. Or find his senior generals if he is no longer there. There is no point waiting in this backwater, however delightful a house with its fine prospects,' he waves at the darkness around them, 'or the attractions of the market or evening *paseo*.'

He looks at Bankes. He guesses this is not the only reason that might precipitate their departure. That Bankes has been indiscreet – that there have indeed been delinquencies. There is talk in town of how the English *Milord* with the red hair is too fond of the boys he engages to help search for *antigüedades*; given everybody knows there are few such antiquities to be found on the coast. For those you must go to the mountains. And Bankes, unusually for Cartagena, is not even nominally attached to a woman, whether wife or mistress, and does not visit brothels, which as a bachelor arouses comment.

He looks at his friend, and at his seemingly innocent green-blue eyes, still as surprising now as when they were students.

'You are right, of course. It is always hard to leave a place where the climate – despite the rain – can be agreeable and society enjoyable.

— 'But by all means. I will confer with the Contessa. I am sure she would like a night at the famous theatre I have heard about in Bogota, with Bolivar's soldiers in their uniforms. Perhaps you could wear one of your embroidered shirts?'

'I am Juan José Francisco de Samano y Uribarri de Rebollar y Mazorra.'

A pause. 'The King of Spain's Viceroy. His Governor and *Capitán General* and *Presidente* of the Kingdom of New Granada, which stretches from the Caribbean all the way to northern Peru.'

It takes a while for the man before them to say this. He appears to be about seventy, his skin parchment white, the cheeks rouged; the vaudeville effect mimicked by the threadbare red jacket he wears over a white linen scarf tied around the neck to mask the signs of ageing. The voice is wheezing and unhealthy, but has a peremptory tone. He is reminded of an old *roué* who has sat at the gaming tables all night – and lost.

The Viceroy is receiving them in what is still the official residence of the Spanish Empire, even though the guards outside appear uncertain of their responsibilities. They had been led across what seemed more a dirty stable-yard – up a staircase on which lounging soldiers with cigars made way for them with reluctance – down long corridors to arrive at this room where the Viceroy has so laboriously introduced himself. To which he now replies.

'My companion, Mr William Bankes Esquire, of Kingston Lacy, Dorset, and George Gordon, Lord Byron – at your service, your' – how does one address a viceroy? – 'Your Excellency.'

The Viceroy gives a pronounced sniff and remains seated behind a large ostentatious desk, empty save for a Spanish flag and some bowls of mint placed in water to sweeten the air from the port odours. His frail body appears shrunk.

'*Vienen a una hora cuando la situación es complicada.* You come at a time when the situation is complicated.'

The Viceroy lisps in the exaggerated Castilian accent favoured by the Spanish court ever since the need to imitate their Habsburg monarchs, who spoke in that manner through inherited cleft lips. Much saliva accompanies '*situación*'.

'The rebels temporarily hold Santa Fe de Bogota and there are reports they are advancing towards us down the river Magdalena.'

The Viceroy takes off a high cockaded hat, which he had assumed when his guests were ushered into the room, to reveal a wig dyed an alarming jet black.

To those same visitors' surprise, he spits copiously into a white porcelain dish beside his chair.

'This is how I would treat Bolivar, Paez, Montilla and all those *desgraciados* who presume on the authority of the Spanish throne. What do they wish for? That the *indios* should rule as well. That they let the Indians *take over*. For that is what will happen if they have their way.

— 'You wish to proceed along the river Magdalena, I understand. Given the *situación,* I cannot guarantee you safe passage. But I will arrange for a small detachment to accompany you – provided, of course, you furnish appropriate emoluments to cover such costs as may accrue.'

The Viceroy stands up suddenly – a diminutive, hunched figure – and skirting the spittoon, comes round the desk to face them.

'This is what I will do to those *hijos de puta* should they come into my hands.'

Taking fresh mint from a bowl on the table, he grinds the leaves under his boots so they disintegrate and the smell is released more strongly into the room. He spits again, directly onto the fragments of mint.

Then he raises his eyes to them, as if there are still some last cards to play, as perhaps there are. For he has a few armed guards outside the door and it only takes one musket to kill a man, or two men.

The Viceroy ignores Bankes and directs his words at the other English *Milord*.

'I have heard many things about you, some contradictory and some absurd – that you are a great aristocrat but also that your title is a young one – that you are not of the first rank.'

If a man had said this to him in England, he would have slapped his face and challenged him to a duel, as with the odious Brougham. Not least because it is true.

But there was a place and time for plain truths. And this was not one of them. Perhaps he would not tell the Viceroy he was indisputably the last of his kind that Spain would ever send across the seas to rule its Empire.

'They tell me too – you are like Satan expelled from the Garden of Eden – or perhaps Adam with his Eve. That you are wicked – but also moral – that you have principles of sorts – that you wanted to fight for the Italians against the Austrian emperor. Do you want to fight with the rebels against *my king*?'

He elects to smile, as if he has not quite understood the question.

'I am travelling with a view to buying an estate.'

'*¿De veras?* Really? I find that hard to believe. *Milord.*' The title almost spat out. 'But if so, you will find yourself in *un mercado de compradores*, a buyers' market, as we say in Spanish.

— 'And now, if you will excuse me, I have other business to attend to.' He puts his hat back on firmly, but with care, so as not to disturb his wig.

Afterwards, as they stand in what is suddenly even brighter sunlight after the shadows of the Viceroy's reception room, he tells Bankes he almost admires the old man's spirit – his obduracy in the face of certain defeat.

'Really,' says Bankes, 'and what do you admire most? The way he summarily executed prisoners in captivity? Many of the best and finest of Bolivar's generals. To the extent that Bolivar has made clear he will show no mercy if he ever captures *his Excellency the Viceroy*.

— 'Do not mistake impotence for clemency. He is his Majesty's dog. Pray Sir, whose dog are you?

— 'Or is it you admire the way he *fled* Bogota after Bolivar made a forced march over the mountains and took him by surprise? When he ran away disguised as one of the poor *indios* he so dislikes, in a poncho and hat – I'm told so abruptly, he had no time to pack the gold he had extracted over his period in office. Perhaps why he is attempting to extract some from us now.'

'You mean his offer of help?'

'His offer of help – will be two boys and a donkey. For a great deal of *emolument*.

— 'If we choose to leave – and I still think we should – it will be under our own protection. What do you think Bolivar would make of us if we arrived with a royalist guard for protection.'

And with an even firmer grasp of his arm than usual:

'Wake up, man! This is a war.'

'Papa, Papa, come.'

Allegra is tugging at his sleeve, insistently, as she does – suddenly proprietorial.

'There is a tree that walks. Come and see.'

He smiles, with indulgence. Bankes is there to tell the child facts; it is for him to encourage her fancy and imagination.

But when she leads him into the forest, with Teresa accompanying them, Bankes is standing by a curious small tree stretched up on long exposed roots, almost as if they were stilts.

'Humboldt and others have written about this strange phenomenon – the tree that can move to find a place in the sun.'

'Like us,' says Teresa.

'Well, up to a point – for this tree cannot move far. It can just *shuffle* its roots along the forest floor in order to gain more sunlight among all the other trees reaching up into the canopy.' And he gestures as if lifting a curtain, a theatrical trick he often uses when displaying paintings or acquisitions.

'So if I stay long enough – and keep still – will I see it move?' asks Allegra.

'No,' says Bankes.

'Yes. Of course you will,' he says, and she gives him one of her rare smiles.

He holds her small hand as they return to the boat. The vessel is smaller than he would have liked, but they needed subterfuge to obtain it, as they had slipped out of Cartagena without the Viceroy's permission.

The captain has plied the five hundred miles upriver to Santa Fe de Bogota many times, he claims, so knows the shifting sand bars they may encounter, which can detain the unwary.

Although the crew sleep on deck, there are not enough cabins for the passengers, so the captain has moored and slung hammocks from the trees – to the delight of Allegra and of all the party, for the novelty of it. Swarms of phosphorescent insects light up the tree-tops like moving clouds, giving off a soft bluish glow. They see this same phosphorescence in the water if they travel at dusk, swirling behind the wake of the boat.

The mules have been brought ashore and graze contentedly under tall, stately mahogany trees, which provide welcome shade and which the boatmen call *palos santos*, sacred trunks.

'That tree is one hundred feet tall,' pronounces Bankes.

'Could you climb it?' asks Allegra.

'Of course he could,' says Teresa. 'And so could your father.'

The mules are for the last part of the journey, after they leave the river and need to cross the mountains towards Bogota over a hundred miles of wild terrain.

His mind works in such a way that while his first impressions are always strong and confused – his memory will over time select and reduce them to order – like distance in a landscape – and will blend them better, although they may be less distinct. So the bamboo forests carpeted by orchids, the snowy mountains, the light mist covering the valleys at sunrise and the bunches of gigantic trees, like green islands above a sea of cloud – he knows all these will return later to haunt his imagination.

They pass through woods thick with evergreen oaks from which parrots emerge to squawk raucously.

'What are they saying?' asks Allegra. 'They sound cross.'

'I know what they are saying…'

He rides with Allegra sitting nestled in front of him, with a cushion against the saddle, so he can tell her stories as they travel. She occasionally attempts to gee up their white mule – although such attempts are futile, as mules proceed at their own pace.

Moretto plods behind him through the Andean forest with the determined look of a bulldog who will always follow his master, however curious his choices. Roaming more widely, Mutz, with sheepdog somewhere in her mongrel blend, snaps at a mule as if rounding up a herd – and prompts a kick which nearly takes off her head. He remembers how she once came off worst when trying to round up a wild pig when they were coming back from Florence. A brave but foolhardy attempt.

Despite her ferocious appearance and foreshortened tail, Mutz has a benign nature and has become a great favourite of Allegra's. She likes to throw small sticks from her position on the horse's neck for Mutz to fetch and carry, an operation which affords both child and dog an unconscionable and simple pleasure.

Bankes is riding the largest of the mules, a grey one called *El Presidente* by the boatmen who have turned muleteers for this last part of the journey and take considerable amusement in the way their passengers – and dogs – jockey for position. Teresa, being the lightest of mounts, finds she can manoeuvre ahead of the others, although Bankes suggests this is not fair – and that, like the Newmarket races, she should be handicapped with additional weights in her saddlebags.

Behind them comes a train of pack mules. A long train. It needs two mules alone just to carry his ninety-two volumes of Voltaire, while Bankes has engaged – at his own expense – an additional mule to carry his Murillo painting. This has been swaddled in blankets and bedded down with acorns inside a wooden case of his own devising, following the model of ones he used in Spain and Syria for such expediencies. Bankes claims he will even reuse the acorns and plant them at Kingston Lacy, once the painting is safely back, as he has done for cedars of Lebanon in the past.

He catches Teresa's eye as she assays a shortcut through the wood that will position her ahead of Bankes – and laughs.

Viva Byron!

CANTO III

They are walking up the few blocks from Bogota's main square – handsome, lined by trees, laid out in some style – to the Coliseo Ramirez.

'They couldn't just call it a theatre,' he remarks to Teresa. 'They had to call it a *Coliseum*. As a theatre it would be impressive. As a Coliseum it is clearly – somewhat lacking in scale…'

The street is too narrow for carriages, so a column of generals – a *desfile,* to use the Spanish military term he has learned, among others – are picking their way through the mud and detritus of the pavements with their women – the men, if anything, with more care for their piped scarlet trousers than the women for their dresses, which they lift up to the thigh without the slightest embarrassment.

He tries to imagine the English equivalent – of London society ladies giving a hint of stocking as they made their way to Covent Garden. He can think of some who might enjoy the excuse – like Caro Lamb. Mad Caroline – how had she had the effrontery to question his sanity? When she had lit that bonfire at Brocket Hall and consigned his effigy – and all his writings – to the flames. She would happily have murdered him in person if given the chance. As would Claire Clairmont. At least Teresa, if Italian and quite capable of throwing plates, was unlikely to put a knife in his back. Which his own wife had done – to his reputation.

Now he is in a world where he knows no one; and few know him. Is it an improvement? He is not sure.

Teresa is flushed, excited in a yellow organza dress that sets off her olive skin and blonde hair, and her *embonpoint*, of which she is proud. As they proceed up Calle de la Fatiga – the 'Tired Street' – a line of Indians wait at a window that sells *chicha*. The Indians do not give them or the generals a second glance.

They join the end of the reception queue at the entrance to the theatre. A tall soldier in uniform so splendid it might be that of a general, with accompanying sideburns and epaulettes, is greeting each couple who arrive.

'Is that Bolivar?' whispers Teresa as they wait their turn.

'It can't be. Far too young. And they told me he is not a tall man.'

The reception line is brisk and military. In short order they find themselves in front of the young officer who sweeps off a cockaded hat as he bows to Teresa and extends a gloved hand.

'Daniel O'Leary – at your service, milady – and my Lord.'

He tries not to look surprised, either at the strong Irish accent or the recognition.

'I am the aide-de-camp to General Bolivar. I look forward greatly to a further opportunity to talk – as does the Liberator.' He glances to an alcove where a small, slight man is watching proceedings – a man who gives the most imperceptible of nods in return.

He does not stare back but has a fleeting impression of a high fore-head and dark eyebrows arched over hooded eyes – wearing not military dress but a black frock and cravat.

'For now,' says O'Leary, taking his elbow and steering him towards the main body of the theatre, 'it is time to dance. I hope the Contessa will allow me later the pleasure of a waltz.'

But the Contessa, later, is almost unable to fit O'Leary's name on her card, such is the press of admirers. As he leans against a pillar watching soldiers swirl past with her, he wonders if – in addition to her natural charms – it is because she is short. Not even the glittering finery of Bolivar's generals, and the quantity of medals on display, can conceal the fact they are almost to a man – with the exception of O'Leary – below average height.

A tall Englishwoman like Lady Hester Stanhope would not be asked for a single dance. But then, given Lady Hester's acid tongue and disagreeable nature, the generals might have been spared.

He stands by a pillar, missing Bankes who has made himself unavailable for the evening on the pretext he has no female companion – not that this is a requirement for admission. In London society, his own disinclination to dance – because of his foot, although he never speaks of it – had been seen as part of his iconoclastic charm. Here, it is seen as a sign of incompetence – as if unable to ride a horse. Or at least this is what Daniel O'Leary suggests in an interval when they go onto a balcony for a cigar.

'He is good at dancing – so he likes his generals to be as well. Particularly the waltz. He spent years in France, remember, when it was not wise for him to be in Venezuela. You will find he likes champagne and claret.'

O'Leary gives him a look. It is not a casual one. O'Leary has already taken a moment to observe his man when he saw him leaning against a pillar.

Byron's appearance had not been quite as he had expected; but then it would have been difficult for anything to live up to the wild rumours.

O'Leary had imagined a more commanding, aristocratic air; that he might play the hero, or try to, like his literary ones. But the man in front of him is modest and self-deprecating in a way O'Leary can see immediately gives him a dangerous charm. And his appearance is still striking. A high, open forehead, exacerbated by having shaved his temples, although his black hair curls a little behind. Eyes greyish brown and full of expression, with one visibly larger than the other. The nose large and well-shaped, and surprisingly *thick*, O'Leary thinks, more like a farmer's than a Lord's.

But the mouth is his most remarkable feature, an upper lip of Grecian shortness, and the corners descending; both lips full, and finely cut. A cupid's bow of a mouth, as the young maids might say in Dublin. True, there is something scornful in his expression – perhaps just what he thinks of the dancing – but this is evidently a natural feature, and falls away as soon as he speaks, revealing white, even teeth and an unexpectedly frivolous tone.

'I'm sure I can manage the champagne and claret. If not the dancing…'

'He wants you to visit him. In his private house above the city. With your Señor Bankes. But without your Contessa. A man's evening.'

'What should I expect of such an evening?'

'I've been with him for years, almost since the start of the campaign. First in the army and more recently as his personal aide-de-camp. And the thing of it is – you will find it very hard to know what he's like. What sort of man he is. Because he has many sides. He is changeable and quick. He can be in the blackest of moods one day – and on *fire* the next.

— 'Bolivar is conscious of how history may remember him. I am collecting his papers. One day I mean to write a memoir – if he permits and I am able – and still alive.' Laughing, in the manner of a young man who thinks it inconceivable he should die in combat.

—'Unless of course that is why *you* have come, my Lord? To write an account of his life?'

'Not at all,' he says briskly. 'There is nothing I want to do less – than write. I want to *live*. I came thinking I would buy an estate. But it would be wrong to enjoy the comfort of such an estate while others are risking their lives for liberty. Even though I would not style myself as a fighting man – and nor would Mr Bankes, although he has many sterling and resourceful qualities.'

O'Leary's face takes on a look that manages to be impassive and attentive at the same time, like a Cork farmer considering livestock.

'What you have, my Lord, is *intelligence*. And what we need, at the present moment, is intelligence. I know the Liberator is minded to ask you to investigate the area to the north-west, on the Pacific coast, where a pocket of royalists may have retreated – in the same way they retreated to Cartagena, as you discovered. It is an area to which we should send – a *reconnaissance* party.'

'To fight the royalists?'

'To establish – whether they are there at all.

—'Perhaps you and Mr Bankes could take a small consignment of men – well chosen – and travel to the area to gather such intelligence? The royalists are reluctant to fight – far less to persecute a small group of aristocratic English looking possibly to buy an estate, as you will give as your purpose. As indeed *could* be your purpose. They may well be interested in selling you such an estate, particularly if they need to vacate the land themselves.' He laughs.

'You may return… with an estate to be the envy of us all.' And O'Leary gives an all-encompassing wave of his hand to indicate that all is attainable in this life for those who dare.

Through the windows from the balcony, he watches Teresa accept yet another invitation to dance – from someone she has already partnered? He thinks so. The man has a raw bulbous face, with hair cut short in a military style and is an awkward dancer; still, he feels the stirring of an unusual emotion within him – that of jealousy.

He turns to O'Leary, in case his attention to Teresa be mistaken for indifference to the proposition. He acts quickly to allay that.

'I am sure Mr Bankes would join me in wishing to help in any way we can.'

'Good. When you see the Liberator, he will not want to discuss *details*. Come to me for that. But he will want to know who you are. Just as you may want to know who I am. You might have wondered why someone so young is in such a position of confidence with Bolivar.'

He had not, but is prepared to be enlightened.

'Colonel James Rooke, of whom you may have heard and who was my gallant commanding officer, died in the battle of Boyaca. The British and Irish troops have been at the forefront of all our engagements, which has given success at times but also brought many fatalities. Colonel Sandes, who now commands the First Battalion of Rifles of the Guard, was so injured he is unable to participate in public engagements such as this – which is why I am deputising. And why, if you will permit, I must return to my duties.'

O'Leary clicks his heels smartly – for all the world as if about to start an Irish reel – and returns to the ballroom.

He is left to patrol the outskirts. He notices – and likes – how fond Colombian women are of laughter. There is laughter coming from many directions. A further cacophony from one group when a stout colonel unpins one of his many medals – or has it been loosened by his exertions on the dancefloor – and attempts to attach it to the shoulder of his equally ample *inamorata,* as a brooch. But he is clumsy and unable to pin the medal above her bounteous cleavage.

'What has she done to deserve a medal?' enquires a lively girl in a white dress with a garland of pale yellow gardenias. 'Or should we not ask?'

'She has danced with a man with two left feet and a *panza* of a belly that must need two horses to support.'

'Give the man another drink to steady his nerves! Then he will pin it with precision.' More raucous laughter.

A staircase leads up to the circle and private boxes that overlook the stage. He ascends, a champagne flute in his hand, feeling light-headed and heavy-spirited at the same time, a combination he remembers from London society. The tiresome round of palling pleasures. The champagne is not quite cold enough and has travelled badly across the Atlantic – he can taste the powdery lees stirred up by the ocean passage.

He circles the boxes, each with their own private entry from the corridor. The sound of flirtatious laughter comes from some; from others, the stuttered noises of consummation. Lines run through his head: '*To look on as a mourner, or a scorner, / or an approver, or a mere spectator, / yawning a little as the night grows later.*' At another time he would have jotted them down, if he were still writing his cantos.

But the door to one box is open and light from the stage shows it to be empty, so he sits alone and watches the dancers below as they part, coalesce and rejoin.

Teresa stands out with her yellow dress and accomplished dancing – surely that cannot have been something she learned at the convent? Daniel O'Leary is leading her gallantly and at speed around the room, the impressive medal on his chest – the 'Order of the Liberators', the highest distinction in the new Colombian army – sparkling under the chandelier.

He has a sudden whim that he could bring her up later to one of these private boxes and behave as many of those to either side of him are behaving. He could position her so she was looking over the balustrade and then lift up her dress from behind and take her, without anyone being able to see – for the architecture of the boxes is designed to give privacy, maybe precisely for this reason. And then they could look down together at the dancers as they made patterns below, with him inside her. They had done far wickeder things with enjoyment. And he knows how much she enjoys a conjunction from behind – the uninhibited relish with which she accepts such an advance, surprising again in one who has attended a convent school; or perhaps a consequence.

But for now he takes astringent pleasure in watching from above – in not being part of the dance.

When he descends back to the long bar, he is struck by how exotically the generals are liveried up – like those tropical birds he had seen by the river dancing along the same branch in competition to attract a mate – in tight trousers with cream piping, and with shoulders so wide and studded with epaulettes that in turning they might knock another man off his perch. He remembers how it was reported Marshals Ney and Junot – those hardened veterans of Austerlitz – had dressed in the finest pink or green silk to attend Napoleon's *soirées* .

His own Hussar uniform seems suddenly dull. In Mayfair it had cut a dash. Here, he is a dowdy pigeon amongst pheasants. The most junior captain has enough medals to cover his chest – indeed O'Leary, it has emerged, is just a captain, albeit a confidant of Bolivar's. He has none to display and feels self-conscious – nor is he used to being *anonymous* at a social gathering.

The custom of the place, Bankes had told him – and as he has seen – is for gallants to bestow some of these medals on their *inamorata* – so the ladies, if popular, become as decorated as any sergeant major –

or even lieutenant if they have performed – as Bankes puts it archly – *valiantly*.

'So did you receive any medals?' he asks Teresa, when much later – for South Americans keep at the dance far past the hour when carriages would be called for in London – the night is over.

'Some were offered, but none accepted.'

'That is considerate of my feelings.'

'I was more concerned they would be clumsy in attempting to pin them to my dress.'

'Indeed. I enjoyed taking you up to our private box at the end of the evening to recover our energies.'

'To recover? I thought that was where we expended our energies.'

They reach their carriage close by the main square – to find Bankes sleeping inside, after his own nocturnal excursions and doubt-less emissions. Their driver is with a cheerful group of other men around a *chicha* stall which has stayed open late for such a profusion of custom as the ball has provided. He buys them all drinks and offers a toast to the revolution and Bolivar and the brave fighting men of his army.

'*¡Viva la Patria!*' they chorus back.

As they drive through the empty streets at night, he looks up to see the mountains above Bogota, the high Andes, rim-lit by a moon against a purple sky, and feels a sudden sense of heady euphoria. Of the impossible becoming possible.

'*¡Viva la Patria!*'

Teresa is startled by his shout.

On another evening, he attends the more impromptu *salon* of a general's wife – so different to the brilliant masquerades of London society of which, by the time he left England, he had become tired. The more he had been lionised in London, the more he slept in the sun.

There, it was fashionable to affect a bored ennui. No one can be more world-weary than an aristocratic Englishman of twenty-seven – unless it be an Englishwoman of twenty-three. Here, there was a vitality that came from the sheer *press* of events, both past, current and those to come. The talk is all of Bolivar's bold and sudden dash across the mountains the year before – a forced march to match Hannibal's over the Alps – which had taken the Spaniards by surprise. The battle of Boyaca, in which the British – and Irish, as O'Leary liked to remind him – had played such a decisive part.

But the talk – after an armistice which has just ended – is also of urgent new deployments in every direction – to hold territory, gain territory, regain it – and ahead the whole bulk of the continent, all still under the silver-tipped Spanish heel. Their huge decaying empire centred around the viceregal capital in Lima, but spreading south to Chile and the Argentine plains; as far as the southern tip of Tierra del Fuego, an unimaginable distance away.

He stands somewhat back, to watch the small groups of generals and military men forming small conclaves in the reception rooms, and then regrouping, like defensive squares who might be attacked. The women meanwhile sit in comfortable ormolu chairs against the walls. He sees Bankes off to one side, wearing the scarlet riding boots of which he is inordinately proud, talking intimately to O'Leary.

General Paez gives a speech – with Bolivar present, nodding approval – in which the shaven-headed, imposing general makes a comparison he senses might be one Paez is accustomed to make – but no matter – that they are 'men trying to lever the heavy presence of the Spanish monarchy – out of the ground'. And the general reaches up in his brocaded jacket, so heavy with medals it must be hard to lift, to mime the action of a man hanging off the end of a pole. An action that would be comical in another, but given Paez's muscularity, the way his collar can hardly contain his straining neck, and the look of ferocity on his face, makes him pity both pole and neck, for one or other will surely give way under the strain.

Applause. Which he joins in. It is the first time he has seen the martial General Paez, of whom he had heard much in Europe; often described as Bolivar's bulldog.

The men bend down to confer with the seated ladies, who may be either official or unofficial consorts – for he has noticed, in the febrile air of Bogota society, petticoats have been loosened just as military uniforms have been pressed and tightened. Then some officers turn to puff cigars the size of bananas – no pretence here they should withdraw to smoke – and try to exude a manly calm, though he can read in their eyes – those who had really fought, not just bought a uniform – a trace of alarm and foreboding.

Bolivar takes the floor, so quietly that no one notices, more like a waiter than a general, fragile in his black frock coat and attentive manner besides the solid brick and mortar of Paez – who signals his master's speech by rapping his knuckles on the table.

'*¡Atención!*'

Bolivar clears his throat as the room goes silent – or as silent as Bogota can ever be, which means they still hear the howls of dogs through the open doors and windows of the reception rooms. It is rare for Bolivar to speak in public – he leaves it to his generals, and O'Leary as his aide-de-camp. There is constant speculation as to when he might begin the advance south towards Peru.

'I propose a toast – to the ladies for whom our honour is at stake.' A phrase that sounds rich and sonorous in Spanish, as such rhetoric always does.

Bolivar gives a pause.

'*A las esposas y las novias*. To our wives and lady friends.

—'*¡Que las dos nunca se encuentran!* That the two never meet!'

The women laugh harder than the men.

He realises, to his surprise, he is enjoying himself. A doe-eyed young woman sashays towards him while Teresa is occupied – as she often is – in a discussion with O'Leary, who has been a regular at their house.

'We met at the ball, *Milord*. Do you not remember?'

He feels as if he is back in Mayfair, where he had defended his amnesia for society ladies with studied indifference. But that will not work – or be appropriate – here.

'How can I not? It would be like forgetting the flowers of spring.'

Has he said that without a blush? But then Spanish, like Italian, lends itself to such phrases, and Colombian women take compliments with more grace than English ones – or does their darker, olive-skinned complexion prevent them from blushing?

'Your eyes, *Milord*, are brown. I thought Englishmen were supposed to have blue eyes. Like Captain O'Leary.'

'He is Irish, not English. A distinction of which he will be more acutely aware than me. And have you not noticed that the eyes of my friend Mr Bankes are a light green?'

'I have indeed noticed Señor Bankes's eyes. Although I am not sure he has noticed mine. He appears little interested in the company of ladies. Perhaps he is of a naturally military disposition.'

'Perhaps… But forgive me, while I remember your face – and of course your own eyes – your name has escaped me.'

She leans close and a wave of perfume flavoured with vanilla engulfs him.

'My name is Bernardina Ibañez.'

A pause, as if he should recognise it.

'I understand you may be leaving for the front yourself. With Señor Bankes and with young Nico Montoya.'

He has never thought of it as the front. But he finds he likes the phrase, if not its full implication.

'Yes – we leave in a few days' time.'

'What a shame. Just when we start to know each other.'

Much later that night, he sees Bernardina again, this time waltzing with Bolivar.

'I told you he liked to waltz,' murmurs O'Leary beside him. 'I have seen him dance for hours if he finds an agreeable partner. And Señorita Ibañez is his most agreeable partner. Then he will stop at two in the morning and go off and write letters, or lie in his hammock for a brief respite. After that – back to the dancefloor!

— 'The waltz is a dance of revolution. It arrived in Paris when he was there – and he embraced it with fervour.'

'And embraced his partners? I have always supposed it a dance best performed by a couple in private.'

'Indeed, I know you do. *Waltz whispers this remark, "My slippery steps are safest in the dark!"* '

'Thank you. Although if our friendship is to prosper, O'Leary, as I'm sure it will, I would be grateful if you never quote my own poetry back at me.'

O'Leary returns his gaze to his commander. 'He finds dancing helps him think. But unlike other men, who need to reflect on their own, far from what he calls the *alboroto*, the hubbub, he has his best ideas in the *very centre* of the revelry – dancing in the middle of the ballroom.'

It is true that Bolivar waltzes well. He envies him that ability.

The Napoleon snuff box is reassuring and familiar in his waistcoat; the box shaped in the triangular form of Napoleon's hat, with a picture of the great man on horseback. Part of his collection of Napoleana: a gold coin with the Emperor's head, a swordstick said – on good authority – to have been his, and Andrieu's medals of Napoleon and Josephine in classical profile as Emperor and Empress, strange yet striking in a way he likes. He had more such memorabilia back in England – a life-size gilt statue of Napoleon in a rosewood canister that opens like an Egyptian mummy – but has travelled with just the smaller items, as touchstones.

Like the medal of Napoleon in a short toga wearing laurel leaves and baptising his infant son as the King of Rome – which has met with derision from his companions. As has the seal he commissioned his agent Hanson to make, with a coronet and the initials N.B. to sound like Napoleon Bonaparte – on the pretext he can sign himself, if he likes, Noel Byron.

But it is the glass locket containing a strand of Napoleon's hair that Bankes and Teresa most bamm and tease him about.

'*A relic!*' says Bankes. 'As if he were a medieval saint – not a despot who tried to impose his will on the whole of Europe! You are *seduced* by him, Byron.'

The piece of hair, black and shining within the glass, as if brilliantined to preserve it – or how the Emperor had worn it in life. Perhaps he used macassar oil? A French brand.

Teresa complains to him, privately, that he should only keep lockets with her hair inside – as indeed he has, from both her head and more intimate hair below – but not the hair of rivals, whether from women or Napoleon.

He has admired Napoleon since he was a boy and Bonaparte first emerged as a force. The more he had been accused of a lack of patriotism – as 'Boney' became the enemy and revulsion was heaped on the newly-crowned Emperor's head, a *boneyman* threatening to invade – the more he relished his contrarian support.

Before leaving England, he had bought Napoleon's fur-trimmed coronation robes, kept now in storage for him at a warehouse in Mayfair. Although he has never seen them – he sailed before they shipped from France – he likes to luxuriate in the thought of the thick velvet draped against him. Perhaps he could sleep under them. Perhaps Teresa and he could have a *liaison* lying beneath them, like the wolf fur he had used for that purpose in Venice, in front of the fire, an idea with which he has acquainted her and which she had supported with both amusement and enthusiasm.

Although she did slyly question whether he wanted her presence or Napoleon's within those robes.

'I think you are more enamoured of him, my Lord.'

Bankes had snorted contempt when he let slip this ambition in an unguarded moment.

'My God man – you'll be frigging yourself to sleep thinking of Napoleon. Has it occurred to you, *Milord*,' – this sarcastic rather than deferential – 'that as your emperor was *short*, like our current general and Liberator, the robes will not cover your feet in such an endeavour as you describe? They will stick out from beneath in a comical and absurd way I think you would agree – may be *unbecoming*. You also need to be careful the dogs do not attempt to bite your toes, or for that matter the Contessa's. Although I suppose, as she is so short, she may well fit more safely under the cover.'

Bankes has a way of bringing his fancies down to earth. And it is hard to resent a man who likes to wear thigh-high red riding boots – not least because of the many opportunities to bamm and rib him back.

A soldier has appeared to fetch them, so he takes his hand out of his waistcoat and tries to put on his most military aspect as they are led towards the house which stands on the hill a little above Bogota.

Bolivar is not at his desk – but beyond, in a *salon* lit by yellow distemper walls which catch any sun that somehow penetrates past damask curtains. Glass cases enclose the small bodies of birds on branches in a taxidermic profusion of brightly coloured finches and seedeaters.

'Do you play? I am told that in England proficiency in *billar* is the sign of a misspent youth.'

Bolivar holds out a cue of inordinate length, which serves to exaggerate the Liberator's own diminutive stature – five foot six, according to Daniel O'Leary, the same as Napoleon.

The first impression on meeting the man, though, is not his physical appearance – but his smell. Warm air from the windows blows a gust of an exotic blend of cedarwood and other spices from Bolivar towards them as Bankes and he enter, a little cautiously, into the *salon*.

O'Leary says Bolivar could use a whole bottle of cologne in one day – and does so regularly. Not least because such scents last longer and are more powerful in the tropics, and more necessary.

There is little time for such impressions as Bolivar faces away briskly and lets loose a shot so violent it produces a cannon of sharp precision – then turns to him as if in challenge.

He has always been good at billiards. Not just because of a mis-spent youth – but as a sport in which you remained stationary, so no chance of being betrayed by his injured foot.

The white cue-ball rests on the cushion, with a red ball close to the pocket and some distance away. The only strike possible – unless he were to find a cue-rest, which seems unlikely and which he does not want to request – is to hold the cue behind his back and, with infinite caution, hit the white so it creeps along the cushion. Done slowly, but fast enough to jump the central pocket and reach the red at the far end – where the ball can be kissed with infinite *ternura* – tenderness – and nudged into the corner pocket.

'*Un beso de billar,* a billiard kiss,' applauds Bolivar, looking at him from beneath the dark hooded eyebrows.

'Palacios,' he calls, and a manservant appears, 'champagne for *Mi-lord* and for *Señor…*'

'Bankes,' reminds Bankes, looking grave. 'At your command.'

'A very military answer, *Señor* Bankes – and one I may have cause to accept.

— 'Do you both know how to play *tresillo*? It is a card game for three players, so perfect for this occasion.'

'Is it like whist?' This from Bankes.

'Then you do *not* know how to play *tresillo*. Excellent. I will teach you briefly – enough so you understand the rules – but not so much you play well – and you will learn as you go along, taking losses as you do. The experience that most have of *military life,* in fact.

— 'I will then have the pleasure of beating you, unless you have the luck of the Irish or of the absolute beginner – both of which Daniel O'Leary enjoyed on first arrival. He defeated me badly, although with tact and the typical consideration of the man, dedicated his winnings to the Republican cause. By giving them back to me. An example I would encourage you to follow, should the situation arise.

— 'The game is also called *hombre*, and for a reason. It is a man's game that calls for daring in the bidding and precision – and ruthlessness in the execution. Although the fairer sex are, of course, quite capable of that. More capable. They just don't do it with their cards on the table.

— 'If you sit here, *Milord*, and Señor Bankes here. We will play against the clock, in every sense, so this way around from the dealer. One suit is made up of cups and coins – the round suit – the other of swords and clubs, the long suit. As you can imagine, I prefer the long suit and will bid accordingly.

— 'Ready? I will explain as we play. Because that is like war.'

'May I ask your Excellency,' says Bankes, 'about the signet ring you wear?'

For a hallucinatory moment, he thinks Bankes may offer to buy it. He would put nothing past his acquisitive friend.

Bolivar takes the large ring from his small, delicate finger and holds it up – but only, he notices, after dealing the last card, as if concerned to do so any earlier might give away advantage. The ring has the *escudo* insignia of the new Kingdom of Colombia: an axe tied in a sheaf of spears and arrows, between horns overflowing with tropical fruit. Bankes and he are familiar with the motif. It is emblazoned all over Bogota with revolutionary fervour – and they have laughed in private over the rusticity and poor execution of the art; although it gives Bankes the excuse to laugh also at the Byron family emblem of a mermaid *encouchant* with prancing horses to either side, of which he is proud.

Bolivar strokes his ring, almost absent-mindedly. 'I chose the fruits myself. I have a particular fondness for fruit – the *guayaba*, the *plátano* banana, the pineapple, the mangosteen. And for passionfruit. My gardeners grow them,' – a gesture at the open window. 'They were what I missed more than anything in France.

— 'Have you tried our papaya, *Milord*?'

'For breakfast. I like it with lime.' This is true. He still eats breakfast standing up, to Bankes's amusement – and Teresa's frustration, as it gives no time for digestion and little for conversation, both of which she considers essential in the morning.

'Good. And *Señor*,' – addressing Bankes – 'do you eat desserts? Like the famous *suspiro Limeño*, the sigh of Lima, made from lemons and the finest spun egg whites?'

'I have not had the pleasure, your Excellency.'

'Your Excellency! No formality needed at the card table. Although of course if you fight for me, *"mi general"* will suffice. But I am pleased you do not like dessert. It is not a manly pleasure.'

Bankes is trying to look his most serious and composed. He can tell, however, that his friend's newly tailored uniform is too tight, around the shoulders in particular, and that he is sweating as his chair is closest to the unnecessary fire. His red-haired complexion is not suited to perspiration. The champagne and anxiety at being in the presence of the Liberator are making Bankes nervous in a way he has rarely seen.

Whereas he feels at ease – far more than he had anticipated. He leans forward to Bolivar, who turns as if such intimacy is welcome – indeed expected.

'Can I tell you, *mi general*, that you have the face of a poet?'

It is true. He has had time to study it – the pale face, the high cheekbones, the black hair.

'A poet! – Of course I am a poet. This has all happened because of letters I have written – speeches I have made – that were needed to make men dream of unconscionable change. Which is what poets do. Or should do.

— 'But what would you like me to tell you in return? Say you have the face of a general? Because you *don't*. You too, Sir, have the face of a poet. Or of an English lord who is proficient at billiards.

— 'How would you be in a battle? How would you feel to kill a man? How would you feel – *aún peor*, even worse – if your own men were killed? Because of course you will have a command. And I could see that men would follow you. Would love you, in the way that fighting men must.

— 'There are moments in which you will discover whether you are men or cowards. This is hard for any man. I had a Scottish general, Sir Gregor MacGregor, who fought for me in Venezuela; who helped me try to liberate that country – my country – the country of my birth.

— 'But what did he do? He was meant to be in charge of a post – and he ran away. Leaving his men to be captured by the royalists – to die. It amounted to the same thing, as that bastard of a Viceroy always killed any prisoners. Then this MacGregor ran away *again*, not once, but many times... Sir Gregor MacGregor. A Scotsman.'

He feels like pointing out that he possesses at least one advantage over MacGregor. Because of his foot, he cannot run away.

But Bolivar continues abruptly, 'Are you not Scottish?

'Only to an extent,' he says – and senses Bankes laughing at him, now the champagne is having a different effect. 'My grandfather was English – Jack Byron. He was a Rear Admiral who sailed up and down the Spanish Main.'

'You mean a *pirata*,' says Bolivar. But he smiles. 'You are all *piratas*, you English. Or Scottish. You pretend to be noble and principled, but the truth is – you are all pirates at heart. So let us see how you play at cards.'

They are riding along a mountain track in a wild exhilaration of leaves and hooves.

Paez and his men head the charge, while he follows with Teresa – Teresa in her brilliant riding habit of cochineal red that has been much admired by Paez's lieutenant – *¡Que traje tan esplendido!* What a splendid outfit! – while he wears the Star of Colombia that Bolivar had personally pinned to his epaulettes – and his fur hat, worn with a securing band devised by Fletcher so it does not fly off in the wind. He hopes the medal is equally well secured. Surely a military medal will have a sturdy pin? Perhaps at some appropriate moment he will be able to pin it on Teresa, with care.

Some of the younger members of Paez's party – still adolescent – fire pistols above them, knowing Paez cannot admonish them, as they are riding so fast, or – as he is leading the charge – identify the culprits.

Even Bankes has lost himself in the moment and is riding hard, with his ragged traveller's cloak flapping round his face. Getting an airing.

That sense of giving your horse its head. Of letting go. Like swimming, one of those energies of motion.

'This is life,' he cries at the top of his voice, to be heard over the gunshots and the hooves, to the alarm of Teresa's horse, who skitters but gets back on track. Teresa has become a far more accomplished horsewoman on the long journey from the coast.

'*¡La vida! ¡Viva la vida! Vivan nuestros amigos y joder a los demás.* Let our friends live long and the rest go to hell!' The drinking toast.

They ride until the sudden darkness that happens in the Andes, as the sun is sheeted out by the surrounding mountains. Then return by the same moon he saw coming back from the ball, now waning, but with the power to illuminate the track which the horses know instinctively. At times, particularly under trees, they are riding blind – Teresa's cloak glowing red in the penumbral dusk, Bankes in his battered blue cloak.

And back into Santa Fe de Bogota, the Sacred Faith of Bogota – a strange name for a strange city, so high in the clouds – clumping down cobbled streets that run precipitously from the mountains towards the cathedral, church bells calling the evening mass and dogs howling from the hills – their horses tired, moving slowly, deliberately, a little majestically.

There are candles lit – perhaps Allegra has her jar of fireflies as well? – in the windows of the house they have taken, a handsome one commandeered from a royalist who fled the capital. A place, according to Daniel O'Leary, who helped find it, suitable for a Lord. It had been O'Leary's idea for them to ride with Paez and he greets them now at the house where he has become a familiar, taking Teresa's reins and leading her horse towards the stables.

He himself remains for a moment with the other riders. Paez turns, the general's broad chest swelling even more with the cummerbund that holds in his waist. There is a toughness to Paez that reminds him of a boxer.

No preliminaries.

'You will take a party of twenty men – large enough to get the work done but small enough to avoid notice. You will head north and west up river, over towards Popayán and then the Pacific coast, and sniff out such *puta madre* royalists as remain. If you find any, and judge them a threat, you will send notice – and we will send a full contingent.'

— 'Is that understood, *Milord.*'

It is not, completely – but Paez has put it as a statement not a question – and he would ask O'Leary to fill in the details.

'*A sus órdenes*, at your command, *mi general.*'

Why does it give him such pleasure to submit his will to others? Like casting loose in a dinghy on a lake and letting the waves take you where they want, as Shelley and he had done once on Lake Geneva. Or giving a horse its head.

Paez gives a curt nod, gathers up his men and rides off with them towards the brothels and bars of the Candelaria.

The house they have acquired in Bogota has advantages. It lies in a narrow side street accessible only by horses or foot, so no carriages pass; a few quadrants from the central plaza, close to the main theatres and *salons* – but distant enough from the fireworks let off in revolutionary fervour throughout the night.

One further improvement over even the Liberator's mansion is an internal courtyard of the sort favoured by the Moors. The courtyard is filled with plants – giant Datura lilies of such potent, narcotic properties any Indian shaman who consumed their seed would trance for days and nights of delirium. White flowers hang heavy and pendulous from the plants, as if too great a responsibility.

He wonders if he should send some to Coleridge. Whether they would survive the journey, or be consumed by idle and curious seamen with demonic effects – who might then witness monsters from the deep. Or whether Humboldt with his companion, fuelled by their insatiable curiosity, had sampled them in the depths of the jungle. Or whether he should suggest to Bankes they do so now themselves.

The internal courtyard has a balcony corridor running around the bedrooms on the first floor, guarded by Moretto, who barks at any outsider. Teresa and he have taken to the custom of an evening *paseo*, when they circle this internal balcony without the whispered *piropos* or distractions of the city – and can have private conversations, with the smell of tropical flowers rising up around them.

From the other balcony, looking out onto the street, the setting sun illuminates the mountains and the twin sanctuaries of Monserrate and Guadalupe; Teresa has visited both with Fanny, to make obeisance to these Catholic shrines. He likes the way Teresa can one moment be such a devout Catholic – and the next suggest their walk around the courtyard has tired her out, so they must retire for mutual rest to the bedroom, to restore themselves and be refreshed before dinner.

Fanny knows enough not to disturb them until he emerges to pass by Bankes's bedroom, where he can enjoy a cigar on his friend's balcony and discuss the comings and goings of the day. Much of which has to do with *intelligence*, for intelligence of what is transpiring is hard to come by, and arrives from many sources.

A young man in the marketplace, with whom Bankes has started up a connection, might have disclosed – on good authority, it is said – Admiral Cochrane is sailing to Chile to help the rebels. With British troops aboard who have proved themselves at Waterloo.

Or Fanny has heard, from a vendor of silks and a trader in gossip, that the Spanish Viceroy is planning to flee Cartagena for the safety of a Caribbean island.

Or O'Leary could tell him confidentially – with the seductive Irish gift of making everything seem a confidence – that the Liberator would *undoubtedly* give him an estate vacated by the royalists, either in Venezuela or this new country of Colombia – if he would take up arms on his behalf; and that Bankes likewise could avail himself of *desirable antiquities* if he contributes to the cause.

He holds the bird in his hand so he can feel the beating heart through the feathers and look closely at its small black eye. The eye appears not to be looking at him, but he knows from Bankes how wide the peripheral vision of a bird can be.

Then he lets it fly – directly overhead and out of the open courtyard – with a shout and a stamp of his good foot.

'*¡Vaya!*' applauds the stable boy in the corner.

He dislikes the Spanish habit of keeping caged birds – and frees those he finds or that are brought to him when he makes clear he will pay for their release, like this one. Particularly when there are so many wild birds in the trees.

A black grackle with a long tail and presumptuous ways likes to sit on the balcony and has become tame, so Allegra can feed it by hand;

the bird rewards the child with squeaks loud enough for Fanny to exclaim it has a human spirit – which may be malevolent and cursed, for it is black with a long tail. But Teresa waves this away as super-stition, and dismisses any idea the shape of a tail should make any difference to an animal's soul. He is not so sure – he has always respected superstition.

Allegra likes the masked flycatchers who swoop the patio pool for their prey, yellow bellies flashing against the water, before they retreat to the mango tree where they make even more noise than the grackle.

'Why are they so noisy?' she asks.

'So that we notice them,' Teresa replies.

'A bit like your father and his writing,' adds Bankes tartly.

There are dogs everywhere, abandoned by royalist owners when they fled the city. Some have attached themselves to the house before they arrived; yet more are now welcomed in. One room on the ground floor has become as good as a kennels, to Fletcher's disgust. Moretto and Mutz, also disgruntled by these newcomers, try to keep order.

He spends a great deal of time with Moretto in particular. Some-times he wonders if he is not at his happiest with the bulldog.

'Moretto, you are no rogue, Moretto.'

'Moretto, thou art an honest fellow, Moretto.'

And Moretto sweeps the floor with his tail as he sits with his haunches on the ground.

Moretto's size commands respect from the mongrels of Bogota, as does Mutz's fierce appearance and her foreshortened tail, a battle wound. Now they have companions to roam the ground floor, which has large quarters backing onto stables and a garden, so perfect for a menagerie – which he wants to extend.

He has made tentative enquiries about a tame jaguar – but such a thing is not easily to be found.

There is talk also of the spectacled bears of the Andes, smaller and less ferocious than the brown bear he kept at Trinity. Perhaps more scholarly, with their spectacles. It appears orphaned cubs are sometimes found and can be brought up by hand. And he has the unusual qualification of owning a bear before, as Bankes reminds him – which endeared him to Bankes in the first place. Indeed, helped Bankes notice him *at all*, his friend remarks, as a little older and a senior figure at the college when Byron arrived in Cambridge; 'still wet behind the ears, from the nursery,' says Bankes, with a gentler tone than usual.

The further they get from England, the more Bankes becomes fully himself, as if he were growing into his own part. The Colombians take a curious view of his 'Greek habits', as Bankes describes them. While they joke about *maricas* and *maricones* – and no man will admit to such feelings publicly – much happens clandestinely in the markets and without prosecution. No case is ever brought to court, on the basis – O'Leary explains – that either the offender is too poor to pay a fine or rich enough to pay off any investigating magistrate. Aside from the odd reference to unnatural practices from the pulpit of the Candelaria – references which its main attendees, the church-going ladies of Bogota, feign not to understand – there is a complacent attitude, far from the uproar caused in Britain by the mere mention of sodomy.

Bankes also, like many Englishmen, enjoys dressing up. He speaks of the freedom he enjoyed in the Levant and Syria when he spent two years wearing nothing but a turban and loose Islamic robes. The tailors of Bogota are employed at full stretch in making him ever more fanciful uniforms and breeches. But the *guayaberas* in bright pinks and oranges from Cartagena have – for the moment – been consigned to the bottom of his capacious trunk; some have been used to wrap delicate pre-Columbian antiquities, along with more acorns.

The sun is streaming over the balcony and Fanny has brought Teresa a tisane of lemon verbena; here called *hierba luisa*, Luisa's herb – she wonders who Luisa was? – which she cradles for warmth, as the mountain air is chill in the morning.

She has woken to find that – as so often – Byron has left the bedroom. Perhaps on one of the shooting expeditions he likes so much, in the hills above Bogota for target practice – just as he did in the woods around Ravenna. He likes to tell how he once almost shot a nun who had wandered out from a convent, when he mistook her wimple behind a rock for the head of a fox.

'But what was she doing behind a rock?' Teresa had asked.

'That, my love, you must enquire of the nun.'

She relishes these moments, when she can advance onto the balcony in her nightdress and a shawl, and look over the city with the sun slanting low over the mountains and the cobbled streets. Bogota is a garden city, arranged in blocks so while houses front the street, trees and plants escape in every direction from the large courtyards behind.

The lemon verbena has come from their own garden, which has mint, rosemary, thyme and coriander, the last of which their cook is fond of using, although she is less accustomed to the bitter taste. But there is also sage, reminding her of Italy, and on the balcony, pots of basil in such abundance she can smell the plants as the day's heat begins to warms them. She brushes the leaves to release their scent more.

Down in the narrow lane below, she can see farmers passing from the countryside. Some wear soft felt hats that flop around their heads –

heads bent with the weight of produce on their backs, so hard to see their faces. The women wear long dresses that sweep the cobbles, gathered at the shoulders and arms, elaborately embroidered. She has taken to wearing such dresses herself – not least so her high heeled boots will not be seen, as she has found a cobbler who can cater for her tastes, albeit at an unusual cost.

When Byron raises an eyebrow at the bill – for someone so rich he can be cautious about money, perhaps because in the past he had less – she reminds him she did not share Bankes's expensive tastes for antiques, let alone paintings – and of the *prodigious* amount the household spends on alcohol, given the preference for fine French wines brought from Europe. And of the amounts that he, Byron, spends on elaborate costumes.

Of these, the most excessive have been the scarlet and gold uniforms he commissioned with Bankes, each egging the other on at the tailors. Despite her comment – as she had been present to advise – that they would just be better targets for the enemy.

Together with an even greater absurdity – helmets.

Helmets of classical proportions from a skilled metalworker Bankes had found, made up to drawings Byron had sketched and the subject of much discussion. They were to be *Homeric*, the two men agreed, to the puzzlement of the metalworker, more used to soldiers concerned whether breastplates could withstand bayonets or bullets.

One huge gilt helmet was ordered for Bankes, with purple trim; another for Byron, just as splendid, with his coat of arms beneath the plume and the motto *Crede Byron*. Both at great expense. As she reminded him when he queried the bill from her cobbler.

'Ah, but those were a necessity. *Crede* Byron. Believe me.'

'Really? They were no more a necessity – than my boots!'

And he had fallen silent. For this had become a complicated area between them. The question of the extent to which he would fight for Bolivar – or just offer tacit support.

Of his bravery there was no question. As he had shown in Italy, when he supported her father against their Austrian overlords. But she could see no need for the dangers and complications of any journey he might make to encounter the enemy, however diminished and in whatever disarray. The Spaniards still dominated the continent, even if enclaves like Colombia had declared their independence. The new country was a fragile one.

It did not help that he felt unable to tell her of his plans – to avoid what he called a scene – and what Italians call *a necessary discussion*. So the only way to elicit information was from Bankes – not reliable – or O'Leary, who affected surprise she had not been appraised by Byron himself and was unforthcoming, preferring to talk of other, more playful things.

Perhaps she should write him a letter? To which he must reply. She had noticed before how the act of writing concentrated his mind and elicited a clearer answer – as when she was leaving the Count. But how was she supposed to deliver a letter when they were living in the same house? Leave it on his pillow? Beside which she slept.

It would be ridiculous.

Still, she composes one in her head; one she has been thinking of for some time, as she stands with her tea against her chest and the sun rises higher above the mountains.

I beg you, Giorgio, to think – of the possible consequences. Would you leave me as a widow before we have married? Or leave your daughters fatherless? There is much you can do in this world without picking up a sword. So much more perhaps by writing instead and inspiring people to liberty.

This is folly and should be addressed as such before you cause harm to those who love you and who in my case have abandoned my husband, family and country to come with you.

The tea has grown cold. She does not send the letter.

He lies awake. Very awake. He is reminded of nights as a boy in the echoing house at Newstead Abbey.

He is due to depart at daybreak. The small hours, and everybody else should be asleep, but the house is not quiet. The open nature of the building and the heat of summer mean the windows and bedroom doors are open to allow a through draught.

He hears Bankes snoring in one room in a *basso profundo* interrupted by stuttered breaths, and Fanny providing more soprano overtones in another. Fletcher – to his credit, and an asset in a manservant given the frequent occasions that force proximity to his master – does not snore. Perhaps because he makes a habit of consuming enough alcohol each evening, bought on his master's account, for sound sleep to ensue.

And nor does Teresa. She lies beside him, her aquiline nose pressed against the pillow, blonde hair cascading down the sheets. They had embraced with all the passion of imminent separation earlier that evening – and while he was never sure of that old wives' tale – that a woman could only conceive if she experiences her *petit mort* – the conditions for conception had been optimal. Would he like to have a child with Teresa? She would like one, she has said.

More to the point, why was he leaving at all? Leaving a beautiful and spirited woman lying in bed who professed to adore him – and had left her husband, however disagreeable, and her family, who were very agreeable indeed, to accompany him across the Atlantic.

Was this folly? To launch an adventure with a ragtag group of Paez's men – men whom Paez might be releasing because he wanted to keep the best back for his own use, understandably. Was he getting the runts of the litter? And what was he trying to show? That, despite a deformed right foot, he could still be a soldier; that he had aligned with Bolivar's cause.

He could not now retract – or risk every woman in the *salons* of Bogota taking him for a coward. Even Teresa might think less of him.

And he is not a coward. His whole life has been about accepting challenges – gloves thrown to the floor. He has surprised himself more often by a *lack* of fear. Frightened himself by fearlessness, if that is not a contradiction.

He wants to swim across all the Hellesponts life provides, with the uncertainty as to whether, like Leander, he might make the return journey.

The noise in the house still keeps him awake. This open living and lack of privacy has been awkward at times – particularly as Teresa can be loud and emphatic in moments of passion. Once or twice, to her amusement, he has used a pillow to stifle her a little.

'Are you like an Ottoman Emperor, my Lord? Who must strangle or suffocate every woman in his harem to make way for the next? Perhaps that could be the subject of one of your poems set in the East. The ones that sell so well.'

There are other sounds. The perpetual howl of dogs on the skyline. The lamplighter who passes to check all are still burning. Calls of sentries, for an armed watch is kept around the capital of this new and still vulnerable country.

For no particular reason – other than a military habit of mind – it has been determined they should leave on a Monday, and so the last revelries of Sunday, in a city where the Sabbath is observed as much with fiestas as with piety, are being played out. Horses and mules with those revellers are still arriving back from the countryside, their hooves amplified by cobbles – although the mules, he learned on the journey from the coast, are quieter than the horses.

He must check with Fletcher how many mules they are taking – and perhaps take more. Large jack-mules of the sort George Washington encouraged settlers to use in the Americas, for strength and stamina. Just in case his smaller white mule feels the rigours of the journey and suffers accordingly.

At least he has got Fletcher to make up a large consignment of Harvey's sauce; however bad the food along the way, a strong sauce will mask the flavour. Fletcher had at first demurred – 'Surely Sir, that may prove difficult to procure in the market. It is not to local tastes…' – but he had insisted, not least because a London grocer in Trinity Street had once given him the supposedly secret recipe. He told Fletcher to dissolve anchovies – easy to get in Cartagena – with vinegar and soy, then add mushroom juice, garlic and a pinch of cayenne.

'Finally, some cochineal to give that familiar red colour, as the easiest dye to hand – and bottle it – a lot, please, as I am sure it will prove of great use. But you do not need to add the orange label with which we are so familiar in England.

— 'If it's any good, you can always sell extra bottles to the local inhabitants as Fletcher's Sauce. *Salsa de Fletcher*. It has a ring to it.'

Fletcher's face had been a masterful mix of doubt, resignation and sorrow at the whims of his master. But he had made the sauce.

So many preparations and considerations for the journey. He calms his unquiet mind by going to Allegra's bedroom, to watch his sleeping daughter quietly by the light from the lamp that has been lit outside her window.

The morning announces itself sharply at six, with military precision, a hard light coming over the mountains and shining past their ineffectual curtains.

He dresses in a white linen shirt and sprays it lightly with cologne, for he has acquired the habit, like Bolivar – because of Bolivar? He does not wake Teresa – who is prone anyway to sleep late – and they have made their farewells the night before. He had told her he would depart like this – quietly – because he knows they might otherwise have an Italian leave-taking of theatrical intensity.

He descends and has a quiet cup of coffee with Victoria, the old black cook, of whom he is fond. She gives him a maize *arepa* – he adds a blood-red splash of the Harvey's sauce to see if it has fully infused – and he eats with surprising avidity, given his normal slender breakfast – but then today is different.

It is as if the whole of Bogota knows they are leaving. Military men he has never met appear at the doorway as the principal door is, unusually, unlocked. Normally kept closed, as the household uses a side entrance from the courtyard, Fletcher has opened it now so they can take out the trunks of clothes and equipment with more ease; and also deliberately, at his master's request, to make public their departure, after consultation with Bankes. He does not want them to slip away like ships in the night.

The familiar sights from their months in Bogota take on a new intensity. The *campesino* farmer squatting on the cobbles to sell small piles of fruit, which he weighs on a portable scale. The large white bowler hat the farmer wears, which in the past has amused Bankes for its sartorial expressiveness, is – he notices for the first time – tied around his neck to prevent the Andean winds from blowing it away. The ribbon makes the hat look like a cake stand. He must make that remark to Bankes, although he can see his friend is occupied with last-minute arrangements and farewells of his own at a street corner, in conversation with a young man.

The distant Andes are covered in a morning mist above the dairy yellow of the old Candelaria church, whose bells ring out for the dawn service. The sky immediately above the city is thin and diaphanous; a mountain sky.

Paez's men wait in the lane. A sergeant – unmistakable as such for build and a certain reassuring confidence – introduces himself as Juan Esteban. A motley assortment of men in tattered uniforms and ragged boots inspire less confidence – what in England would have been called parish soldiers.

There is little he can do about their uniforms – but the boots will be a problem.

'Fletcher, go to the Callejuela de Merced where all the cobblers work who we visited for the Contessa. I'm sure their shops open early – since they close early. Take these men and buy them boots. And tell them to take rifles and shoot any shopkeeper who tries to charge above the odds just because they can see the matter is of *urgency*. In fact, take the sergeant as well – although his boots are fine – as I can't see any-body arguing with him.'

Juan Esteban has not understood this, but gives a broad smile.

As Fletcher leads his incongruous party away to be sized and booted – he thinks of Falstaff, Bardolph and Pistol off to join Henry V – a sound of wailing fills the air as the Montoya family approach.

Señora Montoya, who could almost be in mourning, wears a large, stiff dress of black lace which she is manoeuvring with difficulty along the lane, while her young son Nico strides ahead, to distance himself from his mother's tears, and wearing the pageboy costume that Byron has spent much time and expense devising.

The progress of mother and son is impeded by the mules assembled – and now abandoned – by the soldiers in front of the house. As the alleyway is narrow, and mules by their nature not accommodating, all traffic, both pedestrian and equine, has spluttered to a complaining halt.

The new republican and patriotic air abroad allows beggars and tradesmen to vent their feelings. There are mutterings of resentment against '*Milord*' for causing this blockage.

'*¡Sinvergüenzas!*' shouts Nico unexpectedly. 'Shameless ones! Do you not know that while you are concerned with your *merchandise*, we may be going to our deaths?' His mother bursts into even more hysterical weeping.

Bankes watches all this with amusement, puffing on a cigar.

'Nothing like an early morning departure to cause confusion. And that's before we've tried to load the mules.'

He holds the bowl close to his chest – a bowl of the *panela* they prepare with great ceremony in the Highlands, a sweet, hot blend of cane sugar and cinnamon in some harsh alcohol like cane spirit that burns as it heats. The hut has no chimney, so the smoke swirls round from the stove and the fire, making Bankes look theatrical through the smoke as he leans towards him, also clutching his bowl of *panela*.

'Hail Glamis.' Bankes grimaces as he speaks. 'And Thane of Cawdor!'

'Why do they do that?' he asks Bankes. 'Have no chimney?'

'I have seen the same in other countries – and in Africa. The smoke will escape through the rafters. And look – they use it to smoke the meat and cheese and anything they have, so it will be preserved.'

He can see, now Bankes has led his gaze, such foodstuffs hanging high up.

The old man of the house notices their interest.

'*¿Quieren salchicha?* Would you like sausage?' he asks in a soft, slurred Spanish that suggests it is not his native tongue.

'Yes,' says Bankes immediately. 'Who knows when anyone will offer us food again?' This from a man who told them he survived on nothing but fried locusts when travelling across the Egyptian desert.

He looks at Bankes. His person has become unkempt and dirty. Smoke is passing through his straggling red hair as if it were also thatch. Doubtless he looks much the same himself – although at least he asked Fletcher to crop his hair short again before he left Bogota. A wise decision, as much to keep down the fleas and lice they may encounter – that they *have* encountered. Even if it means Bankes can bamm him for being prick-eared because they stick out so much.

He calls Fletcher and asks him to take off the money belt with which Bankes has equipped them – a stratagem he had used against rapacious Bedouin.

'Buy some of these smoked meats and cheeses for our saddle bags – those the old man will sell – and pay him well.'

What would the Lake Poets – the wretched *Lakers* – those *pond poets* – make of this enormity – this landscape without end? Perhaps finally – and mercifully – they would be lost for words. You could drop the whole Lake District – or the Scottish Highlands for that matter – into these mountains, and both would disappear.

They are on a wide, muddy river between chains of mountains that run like ribs across the country. He likes to lie on the deck of the *lancha* and watch the swirl of the currents pass.

Herds of capybara paddle in the shallows by the living palisade of the green walled riverbanks. The capybara are rodents – the world's largest, according to Bankes, but of a size – around a hundred and fifty pounds – that would deter even the most audacious cat. They look like giant, blunt-nosed guinea pigs. Bankes says they can be domesticated but despite the softness of their fur, something in him, although tempted, shies from the idea of a giant capybara as a pet. Nor would his dogs tolerate them.

Mutz and Moretto have been left behind in Bogota. It was one thing to risk his own life in a war. Quite another to risk those of his dogs.

He has commandeered a wooden daybed. With a few rugs it is tolerably comfortable. He can lie on it while playing a game of passage with Bankes and Nico, rolling the dice on the deck.

At night, he hears river dolphins snoring against the perpetual hum of insects. By day, he sees the dolphins – which the boatmen call *toninas* – patrolling the banks, powerful backs thrashing the water so even crocodiles and the large cattle egrets look alarmed and back away.

He remembers the flying fish on their earlier sea voyage – how they had jumped out of the ocean to escape the dolphins' fierce teeth.

At other, calmer times, he just watches the water swirl by – water they have drunk and even when filtered through linen appears dark and impure. To stay healthy, Fletcher declares, they must mix cane-spirit into the water, so the alcohol will kill any pestilence. Fletcher likes to recount – often – the story of the captain who survived an arduous voyage by drinking only whisky – while his crew drank the ship's stale water and as a result, succumbed. 'To a man.'

He is impressed by the facility with which the boatmen work. How they corral the horses and mules on such a small craft – and navigate the river shoals, for the sand banks extend underwater in ways that could strand the unwary. Sometimes they must moor up if the prevailing wind becomes too strong.

The crew are mostly young. But José is older and toothless, stooped from years of the same task as he stands at the bow with a measuring pole and calls out the depths – a duty that calls for an intimate knowledge of the river and its vagaries and its shallows.

José's voice as he calls is so guttural and rancorous and loud it is like the rooks gathered in the trees near Newstead; the sound that oppressed his spirit when a boy. Yet the old man does his job with such attentiveness and skill, he rewards him with coin to buy gold teeth – much coveted, as a considerable supply is to be had in the towns they pass; many taken from corpses on the recent fields of battle, to be used again.

'This,' advises Juan Esteban, their sergeant, foursquare enough to have satisfied either Wellesley or Napoleon, 'is the time for a man to fill his mouth with new teeth.'

He informs Fletcher of this intelligence, as Fletcher has also not got a full complement from youthful ructions in London, and adventures since, often when drunk; but his manservant is not enamoured of the prospect.

'I would not sleep in a dead man's bed – nor wear a dead man's shirt – so why should I wear a dead man's teeth?'

'But you would have no objection to a dead man's widow?' interjects Bankes.

Fletcher considers the matter while picking at those teeth which remain, as if reminded of their presence. The usual formalities observed in the presence of his master and his master's friend have loosened now they all serve under Bolivar's flag; for which Fletcher has volunteered, attracted by the idea he could be paid twice, once by Byron and once by the Republican army. He had been given the choice to stay in Bogota. 'What, with those bloody dogs to look after!'

'Far from it, Sir. They say a widow is like good mutton or beef that has been well hung. That age and experience give a better taste. And Sir – they have the habit of intimacy and of conjoining – which a young bride does not yet know and may take to – but also may not take to. Virginity is an *overrated commodity*.' He says the last with some satisfaction.

'So Fletcher, should the widows in Lima and Quito – or wherever we reach – wear their best mantilla lace on your approach? Perhaps worn low over the bosom, in the style of country girls?' he asks, with mischief.

'Should the women who are still married wear *theirs* – on your approach, my Lord?'

'Very good, Fletcher! I should have you commandeered for mutiny or insubordination to a superior officer... I would not like to have been a customer in your alehouse who asked for credit – or complained the small beer contained slops – as I understand often occurs and have indeed experienced at some establishments. Or questioned the prove-nance or purity of your gin.'

'My *gin*? My gin, my Lord, was so pure you could see through the glass —'

'To the strumpet beyond,' finishes Bankes.

He watches Nico listen to this banter in English, smiling amiably but without understanding a word – Nico with black curly hair and pre-ternaturally black eyes against a Latin skin that never darkens in the sun, like those of Teresa's relatives near Ravenna. Nico Montoya, from a good family in Bogota, whose care Bolivar has personally entrusted to him.

'He wants to fight for the cause; not die for it,' Bolivar had said. 'He is only nineteen. I know his family, both in Bogota and Venezuela. One of the finest Mantuano families. So I am sending him with you. *Cuídalo bien, como si fuera su hijo – o lo mío.* Look after him well, as if he were your son – or mine.'

Before they left, Bolivar had again summoned them to his house, for a *despedida*, a formal farewell – and in a brief but intense en-counter, delivered a geography lesson, together with their military orders, such as they were. He wore his black frock coat without a single medal, and sat in an upright chair while they stood. Maps and charts were spread across the broad desk in his study. Ignoring these, he took a large sheet of plain foolscap and scrunched the middle of the paper in his small fist, dropping it on a card-table in front of them – then paused for practised effect.

'This is the new country of Colombia, to be written on a blank sheet of paper – but on paper shaped like this, in an impossible series of broken mountains and valleys. This is what you must cross to get first to the west, to see what royalist forces remain, and then up to the Pacific coast' – he tapped the very far end of the paper – 'which is why it is still the most remote of places – and where the royalists have chosen to hide, thinking we will never reach them. But you will.'

— '*Tengo una confianza total en ustedes.* I have complete confidence in you. So I only ask that you repay my trust.'

He had been distracted again by the smell of his new commander's cologne, which O'Leary had said was made to Bolivar's personal specifications in Cuba – the famous perfumiers of Havana – and contained, as well as citrus fruit over cedarwood, elements of tobacco.

This last had surprised him. Why would a man want to smell of tobacco? In Mayfair, the gentlemen retired to a special smoking room so ladies would not be *distressed* by the fumes. And Bankes reeked of cheap cigars. Yet on Bolivar, the tobacco smelled sweet – for now O'Leary had alerted him, he could distinguish it amongst the other notes of the cologne. A honeyed smell, more like night-flowering stock – or *nicotiana*, the tobacco-plants of kitchen gardens. Was the perfume made from the flower or the leaf?

'*Milord*?' said Bolivar sharply. 'You appear distracted?' And he rose up.

'Although words are my profession, they have failed me on this occasion, *mi general* – it is the emotion of the moment. We will do our utmost to fulfil your requirements.'

Bolivar had a disconcerting habit of coming up close to people and peering at them from under large dark eyebrows. Eyes that never seemed to blink. Or blink first. Maybe it was so they could smell his cologne.

'You are beginning to speak Spanish as well as a politician, *Milord*. Better, certainly, than many of my generals. You have a facility for languages. I am impressed. Although have a care your accent is not Castilian – or you will sound like the Viceroy who was lucky to escape with his head on his shoulders and a mouth still to speak with. Do not lisp your 'c's in that affected Habsburg way. You may have learned your Spanish in Europe. But we speak cleanly here.'

Something he has tried to do ever since.

It is magnificent. Absurd. Since they left the river, clouds have followed them for days over the high mountain valleys. But this morning they have lifted and there is a volcano ahead of them, large, snow-capped and dominant, a picture-book vision of symmetrical perfection such as a child might draw.

He looks at Bankes.

'The Nevado del Tolima. One of the highest volcanoes in Colombia – almost 17,000 feet. Higher than Mont Blanc or any mountain in Europe. We will need to skirt its flanks.'

'Why?'

Bankes looks at him as if he is obtuse.

'So that we can get to the other side towards the Pacific which is where – we – want – to – go.' Bankes's voice slows to a crawl, as if addressing a small and stupid boy.

'I realise that,' – with impatience – 'but I think we should climb as much of it as we can.'

A sharper look from Bankes, as if he were not just obtuse but mad.

'Have you any idea what ascending such a mountain might entail?'

'More than you. Do not forget I was in the Alps for some time. I have reached summits.

— 'Juan Esteban!' He calls the sergeant over.

'*Capitán*?'

'We need to climb that mountain. Or as high as we can.'

One of Juan Esteban's signal qualities is his ability to absorb any suggestion with total equanimity.

'*Por supuesto.* Of course. To survey the military position beyond?'

'Exactly. To survey the military position beyond…'

And he turns in triumph to Bankes.

They leave the main body of men beside a small lake a farmer has told them is called Bombona, with instructions to forage for firewood and provisions, with the farmer's help. And pay handsomely for anything they receive.

He rides the small white mule he has come to trust as surefooted and reliable; Bankes insists on walking, and Nico follows suit, while Juan Esteban leads the way, with a sure feel between which is a random track made by cattle or goats and one made by and for men.

They pass Datura lilies, not white like the ones in their courtyard in Bogota, but an intense orange; trumpet-shaped flowers hanging pendulously towards the earth. He never did send those seeds to Coleridge. There are fuchsias of an intense scarlet Teresa would enjoy if she was with them.

He is too far behind Bankes and Nico to hear their conversation. Besides, he is lost in his own thoughts. But Nico is listening to Bankes with attention. Perhaps Bankes is telling him of his travels. He is jealous sometimes of the wealth of experience his friend enjoys – the temples he has seen in the Levant or ancient Egypt, like the oracle of Amun in the Siwa Oasis. He can imagine Bankes on the Nile, sailing on a felucca with the wind filling the white sail, the oldest and simplest of sailing designs; or advancing into a tomb with torch in hand.

Although Bankes has told some of those stories so often, he feels he has experienced them himself.

But this journey now has an intoxicating delight of its own kind. Riding along the shore of a lake towards a snow-capped monster of a mountain, whose reflection in the water is surrounded by palm fronds – as exotic as any vision Coleridge could conjure up with his opium and his Kubla Khan.

How strange Coleridge had not realised how good that poem was – and waited twenty years to publish it – until he, Byron, pressed him to do so, insisting it was not an interrupted failure but a natural expression of his true talent. His volcanic talent.

He feels Shelley beside him as well – tripping with excitement – his ungainly hop, skip and sloping walk. All bony shoulders and thin legs, as when he used to accompany him through the streets of Italy. Skin covered with freckles, his tousled hair threaded with premature grey. Shelley who had supported *Don Juan* – recognised the cantos for what they were when all the others back in England were clucking like wet hens. Murray the worst of the lot, claiming that – as a family man – he could not publish the book as first sent. As a *family man*. What cant. What a cunt.

Shelley had seen the poem as the epic that he always wanted his friend to write – that it expressed his true *character* – that it was astonishingly fine. Wonderful words, given Juan's loose-limbed adventures were so different from the high-toned philosophical verse that Shelley wrote himself.

How Shelley would have been excited at the volcano ahead. Shelley loved a good volcano – not just as *spectacle* – his story of Vesuvius by night – but as a *symbol*. A symbol of the natural impulse for freedom surging out of the ground in countries like Italy and Greece – and above all France and its Revolution – after they had been held down by despotic rulers or foreign invaders.

'Think of the world,' he would say excitedly, in his cracked soprano, 'as just a thin crust, underneath which molten lava is contained – trying to *burst*,' – his voice would almost squeak – 'for that is the state we – are – in. We are living through an Age of Turbulence – when the desire for freedom is forever trying to erupt.'

And he, Byron, had agreed and added he thought the same true of the imagination. The *lava of the imagination* could and should not be contained, but should burst forth and run unfettered in whatever direction it could. Not be checked, endlessly, by the dictates of polite society against which he had so long chafed.

'England may be sleeping,' Shelley would add. 'But it is the long sleep before an earthquake.' Volcanoes were a constant reminder there was always the possibility of change; violent change, which could erupt within the human spirit – ancestral voices prophesying war.

That is reason alone to climb this one – and he had heard Bolivar speak of his desire to reach the summit of Chimborazo, the higher cone further south. For a long line of volcanoes extended down the Andes; a rift under the earth's surface must allow such uprisings. Bolivar spoke of ascending Chimborazo as *a stairway of Titan*, as he called it – an unassailable battlement, as if a military objective; a necessary part of his war against the Spaniards.

As they come over a small dip, he notices an intense smell of sulphur. Nico exclaims in delight, '*Baños termales* – hot springs.' The boy strips off his boots and paddles in the shallow water which spills from the ponds. The sulphur has left the surrounding rocks russet-red.

The water is not deep enough to bathe fully; but afterwards he rides barefoot, enjoying the cool air on his newly cleaned feet, resting the lame one out of the stirrup, though he notices Nico viewing it with curiosity – which normally he would mind but, such is his elation at their surroundings, today he does not care.

They come over another ridge to find camelids grazing, smaller and wilder than the alpaca and llama they have seen before, looking more like deer. Nico turns, his eyes cratered even blacker by the overhead sun. He has never seen the boy so excited.

'*¡Vicuña!* They are rare and impossible to tame, with the softest of fleeces.'

On seeing them, the vicuña wheel away in a great arc, shadows cast wide on the grassland *puna* as if a flock of birds circled above.

He has settled into the rhythm of his white mule, only fourteen or so hands, but nimble and able over the rocky terrain. A female mule – a molly. He had kept her after the journey from Bogota, so knows she is sturdy and strong – and also white mules were rare, and this one had taken his fancy. He is pleased now he had not insisted on a jack-mule instead.

He remembers riding on her with Allegra and telling stories of 'El Guapo and the Saint'. He will write Allegra a letter with another story, and perhaps a drawing of the volcano. Perhaps the story could be about the volcano.

He thinks also of Teresa. When he left, Fanny and she had been experimenting with long rolls of Chinese silk they sold in the market. How they could be swathed around the body in a complicated way that, according to Bankes, was how mummies were wrapped in Egypt.

Allegra had asked what a mummy was – and Bankes said, with unnecessary bluntness, he felt – for Bankes often spoke to Allegra as if she were eighteen not four – that a mummy was a dead person. And Allegra had looked puzzled but also knowing, in the way she sometimes did. And Teresa had woven the blue-green silk around herself in an intricate layering that allowed her to move across the ground as if she were water flowing.

Bankes and he have cut up one of Bankes's old shirts from Cartagena, an exuberant yellow one, into thin strips they can use as turbans – for Bankes has experience of them from Egypt – and they are cooling in the equatorial sun. He thinks wryly of the Homeric helmets they commissioned in Bogota, long since abandoned.

His went to José, the toothless old boatman on the Magdalena, who had fingered it as the helmets lay among the flotsam of their baggage. He likes to think of the old man scaring any capybara in the shallows with the flashing gilt as he calls the depths.

The yellow turbans feel light, although he is not sure he wears his with the same panache as Bankes. Juan Esteban has pointed out – just as Teresa had done – that the two of them will make easy targets for any royalist rifles. The joke is wearing thin. He reminds himself that Napoleon always wore the most distinctive of cockaded hats and survived the attentions of any sniper.

After some hours, the mountain becomes steep. He dismounts and leads his patient mule by the reins. They are high now, an intoxicating feeling, with a febrile quality to the air. When Nico slows his pace, Juan Esteban makes him drink water – makes them all drink water from the saddlebags.

'At this altitude it is necessary,' Juan Esteban declares. 'To prevent *soroche*, mountain sickness.'

Perhaps it is hypoxia, but he is gripped with a wild excitement. The mountain above, its cone extending from the hot earth's core, the way that Mount Olympus should look, a mountain of gods. Standing out against the azure blue of the sky – the snow on its summit – the extremes of heat and cold, like white on black, fascinate and compel him. He does not want life to be *tiède*, as the French say – lukewarm – when it can be like this.

The energy of their approach appears to have transfixed his companions as well. They stride forward with purpose. Bankes has that familiar thrust to his shoulders he recognises whenever his friend feels excitement and determination.

They reach a promontory which gives a view right down towards the last mountains before the Pacific as the sun sinks lower towards the horizon.

'We should turn,' says Bankes. 'Before dark, as it will be hard to find a way back, even with a clear night and the moon.'

Juan Esteban agrees. And they have reached a satisfying place. A *mirador*, as the Spaniards call them, a viewing platform with stones carved and arranged in a way which cannot surely be natural or arbitrary, but has been done by some ancient people.

From the volcano's slopes, they see Colombia spread out below them – pale grasslands, the rich green of the tropical valleys, a blue haze around the mountains that lie between them and the ocean.

'It was from a volcano such as this that Humboldt felt the *interconnectedness of all things*,' says Bankes. 'That nature is a web of life, extending across the globe.'

The prospect is sublime. As beautiful as a dream – solitary and savage – and wholly remote from the affairs of men.

While they make a pretence of scouting the surrounding landscape for signs of royalists, the likelihood seems as remote as coming across a Scottish castle – although it would be a fine position for a castle, he cannot help thinking. Perhaps this is where he should purchase an estate?

Fletcher has given them a hip flask – 'against the cold, my Lord' – and he produces it now from the saddlebag. The raw Colombian brandy spreads to his gullet and his head so he too feels like a volcano and can hardly contain his excitement at the sheer accident of being alive.

'*¿Que piensas?* What do you think?' he asks Nico.

The boy's face is shining.

'*¡Magnífico!*'

To John Cam Hobhouse, from George Gordon Byron

San Agustin, March 21st, 1821

My dear Hobhouse –

The likelihood of this letter reaching you is slight. It will be sent clandestinely to Cartagena, in a packet addressed to Señor Luis Enrique de Palomas – a man known to one and all as *Sangucho* – a soup of the region which mixes ingredients and spices with profligacy – as he is of mixed blood, like most in Colombia – where we have found an array of skin colours to test the palette of any Academician. He is a commendable man, of enterprise and energy – and if anyone can assure the arrival of my correspondence, he will.

On our circuitous travels – to outflank any enemy so we can reach the Pacific Coast – a report came of ancient ruins lying to the south, near a town called San Agustin. This would require considerable diversion – and I at first demurred, as we have had many such reports during our travels and such intelligence has often proved false – or we have been promised a Cleopatra of archaeological riches – only to discover a *Charmian*.

Nothing, however, could hold Bankes back from any possible antiquities – not least if we might be the first to report them – as it appears Humboldt did not – and so we have diverted here – to find the most remarkable of spectacles.

Under the direction of a local superintendent, the inhabitants have dug down where stone objects were perceived to be lifting the ground – and found, not buildings underneath, but giant statues – left long before the Spaniards, by a people of whom there is no record.

The statues are monumental – twenty-five feet high, good enough for a Wellington or Castlereagh – carved in stone and of a style so peculiar I would need a paintbrush, not pen, to describe them – of course Bankes, with his usual attentiveness, has made sketches in his famous *notebooks* that will doubtless never be published.

While Bankes took his measurements – as a learned *Antiquary* – I wandered up to the crest of a hill which gave a view of the river, with more of these statues half covered by the ground. I felt that sense of elegy – and sadness – you may remember I did at the burial mounds of Troy – where the only vestige were the barrows supposed to contain the carcases of Achilles, Antilochus, Ajax, &c. of some civilisation that is past – of which we only have the *disjecta membra* – the fragments – and know so little of the true story.

The statues remind me of Shelley's abandoned relic in the desert – *look on my Works, ye Mighty, and despair*. It is curious to think of him still in Italy – he has been much in my thoughts – though it is possible he may have sailed away – if only to escape the attentions of Claire Clairmont, who no longer has me as her bear to bait.

Did they have poets here? A Homer of their own? Or storytellers? If so, no words survive. Perhaps we should inscribe our poems on stone, not bind them in fine octavo volumes, and then *bury them* – in the hope future generations will still speak the King's English – and can dig and decipher them, as Bankes tells me they are doing with the hieroglyphs in Egypt.

I think I shall write to Murray and suggest he engraves my poems on stone slabs. He might have more success in selling them than my poor *Juan,* which before I left had moved fewer copies than *Childe Harold* – although that appears to me now a mawkish affair. But then, as my sagacious friend Sangucho likes to say – for he is a bookseller among other attributes – what do we writers know of what readers want?

My future here is still uncertain. Please arrange with Murray and Kinnaird for any further payments to be banked with you and kept in trust for my return, or failing that, for my daughters.

Yours ever - N.B.

Sometimes he thinks Shelley should have come instead of him. Tall, skinny Shelley, still wearing his schoolboy's jacket as he did in Italy. The people here might laugh at him – just as he had been laughed at in school, for Eton had no time for a freethinker – but Shelley would have the *idealism* to see this through. Whereas he can see the holes in the enterprise. The absurdities. And deplore the savageries.

Daniel O'Leary had told him how many British soldiers had died at Boyaca – a word O'Leary mispronounced with relish as if an Irish place name – *'Boyo'ca'* – the battle which had won Colombia for Bolivar. Which had sent the old Viceroy scuttling down to Cartagena and spitting impotently with rage.

But those British – and Irish – had died for what? Because after twenty years of fighting Napoleon, nothing was left for them in Europe, with Bonaparte safely on his prison island? Certainly there was no work at home – so Bolivar's agent in London had signed them up and sent a packed troopship here.

Was that all Bankes and he were? Mercenaries who, as officers, were not even paid? Like a pub without a pot to piss in, my Lord, as Fletcher would say. Although Bolivar had said his path to acquiring an estate would be eased if he fought. And doubtless Bankes could help himself with more impunity to antiquities if he had a few medals pinned to his chest.

A movement catches his eye – a fox moving under a small bush. An American fox, larger and browner than those to which he was accustomed back in England. Everything is larger here.

'Halloo! Tally ho!' he shouts at Bankes. His friend looks at him blankly – knowing he hates hunting – as if he is going mad.

Perhaps he is. Perhaps he always has been.

Damn!

How had that happened?

He has lost a second ring – one of which he was inordinately fond. A ruby set in gold, slipped from his finger. A theatrical, ostentatious ring which he had bought in Venice on completing *Childe Harold*, with the reflection the royalties should pay handsomely, as they had.

'You're losing weight, man,' Bankes had said – unhelpful but true. The fingers that looked so puffy in Venice are slender. A diet of being constantly on a horse, the thin gruel of army life leavened by occasional diarrhoea and sickness, and he is becoming a wraith. Or rather, restored to the figure he had at twenty. Military life is proving a better regime than the vinegar and raw eggs he had imposed on himself whenever he got fat. Which had been often.

'Fletcher, would you please store my signet ring in the kitbag? And the Cornelian ring.' The Cornelian ring that a boy he had fallen in love with at Cambridge had given him. 'Or I will lose those as well.'

'Should we look for the ring you have lost, my Lord?'

'No.' He gestures at the landscape behind, a maze of shrubs and small streams. 'That would be pointless. Where would we even begin?'

There are no roads. Now they have reached the coast, they must ride across the sands at low tide. They camp under the stars or – more often – the rain. He likes to lie in a hammock under the tarpaulins they hang from the branches.

Once, while waiting for the tide to fall, Bankes and he walk barefoot up a stream that comes down to the sea. Large blue butterflies of an iridescent sheen sink slowly through the air, wings opening and shutting like the beacon of a lighthouse. Bankes claps his hand close to one and the butterfly's flight alters abruptly into a wild and swooping manner – 'As if I were a bird,' says Bankes, 'attacking it' – and he often does think Bankes is a bird, one of the black frigate-birds that circle them on the shore. 'And if I were a bird, I would be confused by the oscillating colour of the butterfly's wings, the slow flap of bright blue, and then by this rapid disappearance – for when it folds its wings on a branch, it looks like a brown leaf. These are the *Morphos*, all named after classical heroes – so there is a *Morpho hercules*, a *Morpho menelaus* and a *Morpho achilles*.'

'Is there a *Morpho patroclus*?'

'There is. There is indeed.'

He is reminded of the print Bankes had shown him in Humboldt's book – of the great naturalist and his companion, Aimé Bonpland, on the Orinoco River; Humboldt leaning against a tree in an open-necked linen shirt of impeccable tailoring, observing the scene with a contemplative pose and holding a telescope – for all the world like Nelson. Beside him, in a floppy hat, Bonpland examines a specimen, doubtless an insect, his speciality. Lianas hang down like curtains, there are bromeliads in the trees, and the local people have lit a fire and are boiling water while their companions lift a canoe ashore.

What the artist was not able to convey – and perhaps it is beyond any artist – is the startling contrast between light and shade. Intense tropical sun burning through trees a hundred feet tall – and sepulchral darkness that extends beyond the clearings made by the streams as they descend. Who would have thought the jungles of the South American continent would be so Gothic in appearance?

It is the same extreme he liked on seeing Teresa's white body against the black sand of Gomera – or when he cuts the black pith of a mangosteen to reveal the white flesh within. They can keep muted pastels for the reception rooms of Mayfair. He likes the intensity of this – the flashy red of heliconias against the green – the blue of the *Morphos*, lit up as if by one of Faraday's electrical experiments. The irradiating brightness of the sun overhead.

They reach a waterfall whose twin spouts have created a bathing pool below and race to see who can take off their clothes fastest, diving below its surface as if in the Cam at Grantchester.

Then, lying in the water, Bankes on his back so his pego lolls against his stomach; he himself looks at the water descending down towards them and diffracting in the light so it sparkles.

The locals call this beach 'El Tigre', which intrigues him – and is strange as there are no tigers on this continent – or in Africa from where many of the slave-descended locals have come. By tiger, they mean a jaguar, he realises – and wants to see one stroll out in all its glory and survey them from a rock, proudly – although Nativo, the old black man with a grizzled beard who walks with them, tells Bankes they are shy; you are more likely to be taken by the ghosts of the forest, or step on a snake – of which there are many – than come face-to-face with a jaguar.

Which saddens him – he would like to have such an encounter – and also makes him more cautious where he is stepping. Bankes has told him of a wise explorer's maxim: 'Never put your feet down when you can't see the ground.' A maxim, Bankes says, that has wider application than just for making your way through hostile terrain.

He sees no snakes. But they do see bats – many of them – in a cave on the beach. The bats are sleeping as it is daytime and Nativo wakes them – '¡Despierta! ¡Despierta!'

The shapes of the flying bats are silhouetted against the cave's entrance as he stands in the black interior sheltering young Nico under his cloak, as if he were a bat himself with folded wings protecting his offspring. While not alarming, they make an odd manifestation, these silent flashes of wings crossing around them. He thinks at night they could all crowd around you, thus, and you might never be aware of them. Like Dante's spirits in the air – and he remembers the lines

Teresa had recited to him in the Cartagena dusk when they saw bats there:

> *The infernal hurricane that never rests*
> *Hurtles the spirits onward as it seizes them,*
> *Whirling them round ...*

Bankes tells him these are *frugivorous*, fruit-eating bats – but there are vampire bats also along this coast, Humboldt had reported, and one had bitten his dog. He would not like Moretto to be bitten; it is good that he has been left in Bogota. When Bankes mentions Humboldt, he always does so with the verbal equivalent of a genuflection, his voice dipping in admiration, stressing the '*Humb–*' as if a deep note that echoes, which it does even more in the cave, as if summoning up the Baron's ghost.

They rest in the welcome shade. The cave is big enough for the horses and mules to be led inside, to the consternation of the bats.

He thinks of how Shelley would have liked the idea of vampire bats – as would Mary and Polidori and their little party in the Alps, when they concocted such fanciful stories as are designed to keep children awake at nights; and how childish Shelley could be at times – an Adonis, a golden boy.

'You are not *present*, Byron,' says Bankes, solicitously but upbraiding him, on a theme his friend has been elaborating for a while. 'You are thinking of something else. Your mind is elsewhere. And in the present circumstances, that can be dangerous. This is not a time to dwell on other matters. We must attend to the moment – this moment – in which we find ourselves. For do not think because we have not encountered perils so far, there are none. They will not *announce* themselves. This is not a play, with determined acts and entrances, however much you might like it to be one – with yourself as the hero.'

A bat flies close to Bankes's head and his hat is brushed off. He picks it up and rams it back on.

The movement from the sunlit beach into the recesses of the cave – the extreme change from tropical sun to the dark – prompts a memory long kept in the shadows. As a callow fifteen-year-old, he escorted Mary Chaworth – Mary, his *beau idéal*, the local heiress who at eighteen thought him a younger cousin, not a romantic proposition – and a gaggle of Derbyshire girls to the Peak Cavern at Castleton, a cave so grandiose it silenced them. The cavern was entered by a great aperture opening into the earth, like a sinkhole. They needed candles to light their way past stalactites and stalagmites – whatever the difference between them, he forgets – and through a succession of chambers.

They reached an underground stream where a small boat was moored, as if Charon's on the Styx, and only two people at a time could cross to the other side – so at least he had the wit to partner Mary in the crossing – and how he'd remembered feeling like Orpheus with his Eurydice, and even then realising the absurdity of the comparison, but also the pain of it.

A pain that became more acute later that summer at some function in Annesley Hall, Mary's family home – far more endowed than his own crumbling house. He had, as ever, been unable to dance – and overheard Mary make a joke about his crippled foot to her cousin. And he had stood by a pillar and watched her dance – slim and fast and the men paying court to her – and then hobbled his way back to Newstead across the moors by moonlight, furious both with himself and with her.

'You are doing it again!' admonishes Bankes. 'Do not think I cannot tell.

— 'You are everywhere but here. You exist in your imagination, just as you always have – which is both a blessing and a curse – fecund in your poetry but lacking sometimes as a presence *in this life*. You live too much inside your head, Byron. You always did.'

Nico has not understood this, as beyond his meagre English, and looks up at him from within the cape.

'*Vámonos,*' he announces to them all. 'Let's go.'

Bankes stops. A trail of leaf-cutting ants is crossing their path.

The ants carry newly-bitten leaf sections that look like sails. They cut the leaves out with curves, like sailmakers – and struggle, as the leaf sections are so much larger than the ants themselves.

Do they, he wonders, get overpowered sometimes and blown away, like boats at sea? And would they find their way back to the line? He suspects they would.

Coming back in the other direction – empty-handed, having delivered their packets – are more ants in a line, constantly hitting the ones carrying loads in their rush to the source of those leaves. Some ants have detached themselves from the line in confusion and have advanced up the calf-leather of his boot. Like a detachment of soldiers. He removes the ants delicately and places them back.

'In such a manner would the Egyptians have built their pyramids,' murmurs Bankes. 'We are like gods looking down on the futile toil of mankind.'

He would have made a benign and wise god, he thinks, as he steps carefully over the ants. Bankes calls him from ahead, and around a corner of the stream, he finds his friend examining a large boulder covered in an iridescent and intense green. He can see why Bankes has stopped.

'Look at this patina, this natural patina. It would take years of artifice to achieve the same – and I know – for at Kingston Lacy we apply a layer of glaze each year over the paint of the dining room and it has still yet to obtain nearly this depth of lustre – despite doing so for generations. The custom began in my grandfather's time, in the reign of George II.'

'An interesting custom,' he observes. 'At Newstead we have – or had, now it is sold – only layers of dust, not varnish, built up over the generations.'

Above them the trees soar yet higher to a prodigious extent. They hear the constant, floating calls of the oropendola, like large blackbirds with a yellow belly, which make the long nests hanging down from the branches. The birds have a wild, loud cry that sounds like water gurgling from a cistern and then flowing down a drain.

The prolixity and fecundity of everything is overwhelming. Not even James Thomson – let along Southey and the dismal Lakers, with their leech-gatherers and daffodils – could seek to capture such a spectacle in verse.

'The proper study of mankind is man' – that had always been his credo. But he feels on occasions, when seeing some wild, improbable flower – a flower almost obscene with its proboscis and lurid colours – how wonderful it would be to convey it in words. Although perhaps Murray would find such words too offensive to be circulated in polite society – and Sangucho would keep such a book in his cabinet for readers with special interests.

'What colour is the dining room at Kingston Lacy?'

'Dark red. A claret red. Similar to that flower, which is a heliconia.'

'It was unfair of you to tell me that.'

'That it is a heliconia?'

'To remind me of claret. Curious – that in a country so fecund, they have yet to learn how to make good wine.'

'There is nothing wrong with the wine they make. The problem is in the conservation. You need deep and cool cellars to keep wine —'

'Which I suppose you have at Kingston Lacy?'

'Yes – how did you guess? Deep and cool cellars for the grapes to mature to their full appreciation. The climate here is too intemperate – and their temperament too impatient – so they drink the wine when it is young and unsettled by the heat.'

He has been told by Fletcher that while the wine is poor, the brandy and cane spirit are good and have medicinal qualities. But he dislikes drinking strong spirits in the heat. In Bogota, he had developed a taste for *chicha*, the light fermented corn drink – although this is considered a *cosa de indios*, an Indian thing by his fellow officers – who affect a preference for French rather than Peruvian brandy, following Bolivar's example.

A small bright blue bird with a black cap and red legs hops onto a branch close by and examines them with the same intense curiosity that Bankes is applying to all around him. But the bird seems to be looking at him, not Bankes. It has a curious rhythm of flying away from the branch and then back again to do a small display. It beats its wings with impatience, as if trying to communicate something of urgency.

'That,' says Bankes, 'is a —'

'Don't tell me. I will, in all likelihood, forget anyway. I prefer to think of it – as – a messenger.'

There are small trees with low branches over the beach, perhaps because, Bankes speculates, there are not enough nitrates in the soil for them to grow higher – and they shelter in the shade, so he can look up at the broad heart-shaped leaves that have been eaten by caterpillars or some jungle insect so they make a tracery of green; some so delicate it seems impossible they should hold together, much like, he thinks, the human heart.

What he likes about the endlessly long shoreline stretching away along the surf is not that you can see for miles – but that you can't. A sea mist softens and hides the little islands along the coast – *morros*, the locals call them – islands with so much wildlife tumbling up and over that they look like pot plants placed in the ocean. Under other circumstances it would be idyllic.

> *And that this place true paradise be thought,*
> *With me I have the serpent brought.*

Or lines to that effect. He quotes from memory. That curious and unfashionable poet John Donne, upon whom much scorn had been poured for his elaborate conceits – even Coleridge finds him too metaphysical, surely the pot calling the kettle black – was a favourite of Bankes who had introduced him to Donne back in their Cambridge days.

> *Busy old fool, unruly sun,*
> *Why dost thou thus,*
> *Through windows, and through curtains*
> *Call on us?*

He could remember Bankes shouting that out one morning as they woke in his rooms in college in a riot of broken bottles and half-dressed boys.

Donne has a quality that he values above all else in verse. Honesty. Like Shakespeare's 'my mistress's eyes are nothing like the sun.'

The way that Donne proclaims to his own mistress – *get on with it, woman!*

Unlace yourself, for that harmonious chime,
Tells me from you, that now it is bed time.

Lines to which he had introduced Teresa. And other lines he wished he had written, even if Murray would never dare publish them today:

Licence my roving hands, and let them go,
Before, behind, between, above, below.

What he hates is *cant* – false sentiment, of the sort now so prevalent; of the sort those dour Scottish Presbyterians at *Blackwood's* sanctimoniously promote – those reviewers who probably only tool once a year, and then only after first asking dispensation from their church Moderator. Turning out the lights. Who are *outraged* at any suggestion that the ladies could be as salacious and wild in their desires as men – for which they criticised his *Don Juan*. Or not admit that money and the seeking of advantage were just as powerful engines in the world as their pious Christian morality.

He walks down to the waves to feel the sun and wind on his face, with just the lightest of sprays, in the way a woman uses a perfume, of salt water on the breeze.

How did Donne's poem continue?

O my America! my new-found-land,
My kingdom, safest when with one man manned,
My mine of precious stones, my empire…

'This,' he tells Nico, 'is the art of *singlestick*.'

He fronts up to Bankes, who has also stripped to the waist and is grasping his wooden stave in a way that signals a considerable – and worrying – amount of experience.

'Mr Bankes will attack – and I will defend.'

He grasps his own staff and holds it level so he can parry away Bankes's lunges. It is an art at which he takes pride in excelling, having practised for many hours with Tom Moore and Hobhouse back in England – and later in Italy, with Teresa's brother Pietro in the Ravenna woods, where they would also take pumpkins to shoot, pretending they were Austrian soldiers.

But Bankes comes at him with a ferocity to which he is not used; comes at him with the intensity Bankes applies to everything. So he finds himself stepping backwards on the sand and needing to parry Bankes's savage blows repeatedly. The stave may not have a blade but would do considerable damage if it connected.

When he stumbles to one knee – his bad foot giving way – Bankes does have the grace to pause, not least so – from a position of superiority – he can continue the lecture.

'It is a way of training in the use of *backswords* – like the sabre or the cutlass.'

He can tell Nico does not understand, as often, but is intimidated by Bankes so does not want to admit this.

Bankes continues. 'The French call it *canne de combat*. In medieval times it was practised as *quarterstaff* – for it gave no quarter.'

Nico nods, even less comprehending.

'Singlestick may be engaged in with walking sticks. But that is just to *play*, as schoolboys do. What is needed is a heavy stave of oak or ash, although one fashioned from the tropical hardwood of these forests has the advantage for the experienced practitioner of more weight – and therefore *power*.'

And Bankes brings his implement down hard on his own stave, which has the effect of driving him down even more into the sand, and it costs him an effort not to cry out. The sea is washing up the beach and he looks forward to being able to swim once this encounter is over.

Bankes wipes his own brow with his nankeen shirt, at the sheer effort of battering his friend into submission.

As they sit afterwards together on the ground, Nico asks, speaking slowly for intelligibility, if Mr Bankes has ever engaged in a duel?

'No. Such enterprises are for fools.'

'I have,' he says speaking too quickly, before realising he has fallen for one of Bankes's more obvious verbal feints.

'I rest my case!'

Nico looks up at him with surprise. 'You were in a duel, *Milord*? *¿Qué pasó*? What happened?'

'I have been concerned,' he says, 'in many duels as a second, but only in two as principal – and two of the duels I was involved in were with men who later became some of my closest friends. A man called Hobhouse and a poet called Thomas Moore. So it is lucky we did not shoot each other first.

— 'A duel that comes to actual fruition is a stupidity. They can and should always be headed off – which is why they take place first thing in the morning of the following day, rather than on the evening when offence has been given, to allow hot heads to cool.

— 'The best marksmen at a target are not the surest in the field. As that affair of Cecil's and Stackpoole's proved, would you not say, Bankes?'

Bankes nods.

'They fought after a quarrel of three years, during which they practised daily. Stackpoole was so good a shot he could fire a gun from a window to shoot the chickens he was having for dinner, at fifty yards. He wished to kill his antagonist, Cecil, for an offence so nugatory it can now not be remembered – but he received his death blow from Cecil, who fired well, or rather was the quickest, if not most accurate, shot of the two. All Stackpoole said when falling was, "Damn, have I missed him?"

— 'Shelley is a much better shot than I am, but is always thinking of metaphysics rather than of firing. His feet never touch the ground. So I would beat him in a duel, not that it would ever come to that – it would be like shooting a cat.'

'Oh, really?' snorts Bankes. 'And we are supposed to imagine you are not constantly thinking of metaphysics yourself?' And smashes his stave very fast into the sand not far in front of his opponent's injured foot.

Bankes grasps his stave again. 'Come, let us have another game of singlestick. And then you can grapple with Nico. I'm sure you would enjoy that.'

Fishermen are out in boats with small nets. Some younger men are just using lines from the shore, so prolific are the catches along this coast.

A frenzy of birds near the landing stage. Heavy pelicans wheel, then fold their wings like gryphons to drop from above, so their weight takes them deep and fast into the water. White birds with long forked tails swirl past, good at hawking the smaller fish that have been discarded on the beach.

Bankes would know the names of these white birds – Bankes likes to make a taxonomy of the world – but he feels no need to classify; any more than a need to know the names of the young men enjoying the sport of throwing lines in the water and having them return laden with fish.

But he knows the giant frigate birds, black with a slash of red or yellow around the neck like a gypsy's knotted handkerchief, which come loose at times with the emotion of the moment, he presumes, so their gullets swell – the birds the seamen on the outward passage had described as '*men-o-war birds*', that gave them heart as the first they came across before making land. Birds that could range far and wide across the oceans.

It appears one only has to throw bait at the waves and fish present themselves. Those that have not been eaten by whales – for leviathans come here to mate and to sport. They see their spouts blowing high in the air sometimes, like spume blown away by the breeze. Is this the sperm-seed of whales being wasted in the air? Bankes assures him it is not. But it is an image that arrests him.

Even bigger birds wheel higher overhead, as if scouting the horizon rather than the shore. Their wingspan is immense and they cast shadows on the sand. He thinks of poor Coleridge – the only Lake Poet he respects – to the extent of lending him money – whose imagination and arcane erudition are exceptional – and his *albatross*, forever searching; and wonders what he would have made of their journey. Coleridge has an extensive library of books about travel – he had seen them in his lodging rooms near Albemarle Street – although the furthest Coleridge has ever travelled is to study at the feet of German philosophers.

And then back in England, the curtains opening to reveal the extraordinary lecture theatre at the Royal Institution – like a vertical bear pit, steeply raked seats looking down on the lone man at the lectern – this hunched wild figure *descanting* on everything that came into his head, from Kant to Hamlet to transcendental visions in the night – all without notes or at least seeming to be so. A wild ride – like the ones he had been making along the beaches – but through the surf of the imagination; fixing the audience with a glittering eye, like his Ancient Mariner.

Perhaps on his return, wild and bearded himself, if he ever does return, he will arrest Coleridge at the entrance to a wedding – or the Royal Institution – and tell him a tale that will likewise transfix him.

There are elegant, slim white egrets standing near this feeding frenzy of birds, unsure whether they should also engage – diffident, as if awaiting an outcome – thinner than herons but with something of their shy manner.

He thinks of Teresa, and remembers how once on the shore at Cartagena they had watched such egrets together. 'If I were a bird I would like to be one of those,' she had pointed. And adopted a similar position, although she had to raise herself on tiptoes to imitate the egrets – and in her elevated boots almost fell on the sand; but rather than laugh, he supported her. Lifted her by the waist so she could mimic the elegance of the birds.

And he determines when they reach the next isthmus with any settlement, he will have a dress of purest white made for her – why should white only be for brides? It is not their fault they are both attached to nominal if absent spouses – and that it should be trimmed with white feathers that have fallen naturally from the birds when they moult, as Bankes tells him they do.

They ride until dark. They can see by the light of the waves and phosphorescence on the beach – small particles that glow in the dark – food upon which hermit crabs live, Bankes says, which must be true as he has read it in *Hum'*–boldt. Although he, Byron, is more interested in *why* they are called hermit crabs. For unlike St Anthony, they must procreate or there would be no more of them. Perhaps they do it in the dark? – So no one can see them in the biblical act. Like those reviewers from *Blackwood's*. Yielding, unlike St Anthony, to temptation.

That night they eat large slabs, like marble, of a firm fish as big as a porpoise – a bit like the tunny of the Mediterranean – smoked in banana leaves, with rice cooked in the milk of coconuts. A meal Bankes and he agree is as fine as any eaten in Mayfair or Venice – indeed Venice, Teresa has told him, coming from Ravenna herself, is a byword in Italy for poor cuisine, although he enjoyed the way they used squid ink to dye their pasta black, with little gain in taste but much in presence – a Gothic meal that Horace Walpole would have enjoyed. Black pasta against the white of the plate.

And then, replete with fish and *viche* cane-spirit, they sleep in hammocks slung between coconut palms to be high above snakes and mosquitoes. Fletcher has become adept at erecting these – has become an advocate for their advantages, proclaiming his patrons at the Deptford pub would have benefited if they had been slung from the rafters. So much better than the nights coming here, spent on coats stretched out over the cold ground of the *pampa* high in the mountains. Where they would wake to find a ground frost with the iced silhouettes of *espeletia* shrubs the muleteers called 'giant monks' looming over them, and their bones frozen to the marrow. When they had been too cold to think.

They have slung the hammocks in a circle around a campfire. The last white smoke drifts up. It is possible to see stars through gaps in the high trees that rise like a high vault. He can make out the Pleiades, the seven Greek sisters clustered so close to Orion and Taurus, tempting both archer and bull, and the familiarity of such stars he would see from the moors as a boy gives comfort now.

For in other respects, there is little familiar in this new world. He feels like Odysseus adrift and lost, and at the mercy of the wine-dark sea of the Mediterranean – awaking on each new island to find strange delights but also dangers.

When he had been in the Mediterranean, he had been travelling through the classical world of his imagination and school days – revisiting Troy and Athens, or the tombs of Dante and Petrarch in Italy. But here, he has no literary landmarks. It is as if man is still *scratching* at the surface of the planet and has yet to make an impression. Ahead, Bankes has reminded him, lies the great civilisation of the Incas which impressed even brutal and illiterate conquistadors when they arrived in Peru. In the mountains they have come from were mysterious remains, like those buried statues.

But on this remote coast of the Spanish Empire, far from their governing city of Lima, it is as if there were *no such thing* as mankind at all. Just monkeys calling to each other – the sound of animals moving through undergrowth, their probable size amplified by the night – and birds which seek to outdo each other in their patterns of call and response, like fishwives at the Rialto.

He remembers another remark by Humboldt – which Sangucho once quoted, sensing he would like it – that coming to South America had made the naturalist feel 'the infinity of space, as poets have said in every language, is reflected in ourselves.' The infinity of space.

Later, waking suddenly – has a large animal moved nearby? – he is taken by a sudden and alarming thought. A thought that is no better because it could have occurred to him earlier. That Teresa, left in Bogota, may have many of Bolivar's men courting her. That she may dispense favours to some of them, much as she did to him when married to the Count. And this thought grows on him during the night so that he tosses and turns in the hammock – to the extent Bankes wakes and tells him abruptly to stop pleasuring himself. 'And go to sleep, man!'

He takes pride in the clothes Nico wears – some of which he bought for the young man when Bolivar suggested him for a page back in Bogota. A black velvet jerkin with gold embroidery, soft but warm enough for the mountains; it matches the black trimmings of his own jacket, which is dark green with loose cuffs that can be rolled back and has a small collar, like a county parson's – although both Bankes and Fletcher remind him that no comparison could be less apt. But a small collar, he feels, is better suited to the vagaries of life in the saddle – his saddle which has been lined with silk cording for extra comfort. Bankes has eschewed such luxuries as unmanly and unmilitary, and for the pleasure of being able to say so.

What had begun as a game – buying clothes for the boy – had turned into an obsession. He had commissioned another helmet to match his own, one less ostentatious – it would be hard to be more – from a deep green cloth on a brass and black leather base. Fletcher joked – complained – they needed an additional trunk just to transport the lavish pageboy costumes the Bogota tailors had laboured so long over.

Although Nico seems uncertain how to respond. If anything, a surly mien creeps across his face the more he receives. Or is it puzzlement? A sense he might be beholden? Hard to tell, for he speaks little – whether intimidated by the older soldiers around him or naturally shy, although occasionally he can spark into action.

But that doesn't matter. He likes having an engaging, beautiful boy at his side even if – as he assures a dubious Bankes – his intentions are honourable.

While Nico continues to look surprisingly fresh in his jerkin and loose-fitting trousers, ideal for riding, his own clothes have begun to unravel. Buttons are loose and threads have caught in the thorns of bushes – to the extent he worries he might appear *seedy*. Is it Nico's youthful vitality that keeps his appearance so fresh, deep in the jungle? Back in Bogota, he had remarked to Teresa that for Nico, once he had a sky-blue uniform to wear over the black jerkin, all his patriotism seemed to diminish, or at least be satiated.

Perhaps that was all men needed – a fine uniform to wear for a ball and to cut a dandy figure, like the Household Cavalry wearing tight trousers on Rotten Row – a spectacle of which Bankes was fond and that might get him into trouble one day. Bankes had a habit of propositioning guardsmen, not all of whom were receptive or appreciative – and sodomy was still an offence for which you could be transported in fetters to Australia, prosecuted regardless of influence or position.

But what if men could just parade, rather than fight? Have the ball before Waterloo and not the battle, with its grisly mess of bones amputated after the smack of cannonballs into soft bodies – for he is under no illusion about the realities of war.

The Spaniards were fond of cannons. Old ones had lined the walls of the fort at Cartagena; and while they might not be accurate – fired centuries ago at Drake and Raleigh when they made approaches to the Spanish Main – they could still wreak havoc. Even the most dishevelled of royalist rump armies would have cannon.

Some of the sailors on the outbound journey who served below deck during the wars with France had told him stories of the carnage such cannon could cause. Even with the embroidery added to such tales

– and too much time at sea to spin them – he could sense his suspicion of military derring-do was well founded.

So why on earth was he now fighting? When he could be looking over proofs with Murray in Albemarle Street, or carousing with Tom Moore and friends down the Strand? Or taking a *paseo* with Teresa around the balconies of their house?

A kingfisher catches his eye, sitting on a branch and trying to manoeuvre a small silver fish in its beak so the fish is at an angle to slip easily down its throat. Absorbed, it has not noticed him. At least he *assumes* it is a kingfisher, or American version thereof, for the bird has a similarly shaped head – although larger and yet more dowdy than the brilliant blue ones he is used to from England. This has a black cap and breast, like a magpie's colouring.

'The female of the species,' remarks Bankes, appearing beside him. 'The male is more colourful, with a fine waistcoat of red and green.'

'Of course. Wearing a uniform.'

The sea exerts its constant roar. From his hammock he can see fireflies on the sand. They remind him of Allegra – Allegra so entranced by the sound of waves against the ship as they voyaged here from the Canaries; who asked him what would happen if one *enormous wave*, of the sort the sailors told her about and had even experienced – should crash upon their own boat; and could a whale swallow the boat whole?

Then he thinks of his other daughter, Ada, back in England with her mathematical mother – Annabella who has proved so difficult and adept, as his wife still, as Lady Byron, albeit separated, at spreading *rumours* – rumours about him, made easier by the way in which they have substance. Their conjugal relations and the inference he had enjoyed himself 'unnaturally' with her, as you would with a boy – an accusation which has gained currency as one an Englishwoman would not make public unless she had just cause. Added to which, she has made a deposition, as part of the separation papers, about his illicit connection with Augusta who as his sister – half-sister, strictly speaking, but no matter – has led to scandalous rumours of incest.

No, his wife had dragged his name through the mud. And the British public had been ready to believe the worst of him, as if she had said a dog had stolen a piece of meat from the table. That was before *Blackwood's* declared he was Satan incarnate. Good for book sales – but not if he ever wanted to walk down Pall Mall again.

How would they be talking about him in the *salons* of Mayfair? At Palmerston's mansion on Piccadilly? Raising an eyebrow and laughing about him 'lost in some jungle', as they would say, or 'gone to conquer the Spanish Main'.

'Has no one told him what happened to Raleigh – when he did that!'

'Ha ha! – *ha ha* – ha ha – *ha!*' He can hear the chinless young men and anodyne young women laughing as they circle each other like cattle waiting to be paired for breeding. Perhaps only Lady Jersey or Lady Oxford would speak in his defence – the only ones in that fashionable world who did not look on him as a monster.

He should have been born an Elizabethan. Writing sonnets to both men and women – why were the English so shy about admitting Shakespeare's love for a young and wayward boy? His own favourite, Henry Howard, patronised as an aristocrat dabbler in verse – like himself – because he was the Earl of Surrey. Whereas Howard had recast the whole form of English poetry; reinvented the sonnet for English use;

added the keeping of an accent and a beat – metre and rhyme – and had the grace and good manners not to be published, but to circulate his poems privately, among friends.

Strictly speaking, Howard was not an Elizabethan but the last of the age before. He could have lived to become one if he had not made the mistake of annoying Elizabeth's father, Henry VIII – an easy thing to do – and been executed – only *the day before* the King died himself. Over a trifling question of rank; an argument over a coat of arms. At under thirty years – younger than he was. Yet despite being a troubled soul who angered his monarch – or because of it – Howard translated Martial's ode on how to be calm and tranquil in this life. Advice the poet had failed to take himself. He knows the lines by heart –

> *Content thyself with thine estate,*
> *Neither wish death, nor fear his might.*

Had Howard sought tranquillity but not found it? Wanted '*true wisdom joined with simpleness*'? He feels kinship for the man. He too would probably be executed back in England – well, at least prosecuted. Castlereagh was quite capable of putting him on trial. Better to face royalists in the jungles of Colombia than barristers like Brougham with stilettos hidden in their gowns – with a wife who might appear in court against him.

He finds no calm in the voice of the ocean, just a brooding discontent. Why has he come to this wild and empty place with old familiar ghosts for company? They should have stayed in Europe – not embarked with him – or disembarked in this New World – that has such wonders in it. Is he like Prospero sailing with his daughter? Into a tempest.

Bankes is snoring in his hammock. Fletcher, as ever, is quieter but asleep. But he can see Nico awake. He calls him and gestures with a cigar, of which he knows the boy is fond.

They sit against a log washed up on the beach, smoking and look-ing at the white froth of the waves as they recede with the tide. Nico tells him of the girl he is courting in Bogota, and of how her father – and indeed his – thinks he is too young and immature to be doing so; and he tells Nico stories of Europe, and of the canals of Venice, and of how he once swam the Hellespont, like Leander seeking Hero, neither of whom the boy has heard of; but no matter.

He enjoys the boy's company; and of course could ask for more. If he was Bankes he undoubtedly would. But he holds back. There is a strange melancholy pleasure in not taking every pleasure. And if he wanted every pleasure, he could have stayed in Venice where there were girls and boys for the asking. Besides, he has promised both Boli-var and the boys' parents to look after him; and whatever *Blackwood's* or the British public think, he does have principles – just ones he has elaborated for himself, rather than received on his knees in a sancti-monious pew.

They fall asleep on the shore where Bankes, as always the first to rise, discovers them in the morning.

'Surprised to find you fully dressed.'

A pause for effect, before he goes on to declaim, theatrically:

'*Some swore he was a maid in man's attire / For in his looks were all that men desire…*

— 'Lines I believe you wrote.'

Nico does not understand what Bankes is saying – but is alarmed by the vehement tone that Byron now adopts. And not just because he hates having his own poetry quoted back at him.

'That is uncalled for. There is no need for such inference. There is a time and place for such behaviour – and this is not one of them.'

Bankes continues, unabashed – for once, in his vehemence, not even misquoting the lines: '*And such as knew he was a man, would say / Leander, thou art made for amorous play.*'

— 'It is you who play to so many galleries, *my Lord,* including your own. But do not attempt to play to mine. I know you too well. When you have seen a man with his breeches off, engaged in all the pleasures of the chase, as I have seen you, there is no need for such a reproof. Or such *cant.*'

Bankes refuses to talk to him for the rest of the day, although by the following one – for memories are short in the tropics, like the nights, and there is the press of events – no more is said.

It is the vultures which alert them first, some way distant, a tower of them wheeling like a helix up into the sky, just as Dante describes spirits in the *Inferno* – a *vortice,* a vortex.

When they arrive at the bottom of the circling tower, they find a pile of bodies. Plain *campesinos,* countrymen, in simple clothes with nothing but machetes to defend themselves. They have been shot – it is unclear if in battle or if lined up and shot as prisoners. No attempt has been made to bury them. Nearby, more are hanging by nooses from a tree.

'*Pinche realistas*, bastard royalists,' proclaims Juan Esteban. 'And these are not long dead. They may be nearby.'

He has seen few dead people; and certainly not those whose lives have been taken in such a brutal fashion. The positions assumed in the last moments of death – curled up as if in defence, or to find comfort –

move him. He feels an uncurling in his stomach, one that is rare for him. It is a great anger.

That evening, there is an opportunity to send a letter to Teresa; dispatches are being taken back to Bogota with their military position. There is little of substance to report to Paez and Bolivar; but this is the first indication that the royalists may still be holding out.

Nor does he find it easy to write to Teresa with his customary fluency or length. It is difficult to describe the sporadic and random nature of their progress in a way that makes sense – neither the width of the landscape or the slow attrition of their reconnaissance mission, with its diminishing returns, are easy to fit on the page.

He addresses the letter,

> From some godforsaken nameless town on the Colombian Pacific Coast – don't ask me what it's called.

Not least in case it falls into the hands of the enemy.

> My dearest T. – We are all well, which will I hope – keep up *your* hopes and spirits. I do not write to you letters about politics and our military business – which would only be tiresome, and yet we have little else to write about – except some private anecdotes which I reserve for '*viva voce*' when we meet – to divert you at the expense of Bankes and some others.

He tries to describe the pelicans flying along the waves and how they break their line; and the tiny red crabs running for cover into holes in the sand, a spectacle he thinks might amuse Allegra; but not the way in which those same crabs run after baby turtles as they make their faltering steps to the sea and rip them to pieces. Just as he has not described to Teresa the pile of dead villagers executed by the royalists under that tower of vultures.

> Perhaps I was a fool to come here – but being here, I must see what is to be done. If we were not at such a distance I could tell you many things that would make you smile – but I hope to do so at no very long period. – Pray keep well – and love me as you are beloved by yrs. Ever
>
> Dearest T. t. a. a. + + + in e.
>
> N. B.
>
> *Ti bacio 10000 volte.* I kiss you 10000 times. In both our languages.

With satisfaction and a flourish, Fletcher produces red wax from the *sabretache*, so he can close the letter with his personal seal. The ritual of the wax and seal, the black leather of the *sabretache* itself – he has had it since a boy – with its brass lion buckles, faded leather and compartments for envelopes and writing paper; his habitual brown ink, but also the red ink Teresa gave him in La Gomera and which he has just used – these things please him, in the way it does to have his handkerchief smelling of cologne. Just because they are – however notionally – under military command, why not enjoy what small comforts life presents? And given the possibility of imminent fighting, every reason, surely, to savour them more.

He imagines a letter back from Teresa, sealed with a cochineal kiss. He has come to realise how much of military service is spent daydreaming; or appreciating small elements of civilian life once taken for granted.

The lone soldier on his mule trots away with the dispatches and letters – the soldier chosen in consultation with Juan Esteban as the one most easily lost from the detachment, yet trustworthy enough to make the long journey home. For the first time since coming, the soldier has a jaunty air as he sits astride the mule and urges the beast home with a light switch to its flanks. Although the wind from the sea is strong, he consults with Bankes afterwards and they both think they could hear the man whistling as he went.

They ride into a small shanty town by the sea, which does not even have a name; the locals refer to it as just *El Pueblo*, 'the town'. Bright lights come from a long rectangular building with windows and people that spill out onto the dirt lane. It is a billiard hall. At some dozen tables, men are playing with ferocity and concentration. For a while they do not notice Byron, Bankes, Fletcher and the others as they stand quietly observing in the doorway.

Then the table nearest to them makes as if to stop.

'*No, no. ¡Sigue!* Continue.'

This from Bankes. He gestures to the barkeeper to bring *viche* from the shelf and line tumblers up along the bar.

'Tell them,' – to the barman – 'I will buy drinks every time some-one manages to beat myself or my compatriot Lord Byron – or *indeed*, Mr Fletcher here.'

It proves a long evening. By the end, Fletcher has proved his con-siderable ability with a cue, learned during a misspent adulthood as a publican; Nico is drinking at the bar and regaling his listeners with news from Bogota; an inebriated Bankes is surrounded by young men in even brighter shirts than his own; while he, less seduced by their charms, has discovered from various interlocutors the extent and strength of any royalist forces in the area – which sound negligible, but then they may not have visited the town to play billiards.

His last vision before leaving is of Bankes taking off one of his celebrated red riding boots and using the heel as a cue to hit the white ball, roared on by the amused cheers, *viche*-fuelled, of the onlookers.

It will not be long before Bankes begins his chorus. '*Busy old fool, unruly sun / Why dost thou thus / Through windows, and through curtains call on us.*'

As he strides through the town, there is a full moon shining on the mudflats where the fishing boats loll at low tide; beyond are the harbour offices where, Juan Esteban has sent word, they have set up temporary accommodation. He sleeps from a hammock slung on the terrace from which harbour officials would normally survey the shipping that comes and goes. He can hear the rain as it begins to fall outside.

'Are you not accustomed to this from your North Briton childhood?' asks Bankes.

The rain has been coming down for days. There is nothing that is not wet – bedding, clothes, the horses who shiver – although, as he once predicted to Fletcher, the mules are faring better.

'With the difference – there was always a dry roof to come back to.'

They are speaking under the broadest of the banana trees they can find – which gives shelter, but only partial. At times a bucketload descends unexpectedly when the water gets too heavy for the higher leaves.

Fletcher and Juan Esteban have managed to keep kindling dry – and Bankes his cigars. They should have stayed in the small town with the billiard hall which had proved both agreeable and dry. But he had suggested they do this reconnaissance a few days up the coast – out of a misguided need to be shown to be doing something – a decision he is already regretting. They could doubtless have learned as much, if not more, about the enemy's disposition by remaining in their hammocks at the harbourmaster's offices and making further enquiries of the locals.

Now they are sodden and his small band of men look increasingly disconsolate.

Moreover, Nico has been taken ill. They have all had intermittent bouts of fever and diarrhoea, but this is severe.

They have positioned him in a hammock with a tarpaulin draped above to keep it dry. Better than the damp wooden cabin, the only alternative, with its soaking timbers and insects – *bichos*, the soldiers call them, whose bites leave a nasty welt which suppurates.

He knows about fever because he has had so many of his own – and watched his little Allegra almost die of it. He has sat at too many sick beds; recognises that feeling of paralysis in which time moves more slowly. The patient sleeping when he was alert – and then alert when he himself felt tired. The urge to mop the sweating brow, above all when instructed not to by a nurse or some proto-medical quack.

He regrets they have no one with them with medical expertise – an error, he realises. He had brought medical supplies, at his own expense – but not a doctor. Why had he not thought of that in Bogota? Though the concern then was to show themselves *martial,* in every regard – which had overridden considerations as to what might happen if anything went wrong.

Fletcher – inclined in the past to be brisk about his master's affection for Nico – is now sympathetic to the boy. He prepares broiled coconut milk for the patient, holding to the belief that the less one drinks of the water the better – 'unless brought up from a well yourself'.

Nico is disconcertingly direct.

'Am I going to die?' he asks in Spanish.

The boy has an ability to read expressions. It must be clear from Bankes's and his own faces that they are concerned exactly that may occur. Whereas Fletcher, who does not speak or readily understand Spanish, betrays no emotion at the question.

'Should I prepare more soup for the young gentleman?' he asks.

'No peppers or onion,' suggests Bankes. 'Both are equally hard to digest. Better to use one of the chickens.'

While this stretch of coast is too tropical for cattle or pigs, chickens thrive and are found in every small hamlet they pass, so they have plentiful eggs and birds.

'Make a broth.'

After more days, the fever, delirium, sweating, the pallor one moment and extreme heat the next – do appear to signal approaching death, although he does not want to contemplate that – or the thought that it is he who has brought Nico to this place.

They should have stayed in the nameless town, where the greatest danger to Nico was losing at billiards. But as Fletcher points out – he can be reassuring at such moments – the town may be where Nico contracted the fever, so they are better away from human habitation.

'The climate is different from the mountains in Bogota to which he is used, my Lord. This is as *foreign* to him as it is for us. Besides, his *dissipation* in the town,' – for Nico had drunk with the freedom of youth and the intoxication of danger – 'may have weakened his constitution, for he is not sufficiently robust.'

True. While a boy of startling beauty – he has the alabaster smooth skin of an Adonis – Nico has moments of fragility; perhaps why he feels such strong affection for his charge.

'Of course you will recover,' he tells Nico.

Juan Esteban has dug a shallow grave. But because of the rain, it keeps filling. There is little gravel along this section of coast – as Bankes remarks – so it will soon become muddy. Additionally, there is the chance of Nico's body being washed up and then consumed by vultures.

'We will burn him,' and he repeats his pronouncement in Spanish, so the men understand him as well.

'*¿Pero es Cristiano, Milord?* But is that Christian, my Lord?'

'No matter. It feels a more heroic death. I will tell his parents, when I see them, that he died bravely. He did die bravely.'

Which indeed the boy had, in the night. He had awoken to find Nico half-fallen from the hammock, his body hanging down while his legs remained inside it, and had known immediately. Then hours awake as a vigil for the boy, watching the sea as the waves stayed dark.

It is not long since they had been riding through the surf, side-by-side – Nico delighting in the adventure, the spray from the horses' hooves, their cloaks whipped round them, pelicans flying in wavering lines low across the waves to spot fish below. He had shown the boy how to shoot with his walnut-handled pistols; with their demons on the butts, mouths wide open and fangs splayed, made by Jackson's of

Fetter Lane. Nico had handled the pistols well – had consistently hit the target. Even Bankes had been impressed.

There was something so incomprehensible in death, that he found he could neither speak nor think on the subject. Any of them could have died of fever – just as Allegra or he might have died of the tertian fever in Venice. There was no rhyme or reason to it. Was that why poets wrote? To apply rhyme and reason to an unthinking, uncaring world where young men could die in just a few days? When they had a whole life ahead of them.

'We will raise a catafalque in the nearest cave.'

There were always caves to be found along this strip of coast. He remembers how Nico sheltered in his cloak when the bats swirled round them at the first such cave they entered.

They make a litter of driftwood which they then dry in the fierce midday sun – for it has ceased raining – and carry the litter to the cave's entrance in case of further rain, and place Nico's body wrapped in his hammock on top of the wood. Fletcher fiddles with the flint and finds it hard to get the wood to catch. Finally he succeeds. The thick smoke drives out the bats who swirl over the burning body, along with scraps of fabric from the blue velvet dolman jerkin of which the boy was so fond.

Bankes puts an arm around him. 'This is not your fault. Do not for a moment blame yourself.'

But he does.

He is still dazed as he watches the woman hack at a coconut with elegant but strong cuts from her machete, the angle changed slightly each time, the shavings dropped around the log she is using to prop up the shell.

A coconut is remarkably hard – so much harder than a man's head, he thinks. One of their soldiers, originally from this region – why he was chosen – has told them more of the locals die from coconut shells than from snakes, poison frogs or even disease. A coconut shell falling is a cannon ball dropped from a great height.

He has acquired a taste for the milk, sweet and thirst-quenching, and the white flesh that can be cooked to sweeten fish – why he has left the platoon after the ceremony for Nico, to be on his own – to come to this small stall where they cut into the coconuts for passers-by. A black man is sprawled on a hammock, dead to the world; a previous customer who has mixed coconut juice with *viche.* He himself is regarded as odd for wanting to drink the juice pure.

Such is the heat of the sun, it takes him a while to realise another machete is being held to his own neck – so he cannot turn. A figure appears in front of him, although because he is sitting down and cannot move his head, he can only see the bottom half of this man, who is dressed in faded cavalry breeches with a trim down the side, topped by a cummerbund in red and yellow stripes. Which, he realises as the man starts to speak, are the colours of the Spanish flag.

'If you move, my men will cut your head into pieces like the coconut on which you have been gazing so hard.'

The voice is guttural, rancorous, with the harsh glottal stops of mainland Spain. The machete at his neck is tilted up so that he must lift his chin and look at the face of the man addressing him. A face which is unshaven and red from the coastal sun – as, and the thought flashes past, his own must be – but this is a brief reflection as he feels a quickening of fear and alarm.

'We already have your companions. So do not think there is any chance of *rescate*, of rescue.'

Rescate. What a fine word. He will keep it close.

He feels his arms pinned behind him and bound with rope. Then he is kicked and without words dragged upright to his feet.

The woman hacking at the coconut has stopped in confusion.

'*Sigue, sigue, Señora,* carry on,' says – or rather shouts – the Spanish officer for whom a barking tone must be habitual. 'I will drink the coconut milk myself.'

After the officer has satiated his thirst, Byron is led away by the rope, past the black man who has remained sleeping in a hammock throughout, oblivious to the entire affair.

Viva Byron!

CANTO IV

He is remembering the morning after his peculiar wedding to Annabella at the big house near Newcastle, on a black coast with grey sand and a grey sea – in January, what time of year was that for a wedding? – with sleet and rain and Hobhouse looking as if he was attending a funeral, not the nuptials of his best friend.

Waking in the morning to the sound of local miners, employed by Milbanke, Annabella's father and self-appointed grandee – the miners gathered outside to perform a cutlass dance, swords sweeping together.

Heavy boots on the cobbles. A big man with a prize fighter's sideburns and thickset shoulders. Smaller men with rapier figures. A younger man with sensitive, quick eyes off to one side who glanced his way – his senses quickened more at the thought of the young man watching him than at the figure of Annabella in her heavy embroidered nightdress in the newly marital bed.

Was that unfair? For Annabella could be passionate – could surprise him, as women often did – and behind that priggish and meek and sometimes spoilt veneer – 'never marry a woman who wants to *reform* you,' Hobhouse had advised and he had ignored – she had been fond of him, in her way. Had called him *a very bad, very good man*. With her unusual and intelligent mathematical mind. His princess of parallelograms. Before her odious mother, and the complications with his sister Augusta, and a myriad other distractions – and undoubtedly his own clumsiness – had caused the marriage to fall apart like one of the rotting carcasses of whales washed up on Seaham Beach – Seaham Beach, where the only other creatures had been the poor scavengers looking for sea-coal or driftwood that came ashore.

Annabella, wrapped in a woollen blanket, had joined him on the balcony to watch the cutlass dance, a curious affair – although now it reminds him of a dance he had seen here, in that small nameless town on the Colombian coast – perhaps why he is remembering that wedding moment, for the first time in years.

There were ten colliers in shirt sleeves with red ribbons, holding crude swords – and one dressed as the Fool, with a silly hat and fox's tail pinned to his buttocks; another as an old woman, a 'Bessie', Annabella whispered to him, for she takes an amused interest in these things. The Bessie made lewd gestures with his – or her – sword, and swished large billowing petticoats with abandon. A great deal of bawdy play was made when the dancers gripped the hilts of each other's swords – helped by copious beer provided by Milbanke. But then, among other things, the man owned a brewery.

He admired the colliers moving dexterously with outstretched cutlasses to form and reform in patterns: first to make a hexagon, which Annabella – attracted by the mathematical shape – told him was called a rose by the dancers, and that then dissolved as they formed two squares, with the Fool and 'Bessie' outside – dancing faster and faster – colliding and bouncing off each other to much laughter, like Punch and Judy – a show he had always thought the most honest depiction of marriage, if not the most appropriate for a wedding celebration.

The fiddle players were fast and accomplished. To general applause, he threw a purse from the bedroom window. Even greater applause when the purse struck the Fool on the buttocks; and then the dancers dissolved into a melee of drinking and conversation, and he could remember little else of the day's events.

Or for that matter of those to come, filled with the dreariness of provincial life. The tea-parties, polite card-games, showing off the bridegroom, dusk coming early so they were lighting the fires straight after lunch. And in the short interval of daylight, walking the coast to see wild waves mock with their intimation that a wider, more exciting world was possible.

Another odd thought occurs to him. That Bankes, of all people, had also proposed to Annabella – unaware of his, Byron's, possible attachment to her – and had come, almost weeping, to him when Annabella had turned the proposal down. The hardened Bankes, who, it must be said, would have made an even worse husband for Annabella than he had.

Perhaps he should remind Bankes of this now. He opens his eyes. Perhaps not.

Bankes is shackled beside him against the wall, his eyes closed, as his own have been, to keep out the harsh sun that is strafing down. The royalist soldiers are ostentatiously sharpening their cutlasses. His friend is blindfolded and gagged with one of the fine silk neckerchiefs of which he is so proud; his mouth strains as if to say something. He is almost pleased Bankes cannot speak – for surely it would be to issue reproaches – or worse, pretend it is not Byron's fault they find themselves in this predicament.

If they had never sailed to join Bolivar – if they had contented themselves with an agreeable life in Bogota on arrival – if he had been conscientious as the nominal leader of their small reconnaissance group and had posted better sentries – or been more aware of the potential dangers. Rather than distracting himself by buying a coconut.

He closes his eyes, as the day stretches forth into eternity, and he has no idea what time it is, or what will happen to them. He wonders if Teresa ever received his letter – and if she will do as he suggested and commission a dress to imitate the white egrets she had so loved.

And whether she will be wearing that dress on the day they bring news of his death, and the death of his companions – for he is under no illusion, the most likely outcome of their current danger is execution, whether by a gun or from a tree. He knows from everything Daniel

O'Leary has told him – and will O'Leary now be Teresa's companion? – that since the brutal actions of the Viceroy, who instigated the policy, no quarter has been given on either side. All prisoners have been executed. Had not one of Bolivar's generals, Santander, ordered such an execution of royalists in Bogota just before their departure?

Thirty-three is an absurd age to die. Not young enough to be heroic – or old enough to achieve all he intends to do. He will not see the outcome of these struggles in South America. Will the Royalists manage to suppress the Patriots, as they have in previous rebellions, and Spain continue to rule its dominions from afar?

He tries to think of Teresa – every last part of her. Her eyes. The filaments of her hair which he likes to see spread out around the pillow as she sleeps. The rings upon her fingers. The way she looks at him as she leans up on tiptoes to embrace. The way she laughs. When he first saw her in the *salon* of the Venetian palace. When he last saw her sleeping in their bed in Bogota.

And then of Allegra, also sleeping, with her lamp of fireflies beside her. He tries to imagine his other daughter, Ada, whom he has never seen; who he will perhaps never see in the future. His wife looking down at the empty courtyard below the bedroom where they first slept after their marriage.

He imagines news of his death reaching England. The mixture of prurience – an excuse to discuss his every misdeed – and perhaps a little regret to season their piquant pleasure, like a kumquat. It is well known the English only admire their own writers when they are dead.

Of course that would not be the worst that could happen. In death they might try to make him *respectable*. Murray could issue a bowdlerised edition of his works – could get Thomas Bowdler himself to do it, to reassure the public – that it was shorn of all *indecencies* and fit for a Sunday School pew. Castrate Don Juan, as Murray had always wanted with his damned cutting and slashing.

He should have kissed Mary Chaworth when he was paying court to her – when they were going down into the cave. From what he has learned of women, she would have responded – or found a gracious way not to do so. But at least he would have tried.

He should have challenged Brougham to a duel. If only he had known he was going to die now anyway; it would have made him reckless. Enough to put a bullet through Brougham's head. Stop all the insinuations the man had made about how he, Byron, had treated Annabella before she left him. Particularly as some were true.

He should have piled all Southey's lousy books on the pavement of Piccadilly and set them on fire – so the smoke could be seen from Murray's premises – where he could retire for a cigar and a brandy with the proprietor while they contemplated the funeral pyre. Although Murray, like all publishers, would have been horrified at seeing new books destroyed.

He should have enjoyed the pleasures of that chorister from St John's who looked so demure for a grown young man in a white costume with ruffs.

He should have let his bear loose in the Fellows' Garden at Trinity.

He should have bricked up the entranceway to Hobhouse's rooms on Great Court when he came across mortar and the necessary tools some workmen had left nearby, as they went for breakfast and he passed the entrance, having drunk all night on the town with Bankes. The wall would have set by the time Hobhouse woke. It would have made a good story. Is that all one could really do on earth? Leave a few stories that could be told.

He should not have been so unkind to his mother, or Annabella – or even poor, maddening Caroline Lamb. He should have answered Claire Clairmont's letter about their mutual daughter. Dammit, it cost so little to say a few kind words.

He should have tried to swim Lake Geneva as he had the Helles-pont, perhaps with an accompanying boat in case of mishap.

He should have written an epic in the manner of *Paradise Lost* – perhaps about Cain, who fascinated him. His battles with his wandering brother Abel. His incestuous marriage with his sister and his troubled soul. Might he then have stood level on the shoulders of giants like Milton? Not jointly with those drab poets who wrote about the *plashy* earth. The *plashy* brown earth which soon would be open to receive him. Unless their bodies were left in a pile for the vultures.

He should have made one strike for the boundary – at least – when playing Eton at cricket. Made use of the fact he was allowed to have another boy running for him, given that however hard he hit the ball he could not be expected to sprint from crease to crease. And not get drunk in the Haymarket afterwards when he vomited over the shoes of that agreeable, handsome Etonian.

He should not have let Murray cut sections of *Don Juan* to suit the current whimsies of the British public – and left in that stanza with its criticisms of the craven Brougham. Maybe that would have led to a duel? He felt in his bones *Don Juan* would last, like Pope's poetry, simply because it might make people laugh. Wit was an underrated commodity in a newly sententious world.

He should have given a final dinner for his friends in London, perhaps at Bush's on the Strand, so convenient for whoring afterwards, and drunk deep into the night. He could do with a brandy now.

Conscious he is letting his mind wander – however useful the distraction – there is nothing else to do in the current circumstances – he opens his eyes again. Fletcher is opposite, tied beside Bankes. Further along the wall are Juan Esteban and the soldiers, similarly bound. If the royalists want a sacrificial victim, they should choose him alone and leave the others to live. They are, after all, only following his commands. He will petition their royalist captor.

Who he realises later – hard to keep track of time – is standing close, blocking his sun. Like Alexander the Great did to the philosopher Diogenes – although perhaps he will not make the same complaint.

The Royalist officer bends down to stare hard, which enables a better view of the officer's own face – ravaged by tropical sun and smallpox, but that once must have been handsome – covered by sideburns of luxuriant profusion.

'How shall we proceed?' The Spanish is formal and clipped, yet somehow sounds careless as well. As if it were not a matter of great importance.

'Under normal circumstances, we would hold a trial – and after some deliberation, condemn you for sedition and treason against King Ferdinand. And then shoot you. Or hang you.' He pauses, as if this is a choice to which he must give attention.

'But these are not normal times. And given the outcome of any such trial is not in doubt – and in your position I would prefer to *terminar la cosa*, get it over with quickly rather than wait – as anticipation can be worse than the event when it comes to execution. Not that I have experienced it myself,' and the officer allows a smile, which does not flatter his features.

'Are you Catholic? I know you English are usually not. But if so, you can make a final confession. We will find a priest.'

The officer waits, absurdly, for an answer – although his mouth is gagged so he can hardly provide one. The gag is removed, with surprising care, by a soldier attending the officer.

'I am Scottish.'

His captor waves this aside as impertinent and irrelevant.

'I am a Lord.'

This has a momentary effect, but then is greeted by a shrug.

'*Mi coronel*,' – best to assume the highest rank likely – 'I can assure you there has been a misunderstanding. I am travelling through these dominions with a view to purchasing an estate. These are my companions,' – he nods towards Bankes and Fletcher. 'We were provided with these soldiers,' – another nod – 'as escorts through territory we understood had become *turbulent*. I have no intention of harming the interests of his noble Highness King Ferdinand, who the British government holds in the highest esteem and respect.'

He is almost enjoying himself – using the most rhetorical and fluent of Spanish, a language that flatters flattery. Caressing the words. No point being good with language if you can't plead for your own life. He senses – instinctively and with a rush of spirit – that confidence is everything.

Bankes is also struggling to say something – a bad idea, given his friend is capable of losing his temper and can be *injudicious*. He is alarmed when their captor removes Bankes's gag.

'Your Excellency,' Bankes begins haltingly, and with a dry mouth, 'I have papers you should see, in the compartment of my saddlebag.'

The officer barks an order in his abrupt way and their saddlebags are brought, so Bankes can identify which one is his. The papers are produced from a small leather portfolio of orange calf, and handed to their captor, who studies them and only now feels the need to declare his identity.

'I am Colonel Roscoff of His Majesty's army. These papers are from the Viceroy of New Granada, granting you safe passage – how did you come by them?'

The change of tone is noticeable. Bankes presses home the advantage.

'I had the honour of attending Viceroy Samano at his residence in Cartagena when we arrived from the Canaries, whose Governor also entertained us.' Clever of Bankes to mention the Canary Islands, still a Spanish dominion – and not a place to give hospitality to rebels.

'He vouchsafed this letter to me *precisely* in case any misunder-standings should arise during our passage through his domain. Furthermore, would you do me the courtesy, as my arms are tied, of examining the medal around my neck?'

The same soldier who has loosened their gags unbuttons the top of Bankes's shirt to reveal the curious medal that he, Byron, has always assumed is an ostentatious piece of costume jewellery to go with Bankes's flamboyant shirts – an eight-point cross on a blue and white silk band, with the image of the Immaculate Conception and the motto *Virtuti et Merito* – a motto about which he has teased his friend, as virtue is not the first attribute that comes to mind when thinking of Bankes.

'This is a Carlos III medal. Did you steal it?' Colonel Roscoff grasps Bankes by the neck. 'Or did you rip it from the shirt of one of my fellow officers when they were dead?'

Bankes retains his admirable *sang froid*. But then his friend has been in many hot and difficult situations – and can patter like a Bermondsey pickpocket when the need is on him.

'If you look at the reverse, you will see an engraving with my name – William Bankes Esq., Lieutenant – and the date – 1813. That is when I fought with Arthur Wellesley, now Lord Wellington, for the liberty of your country.'

'You fought at Salamanca?'

'No. I joined Wellesley as an aide-de-camp for the second, later peninsular campaign that year as we advanced from San Sebastian and took the battle into France. We were chasing Marshall Soult, ending with the battle of Nivelle – after which I was awarded this medal, as proof of my services against that enemy of both ourselves and your country – *Napoleon*.' Does Bankes shoot a sly glance of reproof towards him?

'It was an engagement,' Bankes adds, with the total lack of modesty necessary for the occasion, 'in which I distinguished myself in combat.'

'The Battle of Nivelle. The engagement of November 13th. My cousin Don Pedro de Sahuquillo fought there. Did you know him?'

Bankes hesitates. He can tell his friend did not. Perhaps wisely – it could be a trap – Bankes keeps to the truth.

'I did not have that honour. But there were many distinguished military men of both nations on that felicitous occasion. As you are aware, the nations of England and Spain were united in their opposition to that despot Napoleon, who had the temerity to place his own brother on the throne of Spain.'

He senses that Bankes really is beginning to enjoy himself.

'For the honour of *la patria* – and King Ferdinand.'

They are sitting with Colonel Roscoff, surrounded by empty glasses which once contained French claret, supplemented by local *viche* to stand in for cognac. Many toasts have been made – including, inadvertently, one of his own to Napoleon, as he is so used to making them – but Roscoff appears not to have realised or perhaps thought he was celebrating Napoleon's defeat. Or being ironic. Or the man was so drunk he had not understood.

There is nothing, he reflects, like thinking you are about to die for appreciating the pleasures of a drink. How sweet and plangent must be that final dinner on the eve of execution. And even better, the thought – after such a stay of execution – that there may now be more to come.

He has time to study Colonel Roscoff over their cups. He sees the dirt that begrimes his collar and his frayed threadbare uniform, one shoulder sodden with sweat. After months on this tropical coast he could benefit from Bolivar's cologne. Perhaps he should offer a swab from his handkerchief, without declaring the provenance? But that might be pushing his luck – which has already delivered much.

The Colonel has declared his intention of drinking as much wine as possible before they leave, as such excellent French vintage should not fall into the hands of those *hijos de puta*, those sons of whores who call themselves *patriotas*.

For the Colonel is about to depart Colombia – or, as he insists on calling it, New Granada – and set sail south with his men – for Peru. Although unspoken, it is clear he feels the battle is lost; but this is a far-flung province and of no importance compared to Peru and the centre of Spanish operations in Lima, where the main Viceroy holds court. Samano in Cartagena had just been an outlier; a junior Viceroy. Perhaps that was why he had stood so on his dignity.

Roscoff admits also to having violent toothache, which he hopes the wine will anaesthetise. As the Colonel explains all this, he listens, befuddled by alcohol and still in the dreamlike trance when he thought they were about to die. So this, then, is an afterlife.

The Colonel follows on with something that brings him abruptly back to the present.

'You will have realised,' – he has realised nothing – 'we will have to take you to Peru with us. '

'It is not that I lack *confianza* – but if you were to come across the *patriotas*, and – inadvertently of course – reveal both our disposition and departure, that would, as I'm sure you understand, be a misfortune.'

The Colonel can tell from their expressions that this comes as a surprise – and not a welcome one.

'You will find Lima to your taste, *Milord*. More than this backward and wayward province going to the dogs and rebels.'

'Do I have a choice?'

Something of Roscoff's earlier snarl returns.

'No!'

After their host has departed, pleading pain in his teeth and leaving them in the tender charge of a corporal, Bankes and he are left among the empty bottles.

He fixes his old friend with a look that mixes gratitude with mild reproach.

'I was not aware you went to Spain to fight with Wellesley?'

'I didn't. I went to Spain to buy paintings. And I did buy paintings, some of them looted first by your adored Napoleon and his brother, and then released onto the marketplace, so to speak, after their defeat. Murillos. And a Velazquez.

— 'But along the way I fell in with the British troops. As Wellesley knew my father, he took me on, as a junior officer. A very junior officer. It must be admitted – although perhaps best not to tell our Spanish colonel – I formed a *particular attachment* to one of the young officers, and so had reason to prolong my stay with Wellesley.

— 'I performed my military duties well, to the extent that he made me an aide-de-camp. A lieutenant. Although in this I was not unusual – half my classmates from Westminster were employed there, the reason

I knew of some of their proclivities. But as this was many years before we met up again – and given your own *proclivities* for Napoleon – I have never chosen to mention it before.'

'And the letter of safekeeping from Viceroy Samano? A man you described to me in Cartagena as being unsurpassed in venality and brutality – and for whom you had no respect. Who spat on our shoes and —'

Bankes cuts him short. 'I have found on previous travels in Egypt and Spain – and the Levant – a letter of introduction from someone in authority has been helpful – necessary – in moments of distress or misunderstanding.'

And with a change of tone, 'There was also a moment of some – *awkwardness* – which I did not apprise you of at the time. When the authorities in Cartagena suspected me of a trifling offence, I was brought again before the Viceroy – and this time felt it expedient to advance some funds towards the royalist cause – an *emolument*, as you remember he described it – to avoid further charges. At the same time, I obtained a letter from him to cover any further difficulties of a similar sort that might occur – although I did not anticipate it might be useful in front of a hanging squad.'

Fletcher appears at this moment, swaying heavily on his feet.

'Just to inform you, my Lord, we are billeted adjacent to the Colonel's room, with a corporal standing duty outside.

—'And may I add, Sir,' – this to Bankes – 'my appreciation for your prompt and quick thinking in extracting us from an unwanted predicament,' – he gave a wave with his large forearm – 'is *unbounded*. I will be – forever – in your debt. Indeed,' – a less admiring look towards his master – 'we all will be. As we could have been dancing the Tyburn frisk.'

The inference is clear. Bankes has saved them from certain death – a fate which Byron had precipitated.

Bankes pauses, as if this is the last he will ever say on the affair. 'I did not like being blindfolded and deprived of my sight. Ever since I experienced ophthalmia in Egypt, I have a horror of not being able to see.'

'So the Duke would never eat between breakfast and nightfall – to the chagrin of his officers, like me, who would have to follow his example.'

Roscoff is hanging on every word – even though, in the days since they set sail for Peru, they must have heard this story – or a version thereof – a dozen times.

'And did you say,' asks the Colonel, 'the Duque would consume several bottles of red *tinto* wine each night – by himself?'

'He preferred the red Navarre wine of your country to all else…'

Shameless. When Bankes wanted to, he could lay it on with a trowel.

'Just as he acquired the taste for your mountain *jamón de serrano*, which he told me once was the humblest food fit for a king.'

If he heard any more of this over the mess table – which they were invited to join for each dinner, held late – being a Spanish one – long after nightfall, with guttering candles stuck to the table – he would vomit as if seasick.

'When we crossed over into France to chase Marshall Soult's tail, he commanded some two hundred thousand men – with thirty thousand of your gallant compatriots, who fought valiantly and sustained heavy losses – but we overcame the cowardly French and were victorious!'

'A toast,' demands Colonel Roscoff, for whom any excuse precipitates another drink. 'To *nuestra amistad*! To our friendship! And to King Ferdinand!'

Bankes drains his glass. He takes just a sip at his. Galling to be reduced to a bystander; moreover, the Colonel has given Bankes a far superior cabin. He was damned if he was going to toast King Ferdinand of Spain, a monarch renowned for his absoluteness and stupidity in a competitive field.

He tries to suggest his own military pedigree to Colonel Roscoff, when the opportunity presents. He mentions his own grandfather had been Admiral Jack Byron. But this misfires.

Roscoff's face darkens. 'Byron the *pirata*? Who followed in the footsteps of *El Drago*, Drake? And of Raleigh? Perhaps it would be best not to mention his name when we arrive in Lima.'

He worries Teresa will have no idea where he is. Colonel Roscoff is sanguine, if not dismissive.

'My Lord, she would have little idea where you are, were you still on the Pacific Coast in Colombia. I have not seen my own wife for three years. I am sure Señor Bankes is not worried about any woman he may have left behind.'

Indeed not. But Colonel Roscoff assures him that somehow – and it is unclear by what method – word will be sent to Teresa they have departed for Peru. Quite how this is to happen – without betraying Roscoff's own withdrawal – and what Teresa should then do – is left in abeyance. As so much else.

He has already noticed that the New World, far from offering a new certainty of opportunity, provides if anything more vagary of choice than even was the case in Europe – the sands shifting, the world turning. Who knew it could have such grey skies?

As they sail down the coast from Colombia, the landscape changes. The abundant forests to which they have become accustomed give way increasingly to desert, interrupted only by fertile estuary mouths where rivers come gushing down from the high Andes.

'Why mainly desert,' he asks Bankes, 'when we are so near the equator? Should it not be humid and productive? Is it because the sun has scorched the earth?'

'Humboldt asked the same question a generation ago – and answered it. There is a cold current that runs up from way to the south, at the very tip of the continent, now called by his name – the Humboldt Current.'

'I would like something named after me.'

'Doubtless there will be. Perhaps *a snuffbox*.'

Bankes pauses as if to lay a right-hander after his left.

'Or perhaps a bat. I can see you discovering an unknown bat. The *Murcielago bironico*, perhaps. There are many types of bat along this coast. They are as numerous as moths in England, which are so profligate a species.'

'Really? I thought there were but fifty types?'

'You are talking of butterflies. And if you are confused as to the distinction between a moth and a butterfly, that is perhaps why there is less likely to be a bat named after you – your credentials as a student of natural history are less impressive, even, than your credentials as *a military commander*. If that were possible.'

When Bankes is animated, he becomes more and more orotund in his rhetoric. It is an irresistible chance to bamm and rib him in return.

'So might we also have a *Murcielago banksiana*? But would that lead to confusion? For the casual bystander of bats might think it had been discovered by your illustrious predecessor, Joseph Banks?'

Over the years, Bankes has often been mistaken for a descendant of Joseph Banks, the great naturalist of the past century – an error, to all his friends' amusement, he is happy to perpetuate, despite the different spelling of their names and the lack of any connection whatsoever. If asked by strangers, he will neither affirm nor deny nor explain, but likes to say, 'I try to follow his methods,' in a manner both proprietorial and modest.

Now Bankes falls silent, uncharacteristically. Almost modestly.

Thwack. He is slammed again the bulwark of his tiny berth that lies towards the bows and receives the full impact of the Pacific swell. The berth is too small to sling a hammock, which would self-right against the waves. Instead he has a cot with a wooden slotted side to prevent the sleeper rolling out. Otherwise there is no concession to comfort. It would be too small for a Newfoundland dog, let alone a human being. Not that he would ever have allowed his own long dead Newfoundland dog to be so contained; even though it had been called Boatswain.

The ship is small – left behind by the Spanish Navy to retrieve stragglers like Roscoff – and not that seaworthy. It ships water like a colander, so a miracle they stay afloat – although, Bankes speculates, as long as the wind blows and they keep moving, the water should pass right through the ship.

But that is of little comfort. Fletcher assures him conditions are worse in the crew quarters, where most of the bedding is perpetually wet.

Additionally, in the rush to leave Buenaventura and Colombia, the ship has not been properly provisioned. The maize *arepas* are rotten and mouldy in the galley. The few chickens on board refuse to lay eggs in protest – a protest he understands, as he would not be inclined to lay an egg himself in these conditions.

The only provisions in excess are *viche* brandy and French claret – not a good combination – after Roscoff's declaration he would not leave a single bottle for the rebel *patriotas* to enjoy. 'Bad enough for them to get the cannons.'

They are heading south, ignominiously, to join the Spanish Navy in Peru, so each night is a drunken, maudlin affair in the officers' mess. The subject of Spanish defeat in Colombia is studiously avoided. Instead Wellington's military tactics are discussed by Bankes and Ros-coff, endlessly. Enough to drive a man to drink – and he has been thus driven, making his small berth in a tossing ship no place to have a hangover, although at least he can make it to the deck rail to vomit.

The little drinking water they have has turned rancid and saline with the heat and the barrel-leaks. Roscoff claims the only way to keep healthy at sea is to drink alcohol, much as Fletcher proposed on land – and the ship's captain, a taciturn Basque with an unpronounceable name, agrees.

As he lies doubled up in the cot – thank God, for once, that he is under six foot – it is hard not to think of the stateroom he enjoyed with Teresa as they crossed the Atlantic – or indeed how he enjoyed Teresa – and how her company lifted him out of himself, and those bleak moments of melancholia that have assailed him since a boy. Some of which he is experiencing again. It does not help he has to lie with such care in the cot to protect his vulnerable bad foot.

While they have survived execution, he cannot argue he has managed affairs well for his friends or for that matter Teresa. They are sailing towards Lima – the royalist Ciudad de los Reyes, 'The City of Kings' as Roscoff frequently reminds them – from whose port the treasure galleons set sail for Europe. Lima, the fortress at the heart of Spanish operations in South America and defended as such – while Teresa is thousands of leagues away in Bogota, in the liberated north, with the swish of balls and the excitement of a new country.

Nor does he trust Daniel O'Leary, now he has time to think more about it, whose intentions to Teresa and love of waltzing and fine conversation make for a dangerous friend. As he should know. Would Teresa take Daniel on as a *cavalier servente*, with the same abandonment she had taken on her English *Milord* in Venice? Of course, one could argue – to use the Shakespearean and naval metaphor – he would then be hoist by his own petard. Although he is unsure which rope in the rigging is a petard. He must get Bankes – or even Roscoff, although he might be puzzled as to the cause of the enquiry – to show him which rope was a petard – and how it was possible to be hoisted by one.

At their final leave-taking, Bolivar had presented him with French brandy – and had also given him a bottle of his own blend of cologne. The brandy had long been consumed, mainly by Fletcher – but he is eking out the cologne in small subversive dabs, to mask his own body smell and as a gesture of rebellion against his royalist captors. If unable to wear revolutionary colours, he can at least smell like Bolivar, with that blend of sweet tobacco and cedarwood. And certainly smell better than Roscoff, from whom he tries to keep upwind.

Later that morning, after black coffee mixed with *viche* to mask its brackish quality – which Fletcher brings to him in his cot, like a nurse-maid to an infant – he has taken up his customary position among the shrouds – when there is a sudden shout from the mizzen mast to announce a ship has been sighted.

By the time he joins Roscoff and the Basque captain on the bridge, she is identified as the *Prueba*, a powerful frigate sent over recently from Spain to assist the royalists.

Roscoff is overjoyed.

'Between ourselves, *Milord*, I was concerned. This ship is not as seaworthy as it should be, you may have noticed. Nor powerful enough to defend itself against the rebel fleet – who are far to the south in Chile, but might venture this way. To have the *Prueba* as a protector is providential. I had heard she was joining the fleet from Spain.'

He can only murmur his assent.

'Besides, I know the commander of that frigate. You will be more comfortable in a berth there – so will we all – and they may have fresh provisions from Lima.'

There follows terse muttering between Roscoff and their own ship's captain.

'We will go alongside and make the necessary arrangements. They have signalled us. We will transfer to the *Prueba* and leave a skeleton crew to sail this ship back to Lima. We will take our last supplies of wine as a gift.'

It is with satisfaction that Roscoff has himself, together with his English prisoner-guests and the wine, transported by tender to the arriving ship. As a newcomer, the *Prueba* sports a remarkably fresh Spanish flag fluttering in the mild Pacific breeze – showing, Roscoff says proudly, they are only lately from Spain and ready to engage with the enemy. The tender is so low on the water he can see the flying fish skimming; one lands on Roscoff who brushes it off fast, as inconsistent with his dignity.

'The Captain of the *Prueba* is celebrated for his hospitality – *un caballero,* a gentleman of distinction, descended from one of Spain's finest families.'

It is therefore with surprise that Roscoff finds himself placed in irons almost immediately upon setting foot on deck – as are they all – and brought to the bridge, to be confronted by an unusually tall commander with sandy hair and a distinctly northern European complexion.

'You are not the Captain of the *Prueba*,' splutters Roscoff.

'Both right and wrong on so many counts,' replies their new commander, in a Spanish lightly impregnated with a Scottish accent. 'This is not the *Prueba*, although you may have inadvertently made that assumption, helped by the false colours under which we are flying as one of the necessary deceptions of war. This is the *O'Higgins*, flagship of the Chilean Navy currently undertaking the liberation of Peru. And certainly I am not the Captain – I am the Admiral of the Fleet, Lord Cochrane – at your service.'

Who of course Bankes and he recognise, once recovered from their initial surprise; can hardly fail to recognise, given that, after Nelson, he has been the most controversial naval figure of recent times. The Spaniards, who feared him greatly, had described him over their mess-table as *El Diablo* – and Roscoff does indeed look as if he has set foot in Hell.

He himself steps forward confidently. Or as confidently as you can when your legs are in shackles.

'My Lord, we should present ourselves. This is Mr William Bankes. And I am Lord Byron.'

'Byron the poet! What the devil are you doing here? And why are you on a Spanish ship?'

'I sent a man to ask him, of course.'

'To ask who?'

'*Napoleon.* Who did you think? On Santa Helena. I sent a good man, one of my best – Colonel Charles – who sailed from Chile round Cape Horn and up to Santa Helena. But when he got there, it was clear Bonaparte was too ill to assume the responsibility.'

He finds, as often with Cochrane, he is struggling to keep up.

'Responsibility for what?'

'To become Emperor of South America. Who else could possibly assume such a mantle of responsibility? Who else has the imperial experience?'

Cochrane drains his glass and places it with a certain delicacy on the table. The Admiral is a strange mixture of the forthright and the reserved, a peculiarly Scottish combination he recognises. And he can tell Cochrane also has what he once heard a Piccadilly whore describe as 'the courage of the very shy'– she told him it was often the men who seemed most demure in their approaches who were most exigent in their final demands.

But when Cochrane does pronounce on anything, it is with vigour and at length.

'We wanted him to accept the throne of South America. All of us who fought for the liberation of Argentina, Chile and now Peru – men like San Martin and O'Higgins – were agreed there was only one *natural candidate* for the role.'

It is rare for Bankes to be nonplussed – or at least show it – yet he can see his friend struggling with this unusual emotion.

'But my Lord —'

'You can call me Cochrane at the mess table. Although the sailors just call me God – the British ones at least. The Spanish call me *El Diablo*, I am told.' A smile of satisfaction. As Roscoff has been confined to his quarters, he is not there to confirm this.

'But my Lord, surely the *patriotas* are fighting to free the continent from the yoke of European territory? Why should they replace the King of Spain – with the deposed Emperor of France?'

Fletcher comes forward with more wine and fills Cochrane's glass, reverently, like a priest preparing a chalice for holy communion. He has confided to his master that of all men, Cochrane is the one he most admires. Yes, *even more* than Prizefighter Jackson. Or Bolivar. Had their new commander not campaigned for the common man – for Reform and justice – campaigned so hard he had been ejected as an MP from the Houses of Parliament? After soundly beating the French on numerous occasions – and then had volunteered to fight for freedom, for a people on the far side of the world.

Cochrane sips his port – strictly speaking, madeira.

'That is a charming and naive sentiment, Mr Bankes. This war is not being fought for *noble* ideals alone. It is also fought for profit. The *patriotas* want, above all, financial independence from Europe. They do not want to send treasure ships to prop up the decaying Bourbon monarchs of Spain, like King Ferdinand. A man who makes the most *bovine* of monarchs, including I dare say – as I am no longer a serving officer in his Majesty's Navy – our *own*, look intelligent. Our Georgie boy.

— 'When that money and silver can be kept for their own use. Any more than North Americans wanted to pay taxes before I was born. *No taxation without representation*. That could well be the cry here as well. That *is* the cry here as well. Of course I appreciate their wish for independence. But also the chance to make more prize money than even Wellington – or Nelson, if he had survived Trafalgar.

— 'The sloop we have captured from your Colonel Roscoff will be auctioned and the proceeds divided – not that it is worth much, being unseaworthy and with no cargo other than a few ragged English prisoners – and the last royalist wine in what used to be called Nueva Granada. By the way, is the wine any good? Or did it ship water like everything else on that excuse for a seaworthy vessel?'

Cochrane does not wait for a reply.

'It is little known or *appreciated* – but back in London I was approached not only by my current Chilean employers – but also by the Spanish Government – who offered me the role of Admiral of their own navy in the Pacific!

— 'I *refused* – immediately – for they could offer little in the way of financial enticement. They thought the sheer honour of commanding the Spanish Navy enough – perhaps why it has been commanded by grandees and fools since the days of the Spanish Armada.

— 'On my way here, I did attempt to stop at Santa Helena so I could – *personally* – persuade Napoleon to accept the position of Emperor of South America. But the exigencies of the campaign – and with Valparaiso under siege – meant the Chileans urged me to make haste to the Pacific and I could not, in all conscience, refuse. So came direct. Which is why I had to send Colonel Charles later.

— 'However, what they need here is a *monarch* – who lives in the Americas, not Europe, but perhaps has credentials from Europe – as these lands need a firm leader.'

'What about Bolivar?' he interjects. 'Surely Bolivar is a republican. He is not looking for a King of Colombia. Or Emperor of South America for that matter. He told me so himself.'

'*Bolivar!*' snorted Cochrane. 'What happens in the north, in Colombia and Venezuela, is their own affair. Down here, San Martin and O'Higgins command. As, I suppose, do I. And what does Bolivar want? To be *Protector* of Colombia – in effect a king by another name, like Cromwell did in England?

— 'I admire Bolivar for his military achievements. The crossing of the Andes before the battle of Boyaca,' – like O'Leary, he pronounces it '*Boyo'ca*' – 'a feat worthy of Napoleon – or Hannibal, though Bolivar had mules, not elephants. But he knows *nothing* of politics and how to manage a country when it is conquered.

— 'And now to more immediate matters. I intend to blockade Callao, Lima's port, where I have reason to believe the forty-four-gun *Esmeralda* is sheltering. The *Esmeralda* is the flagship of the Spanish fleet in the Pacific. She is fast and powerful, and must be contained. There will be no opportunity or for that matter incentive to put you ashore first.

— 'This is a fighting ship of the line. I have no place for passengers, however distinguished or agreeable. Moreover, I understand you took up arms for Bolivar – if not to great effect – so I presume you have no objection to taking up arms on my behalf and that of the Chilean government?'

Cochrane pauses to look down at them. He could swear the Admiral has a chair raised above the others at the mess table, which together with his commanding height makes him a formidable presence, despite the stoop acquired from a career squatting between decks. The pause is like a *caesura* in a line of verse, and Cochrane flows on.

'Mr Bankes, I gather you served with Wellesley on his peninsular campaign – I propose to offer you another commission as *a lieutenant*, of which I have too few.'

Bankes gives a surprisingly polished salute.

'As for you, my Lord, I am mindful of your signal *lack of experience*. On deck earlier, you were unable, unlike Mr Bankes, to identify the halyards correctly. And a concern as to which rope is the "petard" to hoist shows commendable literary interest – but not confidence in your naval ability. Particularly as a petard is *not a rope on a boat at all*. Shakespeare was referring to a small bomb used in his time and the expression "hoist by your own petard" means to be *blown up by your own bomb*, a frequent occurrence in military matters – if not a desirable one. You will understand, therefore, if the only commission I can offer you is as – as *a midshipman*.'

'A *midshipman*!' He thinks he can hear Fletcher give a snort of laughter over the decanters in the background.

'*Nothing* wrong with being a midshipman. I began as one *myself*. And there are midshipmen of all ages, from twelve to forty-five, when sea legs begin to give out for advancing aloft. I am sure if you show the *acumen* you have displayed in other areas, you will advance rapidly.

— 'But first, you must learn to sail – and learn the dispositions of a fighting ship. While I am a great admirer of your *Childe Harold* – I have a copy in my cabin – *Who would be free themselves must strike the blow!'* – he thumps the table, with care not to spill the glasses – 'and while we share a mutual admiration for Napoleon – I cannot entrust the operation of my ship to a man who thinks port is not the opposite of starboard, but a fortified wine.' As if reminded of his own glass, the Admiral drains it.

'You will begin at first bells tomorrow. The master of the watch will instruct you in your duties.'

This is a dismissal.

Over the following weeks, he comes painfully to learn the stations allotted to him when the ship is at quarters, when he is on watch, and how the hands are summoned for setting or taking in sail.

In a curious manner, he feels happier than he has ever been. The rituals of life on a man-of-war suit him, in a way that would have astonished those who knew him in the *salons* of Piccadilly or the *palazzi* of Venice. And the Admiral had been wrong on one account. Having owned a small schooner in Italy – which he had called, of course, the *Simon Bolivar* – he at least knows the principles of sailing – his port – or *larboard* – from his starboard, his close-hauled from a broad reach. Even if the principles applied to a gigantic man-of-war with many masts and sails might take a bit of learning. But it gives him pleasure to do so.

Meanwhile Fletcher has put it about, loyally, that the clubfoot from which he has suffered since birth is instead due to a wound acquired in Bolivar's service. This accords him respect from the crew, many of whom have suffered similar damage during earlier battles Cochrane has fought. The ship is full of blocks and tackles and winches that can trap a man's hand or foot or entire leg – so the phrase 'able-bodied seaman' is an anomaly more than the rule.

While he is, in every sense, shown the ropes on deck – and with tact – given his foot – not asked to climb the mizzen mast, as a more junior midshipman might – he learns much – if not more – from con-versations with Cochrane in the Admiral's stateroom, with its fine windows overlooking the sea and Roscoff's excellent wine on the table.

The Admiral has adopted him as an unofficial aide-de-camp – for he has the signal advantage – Cochrane tells him straight, 'You have no *side*, Byr'n' – of *not* being in the naval hierarchy and so is without axe to grind, unlike other officers. He is also a good listener, prepared to attend to Cochrane's at times meandering stories. To keep up.

For Cochrane's life has an epic wandering quality that makes his own Don Juan look tame.

'Did you know I was captured once? By the French?'

This seems a rhetorical question, but he nods to show encouragement.

'About twenty years ago. When I was in command of a small brig, the *Speedy*. We roamed the Spanish coast and for a while I had success – not that Lord Vincent, the damned fool, had the grace to acknowledge that success – or ensure I received my share of the prize money. Vincent, who let Nelson do all the work and took the glory for himself. Gout-ridden old man.

— 'Once we were surprised by a French line-of-battle ship – to be precise, *three* line-of-battle ships, which gave chase, with one of them, the *Desaix*, most prominent. I tried to outrun them, but we were just off the Spanish coast, so I had limited room for manoeuvre.'

Cochrane looks deep into his glass as if he can see the sea inside. Not for the first time, he is struck by the Admiral's resemblance to Bankes. Cochrane could be Bankes's older and taller cousin. They have the same sandy, almost red, hair and bright blue eyes with a touch of green. But whereas Bankes has startling good looks, no one would ever describe Cochrane as handsome – not with his prominent nose and weather-battered cheeks. Nor, he suspects, would the Admiral care.

And Bankes does not have the slight Scottish accent that emerges whenever Cochrane is speaking with emotion – as he is now.

'We endeavoured to escape by making all sail, and, when the wind fell light, by using our sweeps. This proved unavailing, so we threw the guns overboard – a desperate situation called for desperate measures – and put the brig before the wind. Notwithstanding every effort, the enemy gained upon us fast…'

As if defending himself at a court martial, and using the tumblers on his silver tray, Cochrane illustrates the movements of these various ships, with the edge of the table as the coastline of Spain – and his own glass as the *Speedy*.

'In order to prevent our slipping away, they separated on different tacks – you follow me?' – a sharp glance, distrustful of Byron's grasp of naval manoeuvres – 'so as to keep us constantly within reach of one or the other.

— 'The *Desaix*, being nearest, fired broadsides at us as she passed, at other times firing from her bow chasers and cutting up our rigging. For upwards of *three hours* we were thus within gunshot of the *Desaix*.'

Cochrane lets this sink in. He knows his audience is of an imaginative disposition. Three hours of being raked by cannon across their decks.

'Finding it impossible to escape by the wind, I ordered the stores to be thrown overboard, in the hope of being able, when lightened, to run the *gauntlet* between the ships, which continued to gain upon us. But there was nothing I could do. Rather than have my men cut to ribbons, I ran down our colours – and surrendered.'

He says the word 'surrendered' as if puzzled by his own actions. Cochrane looks up from the wineglass and directly at him. As often with Cochrane's stories, he finds it difficult to react. With absolution, like a priest, or with sympathy, like a friend? With admiration, like a junior officer? And as often, before he has decided, Cochrane has commenced a further broadside of narrative.

'I handed over my sword – on the deck of the *Desaix* – and I have to say the French captain treated me well. With due respect. With more respect, perhaps, than I ever received from the Admiralty – not even perhaps – *certainly*.

— 'And I learned something from my captivity.'

'Really, my Lord? I would have thought the confinement both irksome and frustrating.'

'For some men. But,' – Cochrane gives a glance to signal the denouement of the story – 'I used my time. During my passage as a prisoner, I had ample opportunity to observe the superior manner in which the sails of the *Desaix* were cut, and the consequent flat surface exposed to the wind – compared to the slack reefs, bellying sails, and *bread bag canvas* of English ships of war.'

'In the same way French women dress better than English ones?' he ventures. It is a touch vulgar as a suggestion. But naval talk does not tend to subtlety – and he wants, like a chameleon, to be able to match Cochrane.

'Precisely! Although I dare say the one thing likely to confirm the British public in thinking *both of us* dangerous forces abroad, would be if they knew we were praising the charms of French ships and women – and disparaging English ones!'

He cannot keep up with the Admiral when it comes to naval stories – but he can venture a thought on Englishwomen.

'As you know, my Lord, I have seen a great deal of Venice and of Italian society, and of Italian women. And at times, yes, they can be dissolute – but in my experience nothing compares to the *profligacy* of Englishwomen. They are in an unnatural state of society.'

'You would be unwise to say that to my wife Kitty. Meanwhile remind me to tell you sometime...' – no reminder will be necessary as he is about to hear Cochrane's story anyway – 'about when, as a junior officer, I was sent to parley with the Dey of Algiers – who controlled the supplies for our Mediterranean fleet. He threatened to put me in prison – without recourse to his harem, sadly, as it was extensive, I believe – and told me the British were the *worst* of pirates! Quite something, from the ruler of Algiers, whose galleys have preyed on shipping for centuries.' Cochrane gives a laugh so dry it rattles in his throat.

'But of course the Spanish think of us as *piratas*. In some ways we are. And why not? As a nation, we have constantly lived on our wits. Only pirates could have defeated the Armada. If we had gone up against them ship to ship, we would have been blown to pieces. It needed cunning.'

The ship's bell distracts him.

'Your watch? – In any event I should write a dispatch to San Martin, nominally my commanding officer, although he is not much better than Vincent.

— 'Keep an eye on the morale of the men, Byr'n. These Chilean sailors are stout-hearted, but a crew can shift like the wind and come at you suddenly from a different quarter. I depend on you, Byr'n. Lord *Midshipman* Byr'n.' Said with irony.

He likes the way the Admiral often abbreviates Byron to 'Byr'n', as if one syllable, and as he sometimes likes to do himself. A faster name, running before the wind, rather than a cumbersome two-syllabled, two-masted surname that would probably lumber if close hauled.

'By the way, man, you're not related to *Jack* Byr'n, are you? The Admiral. Who knew these waters better than any Englishman of his time. That's just occurred to me.'

'My grandfather, my Lord.'

'Well, for God's sake, man. Why didn't you say so before? Too late now, of course, but I might have made you a more senior officer.'

Such familiarity does not occur above deck. If he meets Cochrane on watch – or the Admiral is summoned for some necessary consultation – every formality is observed.

All officers know better than to interrupt Cochrane if he is thinking – *calculating* – or looking down at the water, with his large bony hands clutching convulsively at the rail, sou'wester rammed over his head.

One night he watches Cochrane against the ocean from the shadows of the officers' bridge and a memory comes back.

He is ten years old. He is himself looking down at the water from above. He has been told on no account must he swim in the dark lake, for the thick weed and mud could trap a boy – particularly one with a maimed and deformed foot. His mother is not one to mince her words. Had she not once in a temper called him a lame brat?

It is night, so no one can observe him. But there is a moon so he can see the water. The surface has a black and viscous look. It could be just a few feet deep or a bottomless pit. He can just make out the reflection of the great bulk of Newstead Abbey behind, blotting out yet more light. Like the ship's reflection in the ocean now. And he can hear the wind whistling around the empty sockets of the Abbey's façade.

He has brought the nankeen vest and stockings given to him when they lived in Scotland for walking across the moors, as the water will be cold. Also a stout stick, which must have been his great uncle's and was still in the gun room. He thinks if he does encounter a problem with the mud, he might use the stick to lever free. Swans are nesting on the lake and without any means to protect himself, he may stumble on their nest and they may attack.

There is a jetty where the water is deeper so he can launch into the water and immerse immediately, rather than wading through mud. He leaves his jerkin and breeches on the wooden planks of the jetty, together with a rug from the hall.

It is not a moment for fear. He dives headfirst into the lake, holding the stick in front of him like a lance, so the waters open. After a few frantic strokes to overcome the shock of the cold, he turns on his back – to float into the middle of the lake and keep clear of weeds, holding the stick out behind his arms and kicking. The moon shines down.

He feels extraordinary contentment and calm. He knows this is how he wishes his life to continue. Both to do what he is told not to do, and then to know how right that decision has been.

In some ways he feels that now. However insane this might all seem.

Cochrane startles him with a sudden observation.

'Lord Byr'n, would you not agree that the stars of the Scorpio constellation – make an extraordinary impression when they appear above the horizon? A sight rare in the Northern Hemisphere.'

He mumbles assent, though none is expected.

There is a pause. During the watches of the night, when time extends, it can be hard to tell if such pauses are for a few seconds or longer minutes.

'What do you know about coal tar, Byr'n?'

Very little, he admits, and forces himself to concentrate on what Cochrane is saying.

'Thirty years or so ago, my father had an ingenious idea. He wanted to use his Scottish estates to produce coal tar – which he proposed the Navy use for the caulking of ships' timbers to prevent the leakage and decay so prevalent at the time. And now.

— 'But to his astonishment – and concern as he invested a large part of his – indeed *my* – future resources in this project – they *refused*! Despite the obvious sense of what he was proposing. And not just because the Admiralty always oppose anything inconsistent with what they describe as *ancient routine*.

— 'Do you know why they refused?'

Cochrane grips the side rail tightly and carries on without waiting.

'They refused – because it was *too good* an idea. Or rather – let me put it another way. When, as a young boy, I accompanied my father on a visit to a shipbuilder, for him to enquire *why* there was resistance to such an eminently practical proposition, the man replied, "Yes, it was undoubtedly a good idea to pay a hull with tar" – but it would put him and his colleagues out of business! And the clerks of the Admiralty out of the *considerable retainers* they acquired from that business.

— 'For the current system depended – *depended*, mark you – on being able to repair or replace ships regularly because of such leakage. Copper sheeting – or hob-nailing a hull – is vastly inferior and less effective – gaps are always appearing – but has the great advantage for the shipbuilders of being temporary and more expensive. I remember the shipwright saying, in my hearing, that if vessels were made watertight – as they could easily and cheaply be, with the application of coal tar – he might as well *shut up shop*, along with every other shipbuilder in Limehouse.

— 'Indeed, he went further. "The worm is our best friend," he said. "Rather than follow your proposition, I would happily cover ships' bottoms with *honey* to attract worms."

— 'It is the stupidity that annoys me. The sheer stupidity. Even after years at sea when my primary enemy has not been the French – but the gross stupidity of my superiors. I gather now, finally, even the Admiralty are adopting the idea. They are consulting Humphry Davy for advice. Too late for my father, who gave up the patent long ago and is living in straitened circumstances in Paris to escape his creditors. Although of course I assist him with what means I can.

— 'On our arrival in Chile, the first thing I did was ensure all our ships were paid with coal tar, easily obtainable in that country – without O'Higgins demurring in the slightest. What I like about the New World – is how amenable they are to new ideas.

— 'If my father had stayed an inventor – like James Watt or Cavendish – he would be a successful man. But he insisted on trying to *manufacture* every one of his ideas – so had too many irons in the fire.

— '*The British Tar Company.*' Cochrane stares into the black waters of the Pacific night. 'My family fortune lost trying to make British tar. Thousands of pounds poured into the void. When I was seventeen, our estates had to be sold. I was already a midshipman, thank God, and making my way in the Navy. My uncle secured the position for me. But it was not an easy passage.'

'I can imagine your sentiments, my Lord.'

Hesitant, but he senses this is a moment when he can interject further.

'And Sir, is it not a universal truth that we make ourselves? Surely that is what the example of Napoleon shows us? That it is the will to *become* who we *want to become* that determines fate – far more than family or circumstance? My father died young, after rash errors of judgement. I was two years old – and later, our family fortunes were much diminished when I inherited them from my great-uncle. I spent many years trying to restore our estate at Newstead, near Nottingham, which had become as ruined as the Abbey within its grounds – but was forced to sell, to my occasional regret. Although I am told the estate would not bring half as much now as I got for it then.' This with some satisfaction.

He stands beside Cochrane, who has fallen quiet, and he stares into the waters thinking of Newstead again; of arriving there as a young boy. Wandering with his dog though the draughty halls – at least Aberdeen had prepared him for the cold – and reading – reading endlessly – imagining what it would be like in faraway places.

He wonders what that shy ten-year-old boy struggling with a lame foot would make of himself twenty years later – sailing with one of the greatest heroes of the age along the Pacific seaboard to help liberate a nation.

But the boy might well laugh at the man for his failure to grow an adequate moustache – as Bankes does. And for his humble position on board.

'Dammit, that sail is luffing, Midshipman Byr'n. Can you not hear it flapping? Ask the helmsman to bear away a few points, if you please. And *pay attention*, man.'

The next day he spends his watch staring at the long dirty Peruvian coast – its grey, unrelenting desert – and lets his mind wander. Snatches of old songs and new poetry come to him. He can hear that insistent Irish ballad of Moore's in his head, 'The Minstrel Boy'. Since first landing in the Americas, he has not been of a mood to write anything down; but now he feels the old familiar itch beginning to stir, like a rictus in his right hand. Keeping time with Moore's song.

This unaccustomed long period without writing – a holiday which at first was a relief – has become an *absence*. He has come to realise it is not enough to have sensations, however intense – he needs to write them down in some form, to catch them before they evaporate, or he will not feel truly whole and complete. To transmute them into another form. His berth becomes filled with scraps of paper, for he writes on anything he can find. Another canto of *Don Juan* comes easily to him, as his hero voyages the Mediterranean and has adventures at sea. And another.

Cochrane is sympathetic and allows him access to the ledgers and writing materials used for the ship's log – even asks him jocularly one evening if he may not have his own portrayal in verse. And suggests.

'Something like…

— '*Lord Cochrane came down like a wolf on the fold / His ship's colours gleaming in azure and gold…*'

The Admiral pronounces this with a loud snort of satisfaction at the mess table. It is unclear how he means this – in jest or seriousness – whether it is a slab of meat or a trifle – so the others do not know how to respond. Bankes, with diplomacy, speculates aloud on how few poems there are about life at sea that succeed in any measure – a sentiment with which Cochrane concurs.

But before the Admiral can proceed, he heads him off, seizing a rare moment in which he can be said to pronounce with authority – given the lack of opportunity to do so on the naval matters that dominate the mess.

'Those subjects on which poets are allowed to discourse are limited altogether in their scope, my Lord. Poets may talk of love – up to a point, which stops short at the bedroom door – of the pleasures of the sublime and the natural world – of which the Lake Poets do so much they would step over a corpse to admire a daffodil. We may assay some grand classical epic when we compete with the Ancients, although almost always to their advantage – a Hyperion, an Alastor, an Absalom or Achitophel…'

He can tell he has lost Captain Guise, the dull staff captain of another ship who has made Cochrane's life so difficult, and who is nodding in blind misunderstanding. Good. He will try to be even more abstruse. Guise can talk for hours about gaff rigging.

'Only Milton's *Paradise Lost* is the exception which proves the rule – triumphantly – that in general we are not the equal of the ancients when it comes to epics – nor perhaps do our readers have a sustained *appetite* for them.

'— But of war, of commerce, of the daily affairs of men, only one man has felt he could discourse on whatever came his way, and that was Pope, a prince among poets. Pope who could write poems about meeting a dog, or the cutting of a lock of hair, or the machinations of Grub Street. There is ten times more poetry in his *Essay on Man* than in Wordsworth's piss-poor *Excursion*, or any of his dull disciples.

— 'It is only because he was incapable of fighting, due to his physique, that he did not write of Marlborough's victories over our European enemies. Or of life at sea.'

'So perhaps we can expect an epic on the battle for Peru from you, my Lord?'

Cochrane smiles indulgently. He does not wait for an answer.

'Speaking of Marlborough, no fewer than three of my ancestors died fighting in his service. One unnecessarily. Let me describe you one mistake Marlborough – or Churchill as he was then – made in the deployment of his forces at the battle of Schellenberg…' And Cochrane marshals the salt and pepper pots in front of him.

Guise stares on woodenly. Cochrane and Captain Guise have all the politeness in their exchanges that comes from two British men who loathe each other and are conscious of the disparities in their respective positions: Cochrane as commander; Guise as his unwilling subordinate. Cochrane as a radical who voted for reform during his brief and turbulent period in Parliament; Guise as a mercenary naval captain with no interest in politics ('the Dagoes can kill *all* the other Dagoes, for all I care'), but plenty in the acquisition of profit – which he has already made by purchasing the ship he commands at an auction in Britain and then selling it to the desperate Chileans at an inflated price. Only to find, on his arrival in that country, that he had been placed, unwillingly, under Cochrane's overall command.

Cochrane suspects him of mutinous intentions – and confides this later to Byr'n as his aide-de-camp, when they are the last, as often, to be sitting at the table.

'That fool would quite happily see me rammed amidships. He is an officer of little intelligence – and they are the most *dangerous* to have as your subordinates.'

Cochrane pauses. If he did not know his man better, he would say the Admiral was embarrassed.

'The thing is, Byr'n, I have written something myself. An account of my time in the late wars with France.

— 'I wondered if perhaps you could see your way to look over it. To see if the thing holds water. Or needs an application of *coal tar*.'

There is nothing he dislikes more than to give literary advice – to read a tedious manuscript. Surely that is what publishers are for, if they serve any use whatsoever. Which he doubts.

'Of course, my Lord. Nothing would give me greater pleasure. My only counsel would be – that you are studiously honest in your account, without fear or favour. Although I suspect you will be forthright. And of one thing I am certain. You will have a British public avid to hear of your adventures.'

Cochrane grunts. It is the nearest he ever gets to a sign of agreement. Or needs to.

Roscoff has asked to see him.

The Spanish colonel is kept as a prisoner in what, he is sorry to see, looks a squalid and unpleasant cabin. He remembers, with a stab of guilt, how Roscoff did at least treat him as an officer after they had been captured, and invite him to join the mess – something that has not happened on board the *O'Higgins*. But he knows better than to remonstrate with Cochrane, who would never countenance such an idea while still on active operation; in case Roscoff too was able to make useful observations. At least his shackles have been removed.

But otherwise the prisoner is in a sorry state. His uniform, already ragged from the campaign along the Pacific coast, has decayed yet further. The cuffs are frayed and he can see right through the shoulder of Roscoff's jacket to a grimy shirt below. Yet the man maintains a certain aristocratic dignity, even while sitting on a cot smaller than the one he himself suffered on the Basque Captain's boat.

'*Milord*, I have a favour to ask you. You will remember that I did not execute you when I had the chance.'

It seems unwise to leave this as a precursor to any favour.

'Just as, Colonel, we have not executed you.'

'*Por supuesto*. Of course. And in war, things can change with great rapidity.

— 'I wanted to ask – if you might be interested in purchasing my estate. As circumstances may mean I am unable to return to Venezuela – or what the rebels now call Colombia – for a while.'

'Where is the estate?'

Roscoff has prepared what is more a prospectus than an answer.

'My family estates lie to the north-west of Bogota, in the area near Medellin which is particularly propitious for the growing of fruit and produce. They comprise one hundred million square *varas* of land – so around 7000 hectares – and the substantial *hacienda* enjoys both extensive stables and cellars and,' – Roscoff pauses as if this is the detail that will seal the purchase – 'a dovecote.'

It is not quite what he expected. 7000 hectares was the size of one of those great Scottish estates where they throw in a few islands and highlands. Enough to live in a style to which he has not been accustomed. Over fifty times the size of his Newstead Abbey estates.

'You will find the climate agreeable – less high than Bogota and therefore not so cold. Many have described it as *una primavera eterna*, a perpetual spring.'

He thinks of a Botticelli painting.

'And may I enquire how much you might want for such an estate?'

Roscoff pauses, and names a figure that is disconcertingly low – as he must realise from the look on his captor's face.

'I am not in a position to negotiate. And I realise you do not of course have the opportunity to see the estate. But I would only ask – that all respect is paid to those members of my family who may still be living there, and they are given assistance to travel to wherever I may be. My wife and children.

— 'I should add as well that the climate is especially favourable for the growing of roses.'

He remembers how much Teresa and Allegra had enjoyed San-gucho's garden. To buy an estate unseen goes against his judgement but not against his nature.

'Colonel Roscoff, I will consider your proposal carefully. If I do buy it, I will give you a more generous price, as I would not want it said I had taken advantage of your *situación*.' He tries not to lisp as the Viceroy had. 'And of course I will ensure your wife and children are offered safe passage.'

'*Milord*, you are indeed a gentleman.'

Bankes and he are standing together at the rail, part of a line of men who stretch far down the starboard side of the *O'Higgins* and then back along the larboard. They peer conscientiously – not least because their commander is close – into the mist that surrounds the ship, although visibility is limited to a few ship's lengths at best.

He wonders what strange phantoms might suddenly emerge and confront them – a whale, or ghostly ship – or anything else passing un-seen just a short distance away. The whole Spanish Armada could be steaming past and they would be none the wiser.

But that is not their current concern.

'These sea fogs are endemic along the Peruvian Coast, particularly in winter. They are far more to be feared than any storm or military engagement. A ship can founder on an island or rock and be *rent* asun-der.' Cochrane stresses '*rent*' almost with satisfaction at the thought of any captain foolish enough to let such an event occur.

He wonders at the scenes that would follow. The men struggling to get the lifeboats and cutters and jolly boats afloat. The sail that might be wrapped round the transom as a makeshift repair, as the bosun told him once transpired on a boat struck by an iceberg in the southern seas. Although surely no iceberg would reach this high up the Pacific seaboard?

He reels sideways. Cochrane has given him a clip round the ear.

'Lord Byr'n, you are not *attentive* again. Your mind is on other matters. You are a midshipman at this present instance. Not a poet. Pray bear that in mind.

— 'Concentrate on looking for seabirds. For their presence is ominous. It suggests we might be close enough to land for them to reach us. And land can mean shoals of rock out to sea. The charts for this coastline are by no means comprehensive.'

They have struck almost all their own sails – just a working fore jib to give steerage and not come upon any hazard at too great a speed. The helmsman calls the depth as his assistants use the deep-sea line.

Dolphins have chosen this moment to appear and are gambolling alongside the ship's beam, crossing backwards and forwards under its bow. Is this some sort of harbinger, like the seabirds would be? Should he tell Cochrane, who is standing further back on the bridge, swathed in his boat cloak, and cannot see down over the rail? Perhaps not.

He has never seen a sea so flat. The only signs of movement are the fins of the dolphins as they break and ripple the surface, which shimmers in the white light of the fog.

'My Lord.' Fletcher hovers behind his shoulder, with hot toddy for both Bankes and him.

'Have I told you the story of how I once almost fainted on a sailing boat on Lake Geneva?' he whispers to Bankes over the drinks.

'No. Although I suggest you do not faint now.'

'We were in a local boat with a loose-footed mainsail.'

Bankes nods and raises an eyebrow in mock recognition at the technical term. 'Had you remembered to splice your jackstays and strike your topgallant masts?'

He brushes this aside. 'The loose-footed mainsail is part of the story. Because the pole that secured it to the deck came loose when we were tacking and hit me violently on the leg. This leg,' and he delicately lifts the leg that has given him so much trouble since boyhood.

Bankes nods, more circumspectly this time. There are times when Bankes could almost be accused of tact.

'I was with Hobhouse, who was further forward in the boat – he turned to see me prostrate on the floor – like a ghost. He revived me with brandy and Epsom salts – of which the salts were far more efficacious. I felt a sort of grey giddiness first – then nothingness – and a total loss of memory on beginning to recover.'

'A shame the memory loss did not last longer,' says Bankes tartly. 'We would have been spared a multitude of stories.'

More kindly, 'I fainted once myself. In the catacombs of Giza. Perhaps from excitement as much as the dust.'

They turn and look out at the fog. The helmsman's voice calls the depth. Or rather not the depth. 'No ground with this line,' comes the cry. They must be reassuringly deep.

'Full fathom five,' he hears in his head, but privately, so his commander does not know.

The fog has cleared. He can see Guise's ship riding alongside, with others that have joined the fleet now they are closer to Lima. At night it makes for a fine spectacle, the white billowing sails against the blue-black.

The Southern Hemisphere with its different stars – a myriad of confusing new constellations – the Southern Cross – Alpha and Beta Centauri, winking down, or 'the eyes of the llama' as the Incas used to call them; so a Chilean sailor says, who teaches him to chart true south by taking a line some lengths from the Southern Cross and dropping down to the horizon.

Sometimes when not on duty, he lies on an isolated part of the quarterdeck, so he can look up at the stars and get lost in their immense indifference.

One night when they have almost reached Lima and its port, Callao, he joins Bankes on the bridge to take the watch. They repeat an exchange which has become a ritual, with elaborate bows and doffing of hats. Both of them have received the hats of dead officers – although Bankes's fits better than his, which he sometimes has to clutch against the wind. The cocked brims fill rapidly with water from the bow-spray; but no officer would commit the solecism of emptying his hat until the end of a watch.

'Reporting for duty, *Lieutenant* Bankes.'

'Your watch, *Midshipman* Byron. *Lord* Midshipman Byron. Or should I say, Lord Midshipman *Byr'n.*'

They take time before Bankes retires to smoke one of Bankes's foul cigars, of which he has an inexhaustible supply, and to admire the white peaks of the waves catching the moonlight.

A watch during the night gives a different pace to a conversation. As he gazes out at the waters of the Pacific, thoughts come to him like slow drifts.

'Strange to think the Earth may have been destroyed many times…

— 'That floodwaters covered portions of the earth…That this ocean we are sailing across may once have been land with mountains, rivers, people…'

'You have a wild imagination, *Midshipman* Byron. Make sure you do not start to see monsters emerging from the deep.'

— 'But you are referring, even if you do not perhaps know it,' – really, Bankes could be insufferably patronising – 'to the theories of the French natural philosopher Georges Cuvier…'

Of course he knows who Cuvier is.

'He came to a conclusion on studying fossils about the antiquity of the planet, but also that several *catastrophes* have occurred at times in its history. That whole strange species of creatures may have been annihilated.'

'As may occur again.'

'Indeed. As may again. As almost certainly – *will* occur again. *Annihilating all that's made / to a green thought in a green shade.*' Bankes exhales a large cloud of cigar smoke, as if the thought gives him pleasure.

'We are but specks upon the infinite. *Nought may endure but Mutability…*'

Bankes looks at him to continue.

He does so quietly, as he does not want the helmsman or hands nearby to overhear:

> '*We are as clouds that veil the midnight moon;*
> *How restlessly they speed and gleam and quiver,*
> *Streaking the darkness radiantly! Yet soon*
> *Night closes round, and they are lost for ever…*'

Bankes waits to see if he will continue, then speaks.

'Those are some of your best lines. I've not heard them before. Why can't all your stuff be that good?'

'Because they *aren't* my lines. They're Shelley's. So with reluctance, I can't take the compliment – however unaccustomed.

'— But if I ever do come to write my epic on Cain and his fratricidal struggles with Abel – which you know I have long thought of interest – I will incorporate some of the thoughts of Baron Cuvier. His *catastrophism*. Although the word may test even my abilities to scan or rhyme.'

'Baron? Since when did he become a baron?'

'Just before we left Venice. The French ennobled him for his services to science.

— 'Did you not know?'

It is rare for him to be able to take Bankes down a notch. *Lieutenant* Bankes.

Some nights he feels as if the ship is like an enormous horse riding under them with a will and energy of its own – the stays and shackles and hawsers a gargantuan bit trying to rein in this restless tossing animal as it surges forever across the bucking black seas – the snaffly, clinky jingle from the booms – the booming echo like a shot when one of the foresails loses the wind momentarily from some angle of a wave – and then fills suddenly again, the canvas smacking back against itself.

He remembers riding out from Newstead across the moors at night – with his Newfoundland dogs running alongside and the same feeling of letting the horse carry you where it would – of having to let the horse carry you. And of not knowing where he would end up in the morning.

'I have decided, gentlemen, on a plan of attack.'

He can tell Cochrane enjoys the moment. The drama of it. They have blockaded the port of Callao – staying just offshore in the Roads of Callao, to use the naval phrase – so preventing the royalists who still hold Lima from receiving supplies or sending treasure galleons home to Spain; home, as they would see it. But there has not been any talk of attack. Attack what?

Cochrane smiles. 'We will sail into the harbour in small boats and cut out the *Esmeralda*.'

There is a silence.

'My Lord – and pardon the impertinence – but is this prudent or indeed possible?' begins Guise, cautiously. 'The *Esmeralda* is a flag-ship of forty-four guns, the fastest, most powerful in the Pacific. As we have ascertained during this blockade, there are thirty or so gunboats patrolling the entrance to the port – which, furthermore, has a harbour-boom laid across the entrance. How can we penetrate the Spanish defences even to reach the *Esmeralda*? Let alone board, take her and escape under the guns of the harbour's defences?'

Cochrane waves this aside with dismissal. Everyone knows he once boarded a Spanish frigate of over three hundred sailors with an attacking force of less than fifty, from just such an attack of small boats cutting out a larger one. It is part of his legend. Which is perhaps dangerous. For once he has a certain sympathy with Captain Guise.

'Because we will.'

He feels a sense of nausea – but also of excitement – as if about to be plunged into some new experience out of his ken.

Guise presses on. 'But will the men follow us?' He has a point. This is a volunteer naval force, not a conscripted one.

'The value of all the boats we take in the harbour – for we will take many – will be shared equally among the men and among us all. The sort of incentive that motivates a sailor. As it could be said, Sir, it motivates some of us.'

Guise's appetite for prize money is well known. If his bulbous and florid face was capable of blushing, it would.

They are in what, after the overwhelming size of the *O'Higgins*, seem like cockleshell-small boats, each one manned by an officer, of which he is one – although he feels he is masquerading in the role. He still has to ask Bankes what certain nautical terms mean, as Bankes, with infuriating insouciance, has acquired such knowledge rapidly, as if a midshipman since a boy – like their commander, who often reminds them of his own length of service.

Their commander, who he can just make out under the night sky a hundred yards ahead in the lead boat. Extraordinary the Admiral of a fleet should lead such a daring attack even if, at just the wrong side of forty, Cochrane is such a young and virile Admiral. Equally extraordinary that no one should doubt for a moment he would.

The lights of a Spanish gunboat swing towards them. Across the water comes a hail in Spanish asking their business – which could be that of fishermen. To his surprise, he sees Cochrane's small craft steer directly alongside the much longer gunboat.

'Surely he will not surrender?' he stage-whispers to Bankes in the next boat.

A Petty Officer in his own boat overhears. 'Surrender, Sir? He will be going aboard with a cutlass, telling their captain if he does not surrender, he and his men will be dead within minutes.'

Sure enough, the gunboat puts out its lights and the swarm of rowing boats carry on towards the great hulk of the *Esmeralda*, like a warehouse against the night sky, all lights confidently blazing. He wonders idly if the Spaniards have painted their hull with coal tar.

He had worried he might feel an incapacity of fear – but instead feels lightheaded, reckless, even though he has declined the offer of beer or brandy. 'What the crew are taking, my Lord,' Fletcher has whispered beforehand. Fletcher at least is not accompanying them. He would not like to have the possible death of his manservant on his conscience again, having narrowly avoided it before.

Fletcher has pressed on him half a loaf of bread and some cheese, which he has in his pocket, alongside his pistol – he fingers the walnut handles of the pistol which he knows so well. The way the wood has worn to shape his hand – though the pistol, taken together with the cutlass he has been issued, makes him feel ludicrous and piratical. But then some of the Chilean crew are carrying tomahawks, and Miller's marines have pikes.

That this is extreme folly, he is aware. There are fifty men in the rowing boats; many hundreds await them on the *Esmeralda*. Whatever the advantages of surprise – even if Cochrane has carried out such exploits before – the risk of ignominious capture is as large as the sky above them.

The oars have been wrapped in canvas to muffle any noise when moving through the water, so their progress is ghostly and quiet.

He tries to identify the Southern Cross – not as easy as it sounds, for a 'false Southern Cross' lies close to it in the sky and they are easily confused. Nearby, he can see 'the eyes of the llama' winking down, so bright they are indisputable.

What would the Incas have made of this conflict? Their conquistadors about to receive a bloody nose. He allows himself to feel anger at what the Spaniards have done over the centuries – suppress the natural freedom of a people. He allows it to burn. He needs a *necessary anger*. It has often been useful to him. Those lines of the German poet Novalis who died so young – *It only needs one word of command to set whole armies in motion – and that word is freedom.* Lines that Shelley had once delivered to stop him in his tracks in a street in Venice; bellowed, almost in his face.

His boat reaches the *Esmeralda* at the same time as that of Bankes, and they have to secure a line to her main chains. One of the more athletic Chilean sailors – *muy hábil*, very able says the Petty Officer who volunteers him – seizes the moment and jumps across the pitching sea. Then his men swarm up the chains towards the sound of fighting far above. He thinks of Jacob's endless ladder, although this one clearly does not lead to heaven.

But of course, he cannot follow with any ease, his wretched right foot not allowing him purchase. Worse, as the men disappear above him, their weight rattling the chains to which he is precariously clinging, he finds he is unable to hold on with just the one foot. His hat has half fallen and his sword is caught awkwardly in the chains as he grabs at them. He feels both stupid and helpless.

A hand reaches for his elbow. It is Bankes. 'We will support your leg.' Bankes has another of the Chilean sailors alongside. Together, they hoist him upwards, and the noise of fighting intensifies as they get closer to the deck.

They emerge to a confusion of musket shot and smoke. As it clears, he sees, as if in a dream, with unnatural clarity, Cochrane and Guise meeting in the mist and – though barely able to talk to each other over the mess table – shaking hands. As Guise was to board from one side of the ship – and Cochrane's men from the other – the inference is clear. The ship is taken.

At that moment a musket shot rings out. Cochrane clutches his thigh and falls to the deck.

'The soft part of the thigh,' Cochrane tells him later, as they sit together for a reflective drink of the last of Roscoff's best wine, looking out of the Admiral's window at the *Esmeralda* which floats beside them.

'It could have been worse. A few inches aside and it would have been my testicles, dammit!'

It is hard to know how to reply. *That would have been a shame, Sir?* Perhaps not. One thing he has learned during his brief naval experience – and about Cochrane – is that it is better to say nothing than to say the wrong thing – an approach so alien to his usual nature, he finds it difficult to contain himself.

Cochrane makes a grimace, as if in pain.

'I hope that imbecile San Martin honours our prize money. Or does so faster than he advanced on land towards the Peruvians. Any slower and he would have been going backwards.'

There has been much talk of San Martin recently, the Argentinian general who came up through Chile to take Peru with Cochrane's crucial support from the sea. Cochrane feels San Martin has been ineffective on land and it is only his naval actions that have gained Lima – for the city has now surrendered completely, as without a functioning port or flagship to guard it, there was little choice.

'I will stay with the fleet. But I suggest you and Lieutenant Bankes, as trusted envoys, travel into Lima and consult with San Martin as to what his immediate plans may entail, given there are still royalist troops at large in the interior of the country – as you discovered in Colombia.'

To John Cam Hobhouse, from George Gordon Byron

Lima, July 29th, 1821

My dear Hobhouse –

If the packet with this letter ever arrives – improbable but no more than many recent events – not least Lima's fall to the patriot forces – with the royalists retreated to the inland hills – and the coast and capital held at sea by Cochrane – with whom I served! – and on land by San Martin, the general from Argentina – but if this letter does reach you – and I have no idea if my last one did – please send word to my daughter Ada and her mother that I am alive.

As to the vicissitudes that led me here – which were many and often wholly unexpected – suffice it to say they were *testing.*

I know you are not over fond of Bankes – and close proximity has reminded me of the qualities that set others' teeth on edge – like his savage and profane jests – but he has shown himself a true and invaluable friend – just as you did when we travelled to Greece many years ago.

Indeed Lima might well remind you of some of those cities of the Levant and Albania.

As the viceroyalty of Peru commanded the whole Spanish Empire in South America from Lima, the city has been the centre of influence, political intrigue and *dissipation* for centuries. The recent wars have not stopped it from being the favourite resort of the wealthy and the sensual. Much, I dare say, like your Westminster, if they have not yet put you in prison again for loose behaviour.

Viewed from the Roads of Callao – where our ship lies at anchor – its numerous domes and towers give it a decidedly oriental air. The prospect at sunset is *arresting* – you might even say *agreeable* – for when twilight throws the plain into deep shade, the domes of the city are gilded by the departing sun.

The approach from Callao is by a fine road, the last mile of which is shaded by four rows of lofty trees, forming a handsome promenade. Bankes and I travelled here a few days ago with an escort to protect us from local pirates of the road – as such *banditti* are prolific – although like most of the population they may have gathered in the city for the forthcoming declaration of Independence – which is imminent – so the worst we might have expected was a cheer. And after months at sea, we looked like *banditti* ourselves.

More dangerous – much to the alarm of Bankes – are the attentions of the *female population* of Lima whose inhibitions

– never well-developed – have been loosened further by the flush that patriot victory has brought to their cheeks.

As to the persons of the women – for that well may be the subject that interests you most, as I know my reader – the *Limeñas* have black, resistless eyes, delicate arched eyebrows, finely turned arms, prettily shaped hands, and feet bewitchingly small. Their stature is short – and nothing sets off their supple forms more enticingly than the *saya* and the *manto*.

The *saya* is a petticoat of Chinese silk brought across the Pacific – which fits closely – and lessens in circumference as it approaches the ankle – so much so, that – to the amusement of Bankes – the wearer is obliged to take very short steps. The prevailing colour is brown, which shows off the women's olive skin to advantage.

The *manto* is a long black dress, open at the front. This – when the ladies walk out – is turned over the head – and, taking a corner of it in each hand, held across, just under the chin, which forms a complete hood that conceals the whole of the face – with the exception of one eye – an engine that seldom appears to be idle.

It has been remarked by the malevolent that a gust of wind rarely deranges the *manto*, so as to discover the features – unless a stranger happens to be passing – and the face beneath more than usually pretty. This unique dress is the costume of ladies when they go to church – to the promenade – or to pay morning visits. It is of Moorish origin and as a disguise gives opportunities to those who may wish to indulge in *adventure* – without provoking scandal. The Limeñas are esteemed warm in their attachments – but like the Venetians – as I should know – somewhat *inconstant*. If married, they feel they have licence to behave as they will – in that they marry for their parents and love for themselves.

We have ample opportunity to observe the comings and goings of the women – veiled or not – as we are close to the palace of the old Viceroy – who has now been ejected by the seat of his well-cut trousers – on the main square near the Cathedral. A cathedral rebuilt many times because of earthquakes, so of an architecture robust more than elegant – and with dark paintings in the Spanish manner which even Bankes – though a great *afficionado*, not least because he duels against the rest in proclaiming it – finds overbearing and obscure. So it is unlikely he will add to the Murillo he left in Bogota.

He takes more interest in the antiquities freely available in the market – many sourced from the desert where dry sand has preserved them to an unusual extent. Something to do with the nitrate. There are clay vessels with portraits of the inhabitants of these lands long before the Spaniards arrived, which have great vigour.

Along with the faces of these ancients, the pottery is emblazoned with the creatures who still live here – jaguars, great orca leviathans, llamas, deer, foxes – of a greater size than ours – monkeys, bats and above all a profusion of *birds* – pelicans, ducks, seabirds and great vultures called condors to give them a spurious nobility. There are also many of an amorous proposition in which couples embrace each other with little left for the beholder to imagine – including some of an *attic* Greek nature which have pleased Bankes considerably.

It is Bankes who now interrupts him by walking in front of the desk and blocking both the view of the cathedral and the light from the window. His friend's uniform has been cleaned and his epaulettes burnished to a silver glow; the barbers of Lima have been at work, and he looks freshly minted.

'We are to meet San Martin at the opera tonight – which should be illuminating.'

'Really? In the meantime, let me get on – and finish this letter.' Said stiffly – but he has never liked being disturbed when writing.

I am here as the representative of Lord Cochrane – an aide-de-camp, in effect – as is Bankes. Cochrane trusts us – unlike his own officers, we have no naval career to promote. Although I'm not sure I would wish to remain a midshipman for much longer.

But the situation is confused. While we advanced from the sea – San Martin made a peripatetic approach from the land, with great caution – to the frustration of Cochrane who is *not* of such a cautious disposition – as you may imagine. Furthermore the iron Admiral is of the belief it is only due to *his* efforts that Lima has been taken at all – there is considerable truth in this – which does not, of course, lead to San Martin feeling gratitude – or at least able to express that publicly without a loss of face. We are to meet him soon so I will know better how he stands.

We have been told – confidentially, in the way all military matters are meant to be confidential and none are – that San Martin is addicted to opium and this has an adverse effect on his behaviour. Apparently he took it for a wound acquired early in the fighting and has been unable to relinquish the habit.

Cochrane is a singular personality – radical in politics – and of the capacity to have an argument about who should pass the pepper at the mess table – which has not served his career well or made him easy to placate.

So – '*En Avant!*' – The Peruvians are advancing in their public progress – We have had an Independence Day with much shouting from the balconies – San Martin telling all remaining Spaniards to tremble if they 'abused his indulgence' – a fine phrase! – the victors quarrelling amongst themselves – and half the country still in royalist hands.

Bankes and I attended a gathering of junior officers after the declaration of Independence. Like other parties of the kind, it was at first silent – then talky – then argumentative – then disputatious – then unintelligible – then 'alltogethery' – then inarticulate – and then drunk. When we had reached the last step of this glorious ladder, it was difficult to get down again without stumbling.

There is a palpable air of excitement and of a new beginning – but also, it must be said, of *confusion*. Wild dogs roam the streets because there is no one to catch them. I have been feeding one whose royalist owners fled the city. I have called him Argos – because he has a golden fleece.

I have not told you that on Saturday – we had the *smartest shock* of an earthquake I can remember – and I have felt thirty slight or smart ones at different periods – they are common in the Mediterranean. The whole army discharged their arms – as if in defence – upon the same principle that savages beat drums or howl during an eclipse of the Moon. It was a rare scene altogether.

Do not ask me for any future plans – any more than Nausicaa and her handmaidens enquired of Odysseus when he was washed up on her shore. As I would answer I do not know. And in sober sadness, anything is better than England.

If I live ten years longer, you will see, however, that it is not over with me – I don't mean in literature, for that is nothing; and it may seem odd enough to say, I do not think it my vocation. But you will see that I will do something or other – the times and fortune permitting – that, as Goldsmith said, 'like the cosmogony, or creation of the world, will puzzle the philosophers of all ages'.

But I doubt whether my constitution will hold out. I have, at intervals, exercised it most devilishly. Some of the conditions on our journey – I speak particularly of our time on the coast in Colombia – and one great sadness there which I will recount to you in person – tested me greatly.

For the moment it is enough to be alive – to have survived – to have lived a life that has had more of event in the two years since I told you I planned to come here – than five times the length before.

Yours ever –

Byron

He fumbles for a moment with the damned fabric of the *saya* – one of those women's items of clothing too clever for its own devices – for of course unlike a skirt there is no approach from below – until the woman brings him closer to her so that he shields them from view with his greatcoat and pulls down the tight dress towards her knees, at the same time as she takes matters into her own hands by unbuckling his breeches and extracting his pego which after so many months of inactivity is already rock-hard – indeed has been so almost since the moment she called to him a few moments earlier from a side alley between the Cathedral and the theatre for, as they say on the Strand, a *flyer*. Helped by the fact he can see her face, as she is not wearing one of these veils, so there is no need to dissemble – and she has that vivacity he always finds attractive, if *volatile*, in a woman.

These are glory days for the whores, pickpockets and *banditti* of Lima – just as for everyone else, unless you happen to be working for the King of Spain – and they display themselves wantonly, as perhaps they always have, although he cannot help but feel there may be a new *excess* to their behaviour.

There has not even been time to agree a price in the manner he was accustomed to in Venice or London – and something of his urgency has communicated itself to her, for she is stroking his pego with a speed that can only have one result, so within moments he spends profusely all over her hand.

He finds he is apologising as if he has spilt tea on a tablecloth at a vicar's reception.

'*Mis disculpas, lo siento mucho*. I'm so sorry, *Señorita.*' He produces a perfumed handkerchief.

'*Va a manchar,* it will stain,' she says with the briskness of a professional. 'But come back when you're not in so much of a hurry.'

He fumbles for coin.

Inside the opera house, Bankes is waiting for him, professing to be studying the fine two-tone marble of the colonnade.

'What kept you, man? Or rather – *my Lord*?'

'The soldiers are blocking the street.' This should be convincing, as he knows San Martin has arrived in a cavalcade – a state carriage drawn by six horses, attended by a military escort and torch-bearers. Moreover, sentries are stationed throughout the theatre and here, just outside the state-box in which General San Martin grants interviews, stand a corporal and six men carrying arms. 'Asking for papers – which I did not have. You have all our papers of safe passage from Cochrane. As the senior officer, *Lieutenant* Bankes.'

'Really?' sniffs Bankes, as if he can smell the handkerchief. 'Well, never mind. He's ready for us – we should go in.'

The performance has begun, and the muffled voices of the actors reach them in the corridor – one high-pitched female bursts into song. Beside the state box is another, carefully screened from public view by a curtain. As they are led inside by a soldier, he thinks for a moment the curtain might come up to reveal the tableau to the audience below.

They would see a few junior equerries sitting in a circle, their trousers so tightly creased they might cut any dancing partner. And at their centre, a tall, sturdy man with lustrous dark skin – many have speculated he has Indian blood – black hair, luxuriant sideburns and gold brocade stiff about his shoulders so it must give little room for movement. He has a lit cigar in his hand and is the only one standing.

'One of my first proclamations was that everyone should be able to smoke in the theatre. The Viceroy never allowed it. And you know who resented the restriction most?'

This is rhetorical.

'The women. The women of Lima love to smoke. They are as likely to have a cigar as a gardenia tucked behind their ear.'

One of the equerries smiles politely in the manner of one who has heard this before. San Martin makes a gesture halfway between self-deprecation and enjoyment, to show he is fully in command of his own private stage. And there is something of the actor about him, a febrile quality.

'Which of you is Lord Byron?'

'I am, Sir, and this is Mr Bankes, both serving with Lord Cochrane – as you are aware.'

'You *were* serving with Lord Cochrane in the struggle for the liberation of Peru – which has ended. But I would hope you *are now* serving the general cause of the *patriotas,* just as I gather you did with Bolivar in the North.'

'Of course, Sir.'

San Martin looks at him carefully. It is difficult to know what he means by this look. It is frank, but also questioning. Is that association with Bolivar somehow problematic? For he appreciates they have different aims and principles – Bolivar is a republican; San Martin is in favour of a monarchy. And the talk all over Lima is how San Martin has yet to pay Cochrane prize money for the ships the Admiral has taken – his argument being those ships *belong* to Chile, as the Admiral was in command of the Chilean Navy – and therefore Chile should pay for them. An argument Cochranes dismisses as *specious*.

No matter.

'General, I would like to say, on behalf of all of us who commend the cause of freedom, your achievement in bringing the Flag of Liberty from Argentina to Chile – and here to Peru – is one for which the world must be profoundly grateful.'

'You speak Spanish well, *Milord*. I like the way you take care not to have a Castilian accent.

— 'Gentlemen, we should propose a toast. To a great soul, news of whose death has only just reached us. To Napoleon Bonaparte, who has died in exile on Santa Helena. *Que lástima*, what a shame he could not become an emperor here, as we invited him to be. Gentlemen, I give you a hero who believed in *Liberté, Égalité et Fraternité*, a holy trinity.'

San Martin's French accent is perfect. He has been told the general is a brilliant linguist – in fact, Cochrane had warned them never to speak privately in English thinking they could not be understood.

The equerries stand and cluster round San Martin. None reach higher than his shoulders. Perhaps he has deliberately chosen shorter attendants. They raise up their glasses towards their general.

He feels impelled to speak himself.

'I share in your profound admiration for Napoleon, Sir. In fact I have written several poems in his honour. About how *the Eagle's lofty rage / has been reduced to nibble at his narrow cage…* Before coming here, I was a poet.'

'*A* poet. I understand, *milord*, you were *the* poet. Do you think we are provincial here? And have no knowledge of the taste of Europe? That if truth be told, you were the *toast* of Europe and that just as we are toasting Napoleon, you were once toasted in every *salon* from London to Rome.'

He tries to look both modest and embarrassed, although neither expression translates well into Spanish.

'Then let us hear one of those poems to Napoleon. And when I say us – I mean all of us,' and San Martin gestures for the curtains of their private audience box to be swept open, which alerts the audience below to San Martin's presence, hundreds of whom turn their heads towards him. The actors on stage stop.

Sam Martin announces in a voice that could hold a cavalry charge, '*Damas y caballeros, disculpa la interrupción,* ladies and gentlemen, forgive the interruption – but we have a distinguished guest from England…'

'Scotland,' mutters Bankes under his breath.

'…the poet, Lord Byron.' There is a ripple of applause. 'Who has fought on our behalf.' The applause is louder. 'And will now recite an ode to the late departed champion of liberty, Napoleon Bonaparte…'

Thunderous applause indeed.

Feeling this is the literary equivalent of leaping for the grappling irons on the *Esmeralda*, he steps forward to address the theatre.

'*Napoleon's Farewell*' – then adds '*La Despedida de Napoleon*', although he declaims the piece in English – for he knows it by heart – sensing what matters is not the language but the *emotion* with which he reads.

'*Farewell to thee, France! But when Liberty rallies…*'

He pauses for effect, and San Martin bellows, as if translator and chorus, '*¡cuando la Libertad resurge…!*' The rest of the verse is under-pinned by olé's and cheers from the audience.

'*Once more in thy regions, remember me then –*'

He takes his voice down to a projected whisper so he can rise up again for the final words:

'*Yet – yet – I may baffle the hosts that surround us*
And yet may thy heart leap awake to my voice –
There are links which must break in the chain that has bound us,
Then turn thee and call on the Chief of thy choice!'

'*¡Al Jefe que quiere!*' bellows San Martin at the top of his lungs. 'The Chief of thy choice!'

A woman in a nearby box tosses gardenias. Men stand in their military uniforms and clap. Most gratifying, the actors on the stage look up towards him and applaud above their heads.

'*Que sigue la pieza,*' declares San Martin, sweeping his hand as if knocking over a line of dominoes – and the play continues.

They proceed next door into the viceregal box, wide enough for them all to have armchairs at the front to watch the overblown theatrics on stage. When they take their seats – 'Would either of you care to have a cigar? From Guayaquil, where they have the art...' – San Martin collapses in upon himself, as if undone by the energy of all this performance. Now he is sitting close, he can see a pallor to the general's forehead, noticeable against the rest of his dark skin.

Bankes is indecent in the haste with which he reaches for the magnificent large cigars an equerry produces – so large he is still smoking his own by the time they reach the interval, after a play more notable for energy than craft. It would never have passed muster when he helped select at Drury Lane. Although after the reception of his poem, he feels charitable towards the actors and indeed everyone in the theatre. As if he had been dining on lobster and champagne in Covent Garden.

When the interval lights go up, San Martin gestures to a corporal for brandies to be brought and reaches over towards Bankes.

'*Mister* Bankes, is there anything we can arrange for you? – I understand you are a scholar interested in the antiquities of the New World. Which I commend.'

'I would greatly like your permission, Sir, to be able to visit the ruins at Pachacamac?'

San Martin confers with an equerry.

'Of course. I have not heard of them before, but of course.'

He gives a wave of the hand, as of dismissal. 'You will be wanting to return to your lodgings. I must confer with my officers.' But then stops.

'And give my regards – to Lord Cochrane.'

'Is this all there is?' he asks Bankes.

They are surveying a monotony of low brown adobe walls that stretch out and bleed into the dirt-desert plain.

On the walls least destroyed, he can make out niches and some-times doorways of a curious trapezoidal pattern – they might, he thinks, appeal to Annabella's mathematical mind – but beyond that, no trace of any human presence.

'What did you expect?' Bankes replies. 'You have been to the site of all that remains of Troy. What is needed for such places – and why you might succeed where others fail – is *imagination*. The imagination to people such a place and picture the city as it must once have been – these walls rising high, painted in brilliant colours that shone across the plain. The priests chanting.'

'How do we know there were priests? Or for that matter – that they chanted?'

'How do we know anything of ancient Rome? From *history*. Because the first Spanish chroniclers left accounts of this place. Though the native peoples – the Incas and suchlike – left none, for they had no writing, at least none we are aware of.'

'How curious – that a civilisation could leave great cities but no writing.'

'Not curious at all. Writing is, at best, a marginal activity.' Bankes takes pleasure in this pronouncement.

'A palpable hit. I shall consider myself among the *marginal*.'

Bankes says nothing, as if that is the correct conclusion to be drawn. After a pause, he continues.

'This was the Delphi or Sphinx of ancient Peru.'

'And was called Pachamacac?'

'No. Pacha-*camac*.' Bankes gives a look a Cambridge don might bestow on a slow student. 'The Incas venerated the shrine – but it was here long before the Incas came, just as the Sphinx in Egypt anticipated the Greeks. Men have always found wisdom in antiquity, when they were the moderns themselves.'

'Rightly.'

'No, sometimes wrongly.' Bankes could be infuriating. 'The Oracle led the Incas astray. Famously.'

'How so?' It is not famous at all.

'When the emperor Atahualpa was taken hostage by the Spaniards on their first arrival, he was attended by a young cousin of the Pizarros called Pedro, who left a memoir in old age of Atahualpa's conversation.'

'His *table talk* – as with Napoleon?'

'Exactly. As doubtless we will see the publication of *Lord Byron's Table Talk* at some stage – although not written by me. So little of it has made any impression...

— 'Atahualpa had a great deal of time in captivity to talk to this young pageboy, Pedro. And he told him the story of this Oracle. Of how he had come to distrust it. For when his father, the previous emperor, had fallen ill during a plague that swept the land, he petitioned the Oracle as to what to do. The Oracle advised the emperor he should sit outside in the sun. Which he did. And forthwith *died*, almost immediately.'

'Ah.'

'Atahualpa then related how his brother, the legitimate heir, then petitioned the Oracle as to whether he should contest the throne with Atahualpa. The Oracle told his brother he would be victorious – so a bitter civil war ensued that makes our own War of the Roses appear a mere *skirmish*. The Empire was ravaged, millions died, his brother was defeated and killed – and the Oracle again discredited.'

'Which would please Atahualpa, as the victor?'

'Well, yes – but when the Spaniards arrived on the coast, Atahualpa, now Emperor himself, made a third and final petition to this Oracle, to ask if he should be alarmed at the arrival of these bearded ones.'

'And what did the Oracle say?'

Although he can guess.

'That the Spaniards were no threat whatsoever and could be ignored. So he treated them as an amusing diversion – a mistake.'

'I see – so he was taken hostage by the same Spaniards —'

'Who proceeded to ransom him for a room full of gold. That is, he had to fill a certain chamber up to a line with gold from wherever he chose across his dominions.' Bankes gestures at the desert inland. 'At which point Atahualpa took revenge. For he sent the Spaniards *here*, to the Oracle, to strip every last bit of gold they had been offered over thousands of years. Which is why you see it bare today.'

'You could sell tickets and lecture at the Royal Institution! There is even a moral to the story —'

'That you should not believe in false idols? No – the moral is you should not believe the words of so-called Christians. For the Spaniards, having received their ransom from Atahualpa, still went ahead – and executed him.'

There is nothing further to say. While Bankes is busy completing his notes, he unbuckles a flask of water from the saddlebag and shares it with his horse, equally thirsty as he is.

'*Yonder all before us lie...*'

Bankes finishes, '*deserts of vast eternity.*'

They start on the road back to Lima, talking as they ride.

'So the Oracle was positioned to be close to Lima?'

He looks forward to a time when Bankes is unable to answer a question, but it never comes.

'No. Lima was a later foundation – much later – built by the Spaniards on their arrival, perhaps because they had been to this area of the coast when stripping the Oracle of its treasure. So one could say Lima was positioned to be close to the now discredited Oracle – not the other way round.'

'And how do you know all this?' he says in grudging admiration. 'Are these Spanish chronicles available in England?'

'They should be. And are not. Though luckily Sangucho has an admirable collection of the originals. He included some in that trunk he packed for us. Men like Pedro Pizarro wrote their accounts in clear, attractive Spanish which is easy to read – soldierly and with attention to detail. They told the story as it transpired – as should you, if you ever describe this new war in Peru between the last remnants of those conquistadors who still rule the country and the fighters for freedom who would replace them.'

'A war that must be over, given Lima has fallen? One thing for Bolivar to take the far-flung provinces of the north – but with Lima gone, surely the whole Spanish Empire will topple over the cliff, however slowly?'

'Lima may have fallen. The rest of Peru remains in royalist hands. Including – ironically – Cusco, the old Inca capital, now the centre of operations for the Spanish crown. So will the rest of Peru fall?'

Bankes lets his question hang in the air, before answering it himself: 'Perhaps we should have asked the Oracle.'

On reaching the outskirts of Lima, they pass a landscape of desolation – the shattered remains of *campesino* houses destroyed by the earthquake which had torn through the country just days before. The earthquake had been widely seen as a portent of the end of Spanish rule – like a comet – but more directly has brought much misery to the countryside. Adobe walls lie broken open and landslides have engulfed the roads; many of the *campesino* farmers they see look blank, as if in aftershock.

He remembers Voltaire's words on the earthquake in Lisbon – proof all was not for the best in the best of all possible worlds – that natural disasters could devastate without rhyme or reason.

He feels the same desolation himself as he looks at the destroyed homes, some of which look more broken than the ancient ruins they have come from – for the ancients knew better how to build to withstand such earthquakes, says Bankes. And he misses Teresa with a terrible longing. A snatch of verse comes to him, almost taking him by surprise:

> *The earthquake came, and rocked the quivering wall,*
> *And men and nature reeled as if with wine.*
> *Whom did I seek around the tottering hall?*

> *For thee.*

'I have been talking to San Martin about you.'

He is back with Cochrane in the high stateroom of the *O'Higgins*. Cochrane prefers to stay on board, where he has all the comforts of being in harbour, rather than live in Lima or Callao. It puts him in a stronger position to negotiate on prize money or other dispositions if it is known he can take off with the fleet at any moment and leave Lima defenceless.

'About me, my Lord?' He is startled.

His part in the capture of the *Esmeralda* had hardly been distinguished; nor had much transpired from his meeting with the new 'Protector of Peru' at the theatre in Lima, other than his recital of an elegy for Napoleon.

'We have exchanged letters since the formal declaration of Peruvian independence. Some courteous, some not so courteous when it comes to the amounts of prize money which – as you know – are in dispute.

— 'But on one matter we have always been in agreement.

— 'We do not have a titular head of government – a monarch. San Martin is simply a *protector* in command of the military forces while there are still loyalist armies at large in the hills. I do not personally think he is of a disposition – or frankly of a capability – to govern in a civilian capacity once that task is completed. He will undoubtedly retire to Europe with the sense of a job well done.

— 'So we are left with a problem. It is deeply inconsiderate of Napoleon – first to have been so indisposed when we sent envoys proposing he become Emperor of South America – and second, even more, now to have *died*.

— 'You may perhaps not know that envoys were also sent to London — and for a while it seemed as if Prince Leopold – His Royal Highness Prince Leopold, no less – the widower of our own Princess

Charlotte – might be a suitable candidate – having lost his chance of being Prince Consort. But apparently he turned the offer down as too *precarious* a situation. Given the choice of being a prince without a kingdom – and as I understand it, much money – or being the King of Peru, I am surprised at his decision. Although perhaps, after a hundred years of having German Kings in Britain, we should be used to their occasional stupidities.

— 'Leopold sounds a poor sort of a fellow anyway. Unlike Napoleon, he has shown no revolutionary zeal or interest in the promotion of new countries. Quite the contrary. I gather he is what the French call *un réactionnaire*, a reactionary of the worst sort. So best left in his royal apartment in Mayfair.'

'I understand, my Lord.' He understands nothing, as it is unlike Cochrane to have a conversation unless it leads to a point. His commanding officer is being unusually obtuse.

'The thing is, *Byr'n*,' – Cochrane is slowly tacking towards a destination – 'we need a European figurehead who has a certain amount of fame, an aristocratic pedigree and has shown commitment towards the cause of South American independence – who ideally has fought for Bolivar in the north and for Peru in the south.'

He cannot understand why Cochrane is saying this. Does he want to second the Admiral in what would seem the obvious choice?

He looks Cochrane squarely in the eye.

'Sir, if you are looking for my endorsement, then of course I would support you wholeheartedly. Your record is outstanding. Everyone knows it is your military prowess that has secured Lima and hence Peru – and with their fall, the likelihood the whole Spanish empire in South America will crumble away. And your political credentials are —'

Cochrane interrupts. 'Thank you, my Lord. It does not seem the right moment to address you as Midshipman – although I may say, you have been a fine one. I might add, even a *promising* one. I appreciate your sentiments.

— 'But before you continue, you have misunderstood me. I have no interest in staying. Nor do I have any interest in seeking office here. I wish to return to England with my wife Kitty, who is in Chile and from whom I have been apart too long. There are causes in England I wish to pursue, not least Reform, as you know well and as we have often discussed, for we are like-minded, on both that and the Irish question.

— 'No, what I want to suggest, and what you have not appreciated with your own modesty – a quality I have noticed and which might surprise the British public – is that *you* are the ideal candidate.'

This time he finds he is genuinely lost for words.

'You have the title, name, fame and commitment to the cause of freedom.

— 'And more to the point, you can *write*, man. Don't you see that what is needed is as much someone who can inspire a new country – and continent – as run one?'

'But Cochrane,' – this is not the time for the usual formalities – 'surely I would need to be *able* to run a country? Both its military and civil affairs. Let alone taxation and exchequer. These are not matters with which I am familiar, although I am flattered by your offer. And how would the citizens of this new realm take to a monarch who has spent all of two weeks in their country? Surely they would want one of their own?'

Cochrane waves these objections away with much the same air he dismissed Guise's concern about their attempt on the *Esmeralda*.

'That is precisely where you are wrong. The *last thing* they want is one of their own. Far better to have an outsider who comes, as they see it, with a neutral approach, without *favour* to any faction. And more importantly, who is not trying to send their money across the seas to Spain. You would be like a disinterested Viceroy.

— 'All the rest can be *managed*. You would be monarch of the country – not its administrator. You can get treasurers and chancellors – and for that matter generals – to help you. They will doubtless be queueing up.

— 'But think, man. You would have the chance to help shape a nation. To give it voice. How many men can say that? And,' – Cochrane gives a snort of laughter – 'it would be the fastest promotion in military history. One moment you're serving as a midshipman. The next you're King Byron!'

He imagines Shelley's voice in his ear, cajoling, laughing, scornful. 'You always were a champagne radical, Byron. Not a true republican.'

He remembers the many times he has denounced the tired old royal families of Europe – the Bourbons, the Habsburgs and indeed their own Hanoverians, that ridiculous sequence of German kings imported by the British. Fat Prinny, foisted on the nation as a Regent. Now – absurdly – George IV. Is he to join their ranks?

The idea is magnificent, ludicrous, reckless – and irresistible, as Cochrane knows.

'If San Martin and you are agreed – and the offer comes from the new Peruvian Congress – then of course I will take it!'

'I thought you would. So I will arrange for a ship to be dispatched to Colombia to collect your consort. You can hardly be a king without a queen. That said, the news may come as a surprise to her.

— 'And forgive me asking – but are you married?'

'We are both married, but not to each other – separated, for different reasons, from unbefitting spouses.'

'Well,' – and again Cochrane gives that magisterial wave of the hand with which in this life all can be given to those who ask suitably – 'that can be arranged too, I'm sure. You may find, like Henry VIII, that it is useful to have your own Archbishop. And your Peruvian public will not care less about the niceties. But will appreciate a queen.

— 'Furthermore I hear – and forgive me if this news has not reached you – I have the advantage of direct dispatches from Bolivar – who has advised me not to play billiards with you, incidentally – and who sends his regards, along with a bottle of his personal cologne – but I hear that the Contessa is expecting your child – who may be, who knows, an heir now to a kingdom.'

It is all too much. He rings the bell for Fletcher, who has taken over duties in the officers' mess and attends the Admiral as well.

'You called, my Lord?'

'You should no longer address him as "*my Lord*", Fletcher,' says Cochrane with an admirably straight face.

'No, instead you should address him as "*your Highness*".'

But he is not concentrating on Fletcher's reaction, however much it might amuse.

Instead, he can see himself, in his mind's eye, on a throne lined with jaguar fur and with a cloak of the sort Sangucho once told him the Inca emperors wore – of hummingbird feathers. With Teresa in equal splendour beside him.

And moreover, there will be the inestimable pleasure of telling Bankes.

Viva Byron!

EPILOGUE

An observer on one of the high summits of the Andes would have seen a strange sight if they had looked down.

A procession is making its way along the royal Inca Highway of the Sun that runs the whole length of the mountain chain from Colombia to Peru.

There are many mules with heavy packing cases, several dogs and some llamas with their lighter tread carrying the more delicate goods.

A maidservant in luxurious Chinese silks and with a bright orange turban sits on the back of a large mule, on which she sways like an Oriental potentate.

A small girl is carried in a palanquin and is intent on the mongrel dog that follows loyally at her heels, and to which she talks, throwing the occasional stick for it to chase.

An escort of brightly uniformed military men, epaulettes flashing in the sun, ride both in front and behind, jockeying occasionally so they can be closer to the middle.

At the centre of the procession rides the subject of their attention, a woman on a white horse, wearing a costume in the bright cochineal red that the Incas would have recognised from their weavings.

She rides confidently and well. Ahead in the distance, she can see a volcano and wonders if it is the one Byron had described to her in his letter.

She remembers again how Corinne in her novel had climbed the volcano with her lover and resisted all those who tried to keep her as *respectable* and deny her existence as a woman, with all their rules and domestic expectations.

How life is so often inspired by literature and literature so often inspired by life.

Afterword

> I had, and still *have*, thoughts of South America, but am fluctuating between it and Greece.

> Letter to Thomas Moore, Pisa, August 27th, 1822

For any reader who missed it, this is not attempted as a contribution to Byron studies but more what he might have called a *jeu d'esprit*. I have taken as many geographical and historical liberties as Byron himself does in the *Don Juan* he was writing towards the end of his life. So it is a happy hunting ground for any pedants who wish to take issue.

However, for those concerned, the events imagined are based on letters Byron wrote for many years from 1819 to 1822 – some quoted verbatim in the text – expressing his wish to leave 'decrepit' Europe and go to South America where Bolivar was fighting. It was only the accident of a 'sliding door' moment that made the notoriously indecisive Byron determine on Greece instead. (At one point likewise in Venice he prepared to leave for England, packed his trunks, emptied the Palazzo, and then declared that, if everything was not ready by the time the clock struck twelve, he would change his mind. As then happened.)

The Peruvians did search for a king after their independence and sent to Europe to see if there were any candidates – Leopold of Saxe-Coburg, Queen Victoria's uncle, was considered but decided later on Belgium instead – so there was indeed a vacant position for Byron to fill.

The story of how he met Teresa in Venice and their subsequent courtship – and of the Count's 'rules' – is based on letters between them and their contemporaries.

It was the only long-lasting and serious relationship in his life, and his final letters to Teresa, just before he died in 1824, having chosen Greece, were signed off:

'dearest T. t. a. a. in e.' – short for 'Teresa, *tu amico é amante in eterno*, your friend and lover for *ever*.'

This book is an attempt to imagine what might have happened to them both if he had chosen a different path.

Bibliography

Byron was a man of his Regency times and if any of the language quoted verbatim from his letters now offends, it is because our own times have changed, not because I have changed his.

Those magnificent letters are available in several editions, including ones selected by Richard Lansdown, although for the fine grain of Byron's life nothing beats the full unexpurgated twelve volumes of his *Letters and Journals* compiled by Leslie Marchand.

The best books about Byron have been written by women: the incomparable Iris Origo whose *The Last Attachment* detailed her discovery of the letters between Teresa and Byron; and the late Fiona MacCarthy's biography of him which revealed the extent of his bisexuality, something earlier biographers had fought shy of.

I also reserve a soft spot for Peter Quennell's *Byron*, for missing out the boring bits, and Geoffrey Bond's charming book about Byron and his dogs, *Lord Byron's Best Friends*, which shows how Byron was ahead of his time in his attitude towards animals and their care.

I am grateful to Anne Sebba for *The Exiled Collector*, her biography of William Bankes, who in real life was finally arrested for indecency with a Guardsman in Hyde Park and only escaped a heavy sentence after the intervention of the Duke of Wellington, as he could not believe that one of his former officers should be capable of such an offence.

Viva Byron!

Thanks

My thanks to Patrick Atkins, Rachael Beale, Marguerite Evers, Anthony Forbes Watson, Patrick Heren, Adrian Poole, Dominic Welby and Anne Williams.

Also to Dave Sidwell for providing a boat to write on, all those who gave me hospitality in Colombia while researching – *mi casa es su casa* – and Emily Paterson-Morgan and the small but perfectly formed Byron Society.

Most of all to Jocasta Shakespeare who accompanied me on many of the journeys needed to complete this book.

J. t. a. a. in e.

Viva Byron!

Viva Byron!

Milton Keynes UK
Ingram Content Group UK Ltd.
UKHW030700021124
450306UK00001B/1/J